Simon Edge was born in Chester and read philosophy at Cambridge University. He was editor of the pioneering London paper *Capital Gay* before becoming a gossip columnist on the *Evening Standard* and then a feature writer on the *Daily Express*, where he was in addition a theatre critic for many years. He has an MA in Creative Writing from City University, London, where he has also taught literary criticism. He is the author of three previous novels: *The Hopkins Conundrum*, longlisted for the Waverton Good Read Award, *The Hurtle of Hell* and *A Right Royal Face-Off*. He lives in Suffolk.

ANYONE FOR
EDMUND?

SIMON EDGE

Lightning
Books ⚡

Published in 2020
by Lightning Books Ltd
Imprint of EyeStorm Media
312 Uxbridge Road
Rickmansworth
Hertfordshire
WD3 8YL

www.lightning-books.com

Cover by Ifan Bates

British Library Cataloguing in Publication Data
A catalogue record for this book is available from the British Library.

Printed by CPI Group (UK) Ltd, Croydon CR0 4YY

ISBN: 9781785631917

for Ezio,
my treasure in the loamy earth

TIMELINE

c500   The Wuffing dynasty arrives in East Anglia from Jutland

c633   Monastery founded at Beodericsworth by Sigebert, king of East Anglia

c841   Birth of Edmund

854   Edmund crowned king of East Anglia at Bures

865   'Great Heathen Army' arrives in East Anglia from Denmark

869[†]   Edmund defeated and killed by the Danes

c900   Edmund's body brought to Beodericsworth

c925   Beodericsworth's name changed to St Edmunds Bury

c986   French monk Abbo of Fleury writes the first life of St Edmund

1002   Massacre of Danes in England ordered by Ethelred the Unready on St Brice's Day

1010   Body of Edmund temporarily moved to London after the Danes sack Ipswich

1013	Body of Edmund returns to Bury
1013	Swein Forkbeard, king of Denmark, successfully invades England, named king
1014	Death of Swein in Gainsborough, Lincolnshire
1020	Swein's son King Canute founds an abbey dedicated to St Edmund at Bury
c1065	Abbot Leofstan opens Edmund's tomb and is paralysed
1066	William of Normandy conquers England and visits Bury early in his reign
1097	St Edmund declared patron saint of England
1153	Prince Eustace, eldest son of King Stephen, dies in Cambridge after dining at, and then looting, Bury
1173	Forces loyal to Henry II, under the banner of St Edmund, defeat a Flemish mercenary army at the Battle of Fornham
1189	Richard I prays at St Edmund's shrine on the eve of the Third Crusade
1192	William de Burgh founds St Edmund's Priory in Athassel, Ireland
c1193	Abbot Samson tells the Barons of the Exchequer that they can come and strip St Edmund's shrine, to raise funds to ransom the imprisoned Richard I, if they dare. Nobody does.
1282	Llewelyn ap Gruffudd, the last Prince of Wales, killed at the Battle of Orewin Bridge
1296[†]	Edward I massacres the entire population of Berwick-upon-Tweed
1300	Welsh nobleman Rhys ap Rhys surrenders to Edward I's forces while the king is at Bury
1350	Edward I visits St Edmund's shrine for the sixth time; St George named as patron saint of England

1376[†]	Richard of Bordeaux (later Richard II) invested as Prince of Wales
1433	The young king Henry VI makes a pilgrimage to the shrine of St Edmund and stays for four months
c1435	John Lydgate, monk of Bury, writes the life of St Edmund
1539	Bury Abbey shut by Henry VIII, Edmund's body disappears
1914	New cathedral consecrated amid the ruins of Bury Abbey
1992[†]	Windsor Castle badly damaged by fire
1995[†]	Princess Diana goes on national television blaming Prince Charles' adultery for the breakdown of their marriage

[†]20 November

A cry of triumph rose up from the western end of the dig, closest to the abbey ruins. As soon as she heard it, Hannah dropped her trowel, blinked for a moment in the woozy head-rush of standing up too quickly, then hastened over to where Magnus and the other senior members of the team, each with a telltale strap of sunburn on the backs of their necks, squatted around a trench. For once, she forgot about the creaky back that always played up after she spent too long crouching in the same position and made her first few steps into more of a waddle than a walk. This was not the moment to bother about that.

It was day four of the dig, and its leaders had known where to look from the end of day one. Once the mesh fence around the three abandoned tennis courts had been taken down and the top layer of asphalt, with its faded white lines marking out three forlorn sets of baselines, sidelines and service boxes, had been scraped off with a mechanical digger, they had embarked on the geofizz. That was what Hannah called it, after years of watching Time Team, but the professionals stuck strictly to 'geophysics'. Whatever it was called, it involved an electrical probe to measure resistance, a magnetic survey to map all kinds of things in the soil, not just metal, and ground-penetrating radar. The whole process produced three different maps of the site which could be laid on top of one another, providing pointers for anyone skilled enough to interpret them. Hannah, who was one of the community volunteers welcomed onto the dig to maintain good local relations, could not tell one dark shadow from another, but she was digging alongside plenty who could.

Looking for a coffin-shaped object should have been easy, were it not for the fact that they were searching for it in a graveyard. For five hundred years, all the monks of an abbey the size of a town had been buried here, between the east end of the great church and the infirmary. They were not so much looking for a needle in a haystack, as a strand of hay. Fortunately, it was not completely hopeless. From what Magnus, the youthful volunteer coordinator, had explained, the monks tended to be buried in lead coffins, whereas the object they were looking for was a wooden 'feretory' – or portable shrine – adorned with gold and locked in an iron box. The iron would have disintegrated long ago, but the metal would leave traces in the ground that the geophysics could discern, and the gold adornments ought also to have survived.

Sure enough, the geophysics had pointed to the likely place, with iron traces delineating an area of the right shape and size, over by the remains of one of the little semi-circular chapels that protruded from the ruins of the presbytery. That location made logical sense: the monks had not had far to lug their sacred burden as they hurried to hide it from Thomas Cromwell's sixteenth-century Taliban.

The discovery did not mean that Hannah and her colleagues could all simply pile in with shovels, like cartoon pirates racing to unearth a chest of doubloons. As Magnus never tired of repeating, this was a one-off opportunity for the site to give up its secrets before the ground was closed up again and it must not be squandered. There was at least half a metre of earth to be sifted meticulously before they got near the right level, and there was also the rest of the site to be investigated. 'It's an area of approximately one thousand square metres or, in layman's terms, the size of three tennis courts,' he said. Hannah laughed, but everyone else groaned.

She had been given a trench at the north-eastern corner of the site, farthest from the spot that looked so exciting in the geofizz. It was on a small brow before the land fell abruptly away towards the children's playground and the tiny chalk stream that bounded the Abbey Gardens. This river had once been big enough to turn the mill that supplied the whole town with flour, and also to carry the great limestone blocks from the quarry at Barnack, on the other side of the Fenlands, with which the greatest church in Christendom had been built. Those blocks were all gone now, and all that was left of the abbey buildings were the misshapen lumps and towers of flint rubble that had formed the core of thick walls and soaring pillars. The little outcrop where she was working had most likely been built up at some much later stage to create a suitable plateau for the tennis courts. She would therefore have deeper to go before she reached anything interesting, but it also meant she was at less risk of doing any harm. In any case, she could hardly volunteer for a dig and then complain about the amount of digging she had to do.

It was warm work, with the permanent yeasty fug from the town's Victorian brewery sitting heavy in the air. She fretted at first that she might miss something important, given that everything looked much the same when it was caked with earth. Under Magnus' tutelage, however, she learned that there was no danger of that, provided she was painstaking. 'Anything that isn't earth is either a pebble or an artefact,' he told the group of half a dozen volunteers, fiddling with his man-bun as he spoke. It had a habit of falling out and Hannah reckoned it needed a pair of chopsticks to secure it, but that would doubtless spoil the look. 'Just make sure you sift every trowelful of earth and examine every object properly. Remember, your brush and your pail of water are your friends here.'

It was acceptable to hack at a decent lick through the topsoil, which was not so different to digging her own garden. After that, the earth needed removing layer by layer, with each few centimetres kept in its own bucket so you knew which order to put it all back. At her corner of the site, Hannah was following the line of the infirmary wall: to her great relief, no one had the slightest desire to open the monks' graves, and it was the stuff around the outside of the cemetery that they cared about. At first she got excited at every piece of broken pottery, until she realised she had yet to dig past the twentieth century. After that she reined in her expectations and could not quite believe it when she unearthed a copper belt-buckle, an iron key and a piece of yellow-and-black Cistercian ware which Vernon, the most senior archaeologist on the dig, identified as Tudor. She could see why people got hooked on this kind of thing.

She was so caught up in her own discoveries – the extraordinary thought that she was the first person in five hundred years to handle this shard of pottery or the lead bowl she found an hour or two later – that she forgot all about the serious business happening over by the presbytery. Then came that exultant hullabaloo and suddenly she remembered again, and it was thrilling, like being in the Valley of the Kings when Carter and Carnarvon first gazed on the face of Tutankhamun. Hopefully their own find would not come with a curse.

Vernon and another of the proper archaeologists, a thirty-something woman with blue hair called Daisy, were down on the floor of the excavation, about a metre below ground level, with everyone else looking on, either crouched on their haunches or leaning into the pit. They watched as Vernon gently prised an object from the soil and reached for his brush to dust it clean. As he did so, it caught the light of the hot July sun with the unmistakable gleam of gold. Having brushed off the worst of the dirt, he now held it up for them all to see: it was a crucifix.

Meanwhile Daisy was digging on, carefully now, with a brush and the tiniest of trowels. 'Vernon!' she said urgently, and he turned back to see. Those crouching and craning above them collectively leaned a little closer too.

Vernon was using his brush now too, and it was hard to see what the pair of them were doing because first his head was in the way, then hers. Then they both sat back on their heels, revealing their find. A dozen diggers, professional and novice, gasped in unison, and one of the younger volunteers stifled what sounded like a sob. Hannah felt every tiny hair on the back of her neck stand to attention.

They all stared in wonder, and the half-buried skull that Vernon and Daisy had unearthed grinned back at them.

Mark Price peered idly into the window of Suits R U in Victoria Street and was momentarily taken back to his schooldays when he saw his own name, or a close approximation of it, on the promo poster between two pin-striped mannequins. 25 PER CENT OFF MARKED PRICE.

About twenty-five years ago, some bright spark in his class had seen that exact same wording – not twenty percent or thirty – on a school trip to Colchester Castle and had spent the rest of the day calling him Twenty-Five Per Cent Off. 'Oi, Twenty-Five Per Cent Off!' Then shortened to, 'Give us a crisp, Twenty-Five Per Cent.' It shrank still further, first to Twenty-Five and then to plain Twen by the end of the day. With their teenage capacity to find hilarity in everything, this had been the funniest thing in the world for his little group, including to Mark, and he had revelled in the prospect of a proper nickname. Twenty-Five Per Cent was a rap name. How cool was that?

But the trip was at the end of term and everyone else had forgotten about Mark's new name by the start of the next one. He had the sense to know he could not revive it himself; that would reek of desperation. So he remained Mark Price, and only occasionally – it tended to be when he was in the throes of self-pity – did he allow a piece of signage to trigger the wistful memory of the time when he nearly had a nickname.

Today was no exception, mood-wise. It was a sign of his general dejection that he was mooching in shop windows in his lunch hour, rather than working through. On paper, being a special adviser to the sainted Marina Spencer was his dream job, particularly with her career on such a spectacular ascendant. Unfortunately, he had learned there was a strong inverse relationship between the level of Marina's public prominence and his own wellbeing. These days the atmosphere was so poisonous he could hardly bear to be in the office.

After graduating in history from the LSE, he had successfully applied to the BBC. Following a short stint on news, he had spent most of his career producing programmes at the World Service, latterly a thirteen-minute, once-a-week drama set in a diverse street in North London, where all the 'residents' spoke just slowly enough for a global English-language audience to understand. He told people at parties that he produced a radio soap with ten times more listeners than *The Archers*, which was true, even if he had never actually met anyone outside the BBC who recognised its name.

Despite that modest success, he was unfulfilled. He was beginning to feel it in earnest when he turned thirty-five and he promised himself he would get out of his rut before forty came over the horizon. Besides, the pay was embarrassing. He must be able to do better.

He had always followed current affairs and, while his journalistic life was hardly *All The President's Men*, he had long envied those distant colleagues who worked the Westminster beat. They knew how the world really worked, they mixed with those who ran or aspired to change it, and sometimes they jumped the narrow divide between their own world and the one on which they reported. Privately, Mark thought he could do the job just as well as they did, but he had taken the wrong road years ago, if that was his ambition. It had seemed a brilliant achievement to get into the BBC – and it really was, there was no doubt about that – so he did not worry too much about not entering the most exciting part of it. He could move from his backwater to more significant positions, he assumed, but he was mistaken. His soap might be popular among students of English in Tashkent and Ulan Bator – they wrote and told him so – but he might as well have been in Outer Mongolia himself, for all that he impinged on the consciousness of domestic programme-makers.

All this steadily became clearer as the years passed. By the time he realised he was at a dead end, it was too late to do anything about it. He fell into self-pity for a while, then bitterness for a while longer, but eventually made a plan. When redundancy was offered in the umpteenth round of cuts, he felt he had served a long enough stretch to make the terms worthwhile, so he decided it was time to give his scheme a go.

His idea was simple. While younger and smarter men and women jostled for position at the court of the two main political parties, the likes of Mark had a better chance with the minority ones. As fortune would have it, his own sympathies were closely aligned to an outfit in the trough of its popular fortunes. An ill-advised coalition with the Tories after the end of the New Labour years had seen the centrist Eco-Dem Alliance almost wiped out in the House of Commons, with its polling down to single figures, and it was the most reviled political party in Britain when Mark offered his services as an experienced ex-BBC producer. Just as he anticipated, its senior staffers were surprised and pleased; in fact their gratitude was borderline embarrassing.

At first, all went well. With party morale at rock bottom, all the brightest operators were long gone, putting their government experience to lucrative use in corporate jobs or consultancies. Those who remained saw themselves as the true believers, made of too stern stuff to cut and run just because times were hard; everyone else saw them as no-hopers without a chance of getting a job anywhere else. They were in no way energised or optimistic. They toiled on, wearing their new opprobrium with grim forbearance, and entertaining few, if any, expectations of an improvement in fortunes. Veterans of the old days, they had always been content to be a tiny, ill-resourced band of misfits, and now they were back in that comfort zone. Nevertheless, it proved a useful training ground for Mark, who was free to learn his new trade without any pressure to achieve. He settled in easily, enjoying the change of scene and not minding being part of such a diminished political force, because it was all new for him.

Then, suddenly, everything changed. After years of chaos following the referendum that had divided the country in two, a majority Conservative government looked set to hold power for a full parliamentary term. But the mass defections prompted by the Brexit food riots obliged a deeply distrusted prime minister to go back to the country, and the resulting election was the perfect storm of which third parties always dreamed. The wrangling Labour Party and the freshly loathed Tories were each wiped out, allowing the Alliance to come through the middle and form its own government, in coalition with the Scottish National Party (on condition another referendum on independence was held within three years), Plaid Cymru and the SDLP. Its leader, the folksy, teddy-bearish Morton Alexander, took office as Britain's first non-white prime minister.

The party's surprise triumph owed a good deal to the formidable media skills of a politician who had been a member of the European Parliament throughout the coalition years, and was therefore untainted by them. She was largely unknown except to the most committed political trainspotters. A single appearance on *Have I Got News For You* a few months before the election changed all that. Her elegant dismissal of an elderly actor with antediluvian views on race went viral, so much so that her put-down – 'Yeah, no, I really wouldn't' – became an instantly recognisable catchphrase. Her appearance was followed by a star turn on *Question Time*, and the country could not get enough of Marina Spencer.

With her shock of white, pixie-cut hair and her clear, unlined skin, she did not fit the identikit mould, and was a fluent and lucid performer. She had the gift of talking human, as the political cliché had it, and she did it while exuding good humour. While other politicians frowned and blustered, she always had a look of amused benevolence on her face, even when talking about the need to tackle the climate emergency or the wealth divide. This infectiously agreeable demeanour made it seem as if a brighter future really was possible, lifting the mood of a depressed nation. The Alliance's nationalist coalition partners struck a hard bargain, dividing the great offices of state among them as the new government took office, and Marina had to make do with secretary of state for culture. But it was widely understood that she personally would punch above that department's weight, particularly when it came to media profile. As the new government took office, the backroom staff from the previous coalition years flocked back from their corporate jobs and consultancies to take up posts in Downing Street, and Mark was disappointed to find there was no room for him there. Instead, in what he was assured was the highest compliment the party could bestow, he was dispatched to serve Marina.

Inevitably, there was a great deal more pressure. In the Alliance's wilderness years, his job had been a quest for attention, for an acknowledgement, however fleeting, that the party still existed. This was dispiriting at first, but once he understood that any such glimmer of interest would happen no more than twice a month, and that nobody in the party hierarchy expected anything more, he settled into a comfortable working routine.

In government, the situation could scarcely be more different. The pace was frenetic and the scrutiny constant, even in a 'soft' department like Culture. It was exciting, of course, to be at the centre of everything. This was what he had craved, in all his years of frustration. Making waves in Whitehall beat being big in Ulan Bator. The problem was Marina, a workaholic divorcee who showed no trace in private of the good humour she projected on television. Her bad temper was such a permanent feature that Mark could not at first fathom why he had ever imagined her to be infectiously cheerful. It took a week at her side, soaking up her stress, demands and frequent rages, before he realised the source of his confusion: the simple styling pencil that she carried in her make-up bag. By marking her eyebrows half a centimetre higher up her forehead than they naturally were, she gave herself an expression of permanent levity, whatever her actual mood.

This discovery would have been funny, had not laughter felt like an indulgence from a bygone existence. Marina Spencer was the most neurotic person he had ever met. Her anxiety focused primarily on her media appearances, which was unfortunate, since she was the government's star media performer. The fact that she always sailed through, that she could do no wrong in the eyes of the public and was therefore seen as untouchable by journalists, did nothing to calm her nerves. If anything, it made them worse. Every time she triumphed, she became all the more certain that she was heading for calamity the next time – like the terrified air traveller who thinks they have cheated the odds with every safe landing. Mark had a private theory that, somewhere in her childhood, she had been told pride always came before a fall, and she was now a permanent hostage to that dictum. All her staff were hostages to it too, for her way of dealing with anxiety was to carry out endless rehearsals before each appearance, demanding briefings on every conceivable subject. It fell mainly to Mark to prepare them. She would demand them at all hours of the day and most hours of the night, since she was also an insomniac and expected her staff to be the same. In public, she was a passionate champion of workers' rights, making an attractive case that collective wellbeing ought to be taken just as seriously as economic prosperity when assessing the health of society. In private, she was apt to berate her own staff for laziness if they sloped off before midnight. 'But Marina,' protested Mark, on one of the few occasions when he dared stand up to her. 'It *is* New

Year's Eve.'

He naively assumed he could share his frustrations with his two closest colleagues, who were at similar beck and call and exposed to all the same caprices. This was a mistake. To twenty-something Karim, slim, intense and precision hair-gelled, who had come back from Brussels with Marina, and Giles, a perma-vaping, thirty-five-year-old veteran of the old coalition, Mark's exploratory eye-roll of exasperation at her latest unreasonable demand was a sign of disloyalty. It branded him as Not On Marina's Side, the worst of all faults. Their fealty to their queen was ostentatious and absolute. Karim trotted half a pace behind her, clearing the unworthy from her path with a ferocious death-stare. Giles, with a hipster moustache that lavishly outgrew his beard, giving him the look of a ginger King George V, was more outwardly affable, but his smile had an unnerving tendency to vanish once his mistress was no longer there to see it. Between them, they froze Mark out, casting him back into a metaphorical Outer Mongolia, without the consolation of his soap fan base.

Karim and Giles were competitive with each other, engaging in constant one-upmanship over who took the fewest days' annual leave. They were all entitled to six weeks, but the pair of them both claimed to have taken three or four days, at most. Even then, Karim maintained he only took his because his grandmother died. They were also determined to expend the maximum possible effort in Marina's service, to show they were doing her bidding. Thus it was not enough for Mark to secure coverage in *The Guardian* for Marina's thoughts on national parks, television licensing or local arts funding. As far as they were concerned, when the story appeared, it had to be press-released.

'But…why?' said Mark, genuinely puzzled.

Karim and Giles looked at each other, puzzled that he should be puzzled.

'Er, so that journalists know about it?' said Karim.

Like any true millennial, he communicated in up-speak, but his was not a solicitous, are-you-with-me? upward inflection. In Karim's delivery, it had far more of an accusatory, how-can-you-not-know-that? edge.

'They know anyway,' said Mark. 'It's in *The Guardian*.'

'I'm talking about journalists who don't actually work for *The Guardian*?'

'Trust me, they'll see it. It's a journalist's job to read the papers. And honestly, in fifteen years working for the national media' – *inter*national, he might have said, never forgetting Ulan Bator – 'I've never seen a press release announcing that there's been a story in a newspaper.'

'Just do it, buddy,' said Giles, making it two against one. 'It's what Marina wants.'

That was always the killer line, the argument that brooked no dissent. Mark was forced to swallow what little was left of his pride and do their bidding.

Karim, by virtue of having worked for Marina the longest, behaved as if he was Mark's superior. Mark was wary of challenging this, because it would have meant appealing to Marina, and he had no confidence that she would take his side, even though his contract made it clear that he reported to her alone. When Karim decreed that Mark should attend a training course designed for newcomers to public relations, called 'How to Spot a News Story', he acquiesced for the sake of a quiet life, because it would at least mean a day away from the poisonous environment of the office. The trainer was an amiable ex red-top hack who treated Mark as a colleague rather than a student, mining him for anecdotes from his BBC career for the benefit of the genuine rookies on the course. 'What the hell are you actually doing here?' he asked discreetly, during a mid-morning break for coffee and biscuits.

'Don't ask,' said Mark, and the guy seemed to understand.

A few weeks later, Mark broke his leg when he tripped and fell down a wet flight of steps at Westminster tube station. He knew as soon as he landed that it was bad, and he lay in a bedraggled, painful heap for half an hour before an ambulance arrived to take him across the bridge to St Thomas's. Inwardly, he was rejoicing. The fracture would earn him a couple of weeks away from the hell-hole.

But bones heal, and now he was back, more ground down than ever by the snarking, finger-pointing and competitive presenteeism. He took refuge in long lunch breaks, even though he knew they reduced him further in his colleagues' esteem. Lunch hours were for clock-watchers who did dull jobs, for whom sneaking a read of a car magazine in WH Smith's or browsing the masonry screws in Robert Dyas were the highlight of the day. They were not for the gilded few who had the honour of walking the corridors of power, still less for the chosen ones who served Marina Spencer. But Mark did not care. For the sake of his sanity, that last honour was best enjoyed in doses of no more than three hours at a time, with a decent break in the middle.

Glancing at his watch, he saw that it was nearly two o'clock already, and he turned away from the MARKED PRICE sign to make his way back along Victoria Street. He was swiping his pass through the security gates at the Department of Culture when his phone rang.

'Ah!' said his mother.

This was her own personal shorthand for 'so you've

actually picked up for once', and it was true, he could be deliberately elusive. That did not make the greeting any less irritating.

'Sorry, I won't be able to talk. I've been out for a while already and I'm just about to get in the lift.'

'Can't you take the stairs for once so I can tell you this news? It's something very big and I wanted to tell you before it…'

'All right then, I'll take the stairs. You've got five floors to tell me.'

'It'll do you good.'

Pushing through the swing doors into the stairwell, he was surprised to see how many colleagues took this route, some of them leaping two steps at a time, like it was part of a workout regime. Who knew?

'Go on then.' He could hear himself panting into the mouthpiece before he had even reached the first floor. 'What's the big news?'

'It's Hannah.'

'Oh yes?'

Hannah was his cousin. They were not close, either in years or friendship. Mark had nothing against her – he had no strong feelings one way or the other – but his mother wanted them to make friends and was under the misapprehension that he would grow to like Hannah better the more he heard about her.

'You know I told you she's doing this dig?'

'Did you?'

'In the abbey at Bury. I remember distinctly telling you about it. Anyway, I know you're in a hurry, so the point is – they've found him!'

Sweating now, Mark stopped at the second landing.

'Found who?'

'Found who! Edmund, of course. *Saint* Edmund. I told you.'

He did vaguely remember, but he had never quite been sure who St Edmund was. Rather than ask, he had just let her run on.

'And where was he?'

'Under the tennis courts. Just where they were expecting.'

'How did he get there?'

'The monks must have hidden him there. It's very close to the ruins of the church itself.'

'Why did they do that?'

'Do what?'

'Hide him.'

'To keep him safe, I suppose, after the abbey was shut down. In the Reformation, you know. Fifteen-something. You'll know the details better than me, with your background.'

'You know that most of my degree was about imperialism and decolonisation, right? Not a lot of Tudors.'

'You must have done them at some stage. Anyway, that's how long he's been there. Nearly five hundred years.'

'And what does a five-hundred-year-old corpse look like?'

'He's more than five hundred years old, you clot. That's just how long he's been under the tennis courts. Well, the tennis courts haven't been there all that time, but you know what I mean. Before that, he was in a shrine in the abbey for five hundred years, so that makes a thousand, and I think he died quite a bit before that. In Saxon times. Are you sure you don't know all this? If you don't, you can look it up yourself. I'd have thought you might be googling it already.'

'I need my phone to google, and I'm using it to listen to you.'

'Well, you can do it when you reach your desk. It's a very exciting development. It'll be all over the news, when they announce it. They haven't done that yet, and I thought you'd like a...what's that horrible expression?'

'A heads-up?'

'Yes, probably.'

'Thank you. I appreciate that.'

'You working for the government, and all that.'

'What's that got to do with anything?'

'Well, he was England's patron saint, until we got St George.'

'Was he?'

'Didn't you know that either? Are you all right, by the way? You sound badly out of puff.'

He was on the fourth-floor landing now, and he was aware of wheezing into the phone. 'I'm fine. It's just that I usually take the lift.'

'From the sound of it, you should take the stairs more often.'

'It's not so long ago I broke my leg, remember.'

'Is it still giving you gyp?'

'Sometimes.' He had certainly become more cautious about exerting himself. 'Look, I'm nearly there, so I've got to go, OK? But thanks for letting me know. It's a very impressive heads-up.'

'I thought so too. Quite a turn-up, for your old mum to know what's going to be on the news before you do, eh?'

'It may only make the local news.'

'No, Hannah says they're getting ready for a big press conference. All the big ones are there – BBC, ITN, Channel 4 News...'

'Fair enough, I believe you.' He had reached his own floor

now. 'I really have got to go. Thanks for ringing. And yes, I'll look him up. St Edmund. Got it. Bye now. Bye…yep, and you…bye…'

He swiped through his messaging apps as he made his way to his desk. There was an alarming stack of new emails, plus texts from Karim, Giles and Marina herself. And now here was Karim, ambushing him before he could reach his desk. His eyes were bright with adrenaline, as if he had been mainlining whatever drama was under way. 'Where were you? Marina's been looking for you. We all have.'

He would not rise to it. 'I'm here now. What's the crisis?'

'She needs eye-catching ideas. Every department needs to come up with five before cabinet.' Karim clearly considered the situation so grave that his voice was not even going up at the end of the sentence.

'Before cabinet? That's not till tomorrow morning. Why the big panic?'

Karim's nostrils flared and his eyes rolled, as normal, upwards-inflected service resumed. 'Because they need thoroughly thinking through? Like, war-gamed, before she can take them to the actual prime minister?'

'War-gamed?' Mark did not bother to hide his smirk.

'Do you really want to send Marina naked into a hostile cabinet, with everyone just waiting for the chance to stab her in the back?'

'I think she'll be wearing clothes. We can all agree on that. There may even be rules about it.'

Karim had his mouth open to reply when the door to Marina's office flew open. Mark could hear her before he could see her. 'So where in Christ's name is he? And don't tell me "at lunch". He isn't paid to be at blasted… Oh, there you are, Mark. At last. Eye-catching ideas! Got it? Christ, I'm going to go naked into that cabinet tomorrow, with everyone just waiting for their chance to stab me in the back.'

Anyone else would be embarrassed to find that the person they were loudly bad-mouthing was in earshot, but that was not how Marina worked. She folded her arms, waiting. Karim mirrored her stance.

It was perhaps not the time to ask why Karim could not come up any eye-catching ideas himself. Instead, Mark said: 'How about a new patron saint for the whole of the UK? Bringing all four nations together, after the trauma of the past few years?'

Marina's artificially elevated eyebrows rose a fraction. 'A new patron saint? Who?'

Until the moment he opened his mouth, Mark had no idea he was going to make this suggestion. As ideas went, it was not so much half-baked as still in the mixing bowl before he had turned the oven on. However, it was entertaining to see Karim swap his look of perma-scorn for grudging attention. 'St Edmund. They've just found him under the tennis courts next to the ruins of Bury St Edmunds abbey.'

'Why haven't I been told about this?' demanded Marina, wheeling on Karim. 'It's heritage. I should have been told.'

Even if nothing came of the idea, it would be worth it for that moment alone. Stuttering, Karim plucked his phone out of his pocket and started stabbing at it, as if it might help him defer the blame.

Mark came to his rescue, enjoying the chance to be magnanimous. 'They haven't announced it yet. I've only just heard it from my, er, contact on the dig. I was talking to them while I was out. Obviously, you know that St Edmund used to be the patron saint of England until he was replaced by St George?'

'Obviously,' said Marina, and Karim nodded briskly. Neither of them had any idea.

'And he's been hidden for five hundred years, so it's an occasion for national celebration, and not just for England...'

'...but for Wales, Scotland and Northern Ireland too,' said Marina. 'Yes, I can see where you're going. A unifying figure could be just what we need, especially with another Scottish independence referendum on the cards. But is there any kind of connection? I mean, wasn't he English? Why should the Scots care about him?'

This was a fair point, and one that Mark himself might have anticipated if he had considered the matter for two seconds, rather than just the fraction of one.

'Of course we'll need to build the case. Leave that with me,' he said. He added a silent prayer to St Wikipedia that he could find some adequate connection.

'Good. Prepare me a briefing. And copy it to Karim and Giles, naturally.'

'Naturally.'

'I'll need that in an hour.' She gave him a nod, the closest he had ever seen her come to gratitude, and turned on her heel. Karim trotted after her, leaning his head in to receive her private thoughts, even though she was not actually speaking.

Mark dropped into his chair, pushed it back from his desk and closed his eyes. His immediate emotion was relief at having escaped from a tight corner, but nagging worry was not far behind it.

What the hell had he done?

Gōdne morᵹen. Gōde ofernōn. Gōdne æfen.

That is my greeting in the old tongue. Depending on the time of day, of course.

I am croaking, I know. I sound weak and reedy to my own ears, a feeble shadow of what once I was. A voice forgets how to function, after centuries out of use. But this is mine, such as it is, for those who can hear it.

Most cannot, I know. Only a select few could know my words when last I was in this place and now, after so much time gone by, their number is even fewer. Even so, I use it to make my presence known. To introduce myself, no more, no less, and then go quiet again. My part in this tale is small now. It becomes much larger later.

I want only to state at this early point that I am not proud of my role in what is to come. All I can say in my defence is that it is not a simple thing to reconnect with this mortal world above the ground after being so long neglected and forgotten below it.

If that sounds like a whining plea for indulgence, it is not meant that way. Rather, it is an explanation. It does not mean I have no remorse over what happened, for I do, in great measure. I ask merely for some understanding of what it means to be lost to the world for half a thousand years and then of a sudden to be found again.

That is all for now. I have spoken enough.

Although Hannah hardly knew her cousin, she knew a great deal about him. Or she had heard a great deal about him, which was not, perhaps, the same.

She had never known her own father, not even his name. Having an unmarried mother was a big deal in the mid-Sixties, before the Summer of Love had even happened, let alone reached Chelmsford, and she spent her earliest years living with her grandparents. Her mother's younger sister Pauline, in her early teens when Hannah was born, was more like a big sister than an aunt.

Then her mother got her social-work qualification, and she and Hannah went off to live in Ipswich. Hannah grew up, went to college, became a teacher and eventually settled into a nineteen-year relationship with a colleague from her first school, which creaked to a just-about-amicable halt when they discovered that neither of them much wanted to celebrate their twentieth anniversary. The end of that chapter coincided with her mother's illness. Hannah took redundancy, which was effectively very early retirement, to be able to nurse her mother through the cancer, until the burden became too heavy and the local hospice stepped in. When it was all over, she inherited a three-legged cat called Arnold as well as the mustard-washed, oak-beamed cottage in the highest village in the county – a giddy four hundred feet above sea level – where her mother had spent her final years.

In those last, dreadful weeks, after which her mother's death came as a merciful release, she and Pauline, who had married an accountant from Swansea but had been divorced since Mark was in his teens, became close once more. Six years on, this bond endured. Having each other in their lives brought them solace: it was a way of keeping Hannah's mother's memory alive, even if they mentioned her less often these days.

Hannah always asked after Mark, which meant she heard all about his frustrations at the World Service, his bold decision to throw in his lot with the unpopular Alliance, and the extraordinary way in which that gamble had paid off, propelling him to a position of genuine power and influence in Whitehall. Pauline was as proud as could be, and rightly so.

Despite that detailed grasp of his career history, Hannah had no real idea what her cousin was actually like. Pauline did not have much to say about Mark's personal life, because he did not tell her. Neither did he often visit, even though his mother was only half an hour from Liverpool Street. Hannah took this as a sign that he was probably gay. She was as proud of her important cousin as his mother was. She searched the screen whenever Marina Spencer was on the news, hoping to see Mark at her side – although it was so long since she had seen him in person, she was not sure that she would recognise him. That was the limit of it, and they had no direct contact.

She certainly did not expect him to call – from his office in Whitehall, no less.

When her phone rang she was having a breather from the dig, perched on a block of flint rubble that had once been a corner of the infirmary hall and which now sprouted little clumps of wild red saxifrage. Her screen showed an unfamiliar mobile number.

'It's Mark,' he said, and she spent a panic-stricken moment scrolling through a mental list of possible Marks, which this clearly was not, before he clarified, 'Cousin Mark.'

'Mark!' she cried, relieved not to have asked, 'Mark who?' Then she panicked once more. It must be Pauline. Why else would he call? Heart pounding, she made an effort to act casual. 'How are you? I hear such great things of you. How are the corridors of power?'

'Covered in really nasty carpet tiles. The one I'm in at the moment is, at any rate. And coffee stains.'

'That sounds reassuringly normal.'

'I wouldn't go so far as to say "normal". Nothing is really that, around here.'

'Oh well. I don't suppose it's dull, that's the main thing.' She was waiting for him to get to the point, while at the same time dreading it, in case something really had happened to…

'Anyway, the reason I'm calling out of the blue…'

'Yes?'

'It's about your discovery this morning.'

Wow, so not Pauline. 'Really? Your mum has already told you, then.' She had called Pauline at the first opportunity, knowing how pleased her aunt would be to hear of their great find before it was officially announced, and also because she really wanted to call her own mother, and calling Pauline was the next-best thing.

'Yes, she called me just now. Amazing news. Congratulations to the whole team. How's the atmosphere there? You must all be very excited.'

'We're still digging away, so we're achy and sweaty, but yes, pretty pleased. Are you interested in archaeology? I didn't realise.'

'Not as such. Just in this particular dig. It's not every day we find a lost patron saint, is it?'

Where was he going with this? While he was clearly making an effort to sound chatty, there was a definite businesslike air to his questions. Surely this was not an official call?

'How certain are you that it's really him?' he continued.

'How certain am I?'

'Well, you and your colleagues.'

'They're not really my colleagues. They're proper archaeologists and I'm just along for the ride. So you'd really have to ask them.'

'Yes but… I mean…do you know how strong the evidence is?'

He sounded agitated. Not that she knew what he normally sounded like. Perhaps he always asked questions in an edgy, badgering manner and that was just the way of things, in his world. 'I think all that will be announced later, by people who know much more about it than I do.'

'Yes but… Sorry, I know this may sound strange, my just calling you out of the blue. But I kind of need to know *before* the announcement.'

He was right; it did sound strange. 'Can I ask why?'

'It's because Marina's very interested. You know, Marina Spencer, the culture secretary. I work for her.'

Hannah laughed. 'Mark, I know who you work for. Your mum and I do actually talk quite a lot.'

'Yes, of course. Sorry.'

She took pity on him. Besides, it was not every day that she was grilled for information on behalf of a cabinet minister. 'Look, here's what I know. St Edmund was a king of the East Angles who was killed by an invading Viking army in the ninth century after he told them he would only submit if they converted to Christianity. His head went missing for a bit. Then it was found again, in circumstances which were either prosaic or miraculous, depending on how willing you are to believe the legend. His body eventually ended up in the abbey of the town they named after him. Here it stayed, in its own shrine, for five hundred years, until Henry VIII closed the monasteries, when it disappeared.'

'So it could have been removed?'

'It was more likely hidden, to stop Henry's enforcers getting their hands on the relics. The whole shrine disappeared, as well as the body. Because the container was so heavy, the historians' best guess was that it would have been buried as close as possible to the abbey itself. Lo and behold, that's precisely where we've found it. At least, we think we have. The casing corresponds to the pictorial records of the shrine, so that's what they're going on for the moment.'

'What about DNA evidence? Will you be able to prove it's really Edmund?'

'No, that's part of the difficulty. With DNA, you need a definite family member for the comparison, and that's never going to happen in this case. The records are virtually non-existent – they were called the Dark Ages for a good reason – and we don't even know for sure who Edmund's father was. Edmund also died unmarried, apparently a virgin, so there wouldn't be a direct line of descent. Aside from all that, even if he did have descendants, he was so many generations back that it would be very hard to pinpoint him for certain.'

'So that's good, right? It means the find can't be disproved by DNA.'

'That's one way of looking at it. It depends what you want to get out of the discovery. So come on, tell me: what does Marina Spencer want with St Edmund?'

The silence at the other end was so long, she thought she had been cut off. 'Hello?'

'I'm still here. Look, you have to understand I'm in a bit of a, er, pressured environment. Marina wants an eye-catching policy, and she wants it yesterday. As you probably know, the Department of Culture has responsibility for national heritage, so it made sense to flag up to her the discovery of a long-lost patron saint. He was the patron saint, wasn't he? I haven't got that wrong?'

'Technically I think he still is. He went out of fashion under Edward the Somethingth – the Third, I think – who decided he preferred St George. But I don't think Edmund was actually sacked. Just quietly abandoned.'

'That's good to know.'

'Does Marina Spencer really want to revive St Edmund as the patron saint of England? That's not a cause I'd associate with the Alliance. It usually goes down best with people who think St George was too foreign and who would rather have a true-blue Englishman. Aren't the Alliance all about touchy-feely cultural diversity?'

'I'm not sure we'd put it like that, but yes we are, and I get that concern, absolutely. That's the other thing I wanted to ask you about. The idea is to adopt Edmund as the patron saint of all four countries, something that can bring us all together, as the union faces more and more pressures pulling it apart.'

'I see. And do you think Edmund will bring them together?'

'I've told Marina he will.'

'And it's not too late for her to drop the idea?'

'Why do you say that?' There was fear in his voice, and Hannah felt bad for not showing more enthusiasm. On the other hand, it sounded a thoroughly daft proposal. 'It's just that, from what I know of the Scots, they may not take kindly to venerating an English king.'

'I understand where you're coming from. But St Andrew wasn't exactly from the Gorbals. I just looked him up: born in Galilee, died in Greece. Besides, we're not asking them to renounce St Andrew, just to accept Edmund for the United Kingdom.'

'I suspect being born in Galilee and dying in Greece makes him more palatable north of the border than being born and bred English.'

'Ah, but was he? That's what I wanted to explore with you. How much do we really know? Isn't there a suggestion that Edmund may have been born in Germany?'

'I honestly don't know, Mark. I'm just a grunt with a trowel. You'll have to ask a proper historian.'

'No time for that.' He sounded more agitated than ever. 'Sorry, I know I'm putting you on the spot. It's just that things are quite intense here. It's hard to describe if you haven't experienced it. When Marina wants you to make a case for something…'

'You have to make the case. I can see it must be difficult. Look, as far as I understand it, the life of St Edmund is a bit of a blank canvas, which has given people in the past a certain licence to do their own colouring in. I imagine it's all about how you sell the idea. From what I've seen of your Marina, she's very persuasive. I'm sorry, I didn't mean to sound negative just now. I'm sure everyone on this dig will be overjoyed that our find is being taken so seriously, and at such a high level. Think it through, that's all I'm saying, because you don't want a backlash. You can always come and see the dig for yourself, if you like. You're more than welcome to use my spare room.'

'Yeah, thanks, that's kind of you. It's just... It's more urgent than... Sorry, I'm going to have go in a minute. Oh, Hannah? One other thing. What time is your announcement this afternoon?'

'I think I heard someone say five o'clock, in time for the early evening news. But don't quote...'

'Five? That's great. I really have got to go. Thanks a lot, Hannah. Bye.'

Before she could even say goodbye, he was gone. She blinked at the blank screen of her phone for a moment. Being pumped for background information on any new government initiative was a novelty for her, let alone a plan to announce a new patron saint. The adrenaline rush surprised and embarrassed her. So this was the attraction of Mark's world: the self-congratulatory buzz of being on the inside track. She wondered if she should share the news with the rest of the dig. Best not, she reflected. It might backfire on her. By rights, she ought to have been more discreet.

In any case, it was time to get back to work. She got down from her block of rubble and tucked her phone into the shapeless canvas shoulder bag that she hauled everywhere with her. Edmund as patron saint of the battered, bruised, far-from-United Kingdom? She hoped her cousin knew what he was doing, as she lowered herself back into her ditch and picked up her trowel.

Although his memory of ordinary, pre-Marina life faded further every day, Mark was still aware that most people considered it rude to end a phone conversation without giving them a chance to say goodbye.

Such civilian etiquette was, however, an impossible indulgence in the world he now inhabited, where crisis – real or imagined – was a way of life. And these crises, real or imagined, were always of world-shaping importance. Since Marina, in the eyes of her party and her voters, was Virtue Incarnate and had been granted an unexpected opportunity to Do Good in this finite period, every second of her time was precious. Every instant that Mark wasted on the phone, when she wanted to speak to him, risked handing victory to the enemies of Virtue. She did not need to call his name or waste valuable energy on a wave of the hand to let him know his presence was required. A glance in his direction, her eyebrows hefted even higher than usual in surprise that he was not in attendance, more than sufficed.

Having summoned him in this manner while he was speaking to Hannah, she returned to her own inner sanctum. He put his head around the door to find Karim sitting across the desk from her, nodding vigorously at whatever she was saying.

Mark coughed. 'Did you need me?'

She looked up and frowned, as if the very idea were preposterous. Then she seemed to remember. 'No, Karim's on it now.'

Even after all these months, Mark entertained the hope that, just once, she would treat him with ordinary civility. In this instance, she might say, 'Sorry to have troubled you, Mark, but thanks anyway.' He lingered in the doorway, willing her to say it. But she had already resumed her conference with Karim – 'It's essential that we're completely across the resource implications from the get-go' – and he had no option but to back out.

It was irritating to be ignored, but it did at least give him the chance to focus on the difficulty at hand. Returning to his desk, he dropped into his chair and hunched over his phone, which was always a better way of pursuing a discreet project than displaying it to the rest of the open-plan office on his desktop.

King Edmund, he now read, was thought to have been born in the year 841. If English history officially began with the Norman Conquest, this was more than two centuries before that. Mark was vaguely familiar with the names of some kings before 1066 – Harold, Edward the Confessor, Canute, Ethelred the Unready – but they were all Saxons. Edmund was an Angle, one of the people who migrated from the neck of land between Germany and Denmark in the fifth century and established various settlements in England, including the kingdom of East Anglia. He was crowned king of this small realm on Christmas Day 854, at the age of fourteen. This followed the death of the old king, Ethelweard, who was therefore assumed to have been his father. However, there was a rival claim in the history books that Edmund was really the son of a German king, Alkmond of Saxony, and his wife Siware. This first emerged in a biography written in the twelfth century, three hundred years after the event, so it could be taken with a pinch of salt and it was certainly no use to Mark: claiming that Edmund was really German might be helpful if he was trying to reinforce the legitimacy of the House of Windsor, but it would not convince the Celtic nations that Edmund was a good choice as patron saint.

According to another account, Edmund's dynasty was descended from the god Woden, originally hailing from Sweden before it settled on the Suffolk coast at Woodbridge. Again, it was not much use to Mark. He needed to show that Edmund was partly Scottish, Welsh or Irish, not Scandinavian.

This was not going well.

If there was nothing plausibly Celtic in Edmund's biography, perhaps the solution was to go negative on the existing patron saints. Marina would hate it, because she disliked negativity – in her public persona, at any rate – but, in the absence of any better ideas, he was not sure he had much choice.

St Andrew, the Galilean Jew who was martyred in Greece, was a well-travelled apostle: he was said to have preached the gospel around the Black Sea and as far north as Kiev, as well as being shipwrecked in Cyprus, but no myth-maker, however fancifully inclined, had ever put him in Scotland. The most the Scots could claim was ownership of his relics, which were brought to the Scottish village of Kilrymont in the early fourth century. It was not the whole body – just an arm, a kneecap, three fingers and a tooth – but that was enough to impress the locals. They built a church to house the relics and changed the name of their settlement to St Andrews.

It was only in later centuries that the Galilean began to earn his keep. In the year 832, not long before the birth of Edmund, a Pictish king called Oengus II prayed to St Andrew for assistance on the eve of a battle against the Angles. The next morning, white clouds formed the shape of an X in the blue sky and Oengus' badly outnumbered forces triumphed over the enemy. St Andrew was venerated from then on as Scotland's patron saint.

Mark sighed. Again, not good. Perhaps St David would be easier to discredit.

Two minutes of searching made it clear this was an equally forlorn hope. A good deal was known about St David, and all of it involved Wales. Like St Andrew, he had a town named after him, but not just in honour of a few bones of dubious provenance: St David spent his entire, long life in the place that came to bear his name. His mother was the daughter of a Pembrokeshire nobleman, and she was also a saint in her own right, so the guy was not just a Welsh-born saint, he was also the son of a Welsh-born saint. St David's Cathedral was built on the site of the monastery he founded, and his bones were eventually buried in it – not just a patella and the odd molar, but every last vertebra, rib and metatarsal. True, these remains had since been carbon-dated to the twelfth century, so all was not quite as perfect as it seemed, and St David's best-known miracle, creating a hill on the ground he was preaching on, could hardly be said to fulfil any great need, in a country with no shortage of high ground. Nevertheless, these were serious credentials.

He called up St Patrick's biography but gave it only a desultory read, sensing already that this was a fruitless line of attack. On the upside, Patrick was actually English, or perhaps Welsh – a Romano-British aristocrat, anyway – and he only ended up in Ireland after being captured by pirates and put to work as a slave. He eventually escaped and got home to Britain, and then moved to France, but his heart was clearly in Ireland, because he returned as a missionary, bringing Christianity to the country and becoming Primate of Ireland. Unless you wished Ireland had stayed pagan, Patrick was clearly the business. That was quite apart from his even more enduring legacy, namely the custom of drinking gargantuan, religiously sanctioned amounts of alcohol on March the seventeenth. Against that kind of competition, Edmund did not have a chance.

Mark closed his eyes and massaged his temples with the hand that was not holding his phone. He pushed out of his mind the dread thought that Hannah was right and any attempt to foist an English patron saint on the Scots, the Welsh and the Northern Irish was sure to lead to a bitter backlash. Instead he focused solely on his breathing, a technique he had learned in a brief flirtation with meditation. It was designed to be soothing at stressful times like this. In and out, in and out. Nothing else mattered or existed...

'Mark!'

His whole body twitched as he was jolted from his trance. He opened his eyes and the fingers of his right hand at the same time, dropping his phone. He bent to retrieve it before turning to face Karim, who was looking down at him with unconcealed disdain.

'Sorry, Mark. Didn't mean to wake you.' In another

place, from any other colleague, that might have constituted friendly banter. From Karim, it was undiluted poison.

'Can I help you with something, Karim?'

'Message from Marina? She's very keen on the Edmund idea and she wants to make it work, but it's got to be across the whole UK and she'll need a briefing paper from you so that she can convince the PM, not to mention all the Nats in cabinet. All the facts to make the case? Before you go home tonight.'

While he was talking, Mark turned back to his desktop. If he was to be given orders by a twenty-eight-year-old pipsqueak, he could at least retain a morsel of dignity by refusing to look him in the eye. 'Right,' he muttered. 'No problem.'

Ordinarily, it would bother him that Marina had called in Karim to discuss his idea. He might end up in an angry internal debate as to whether it was a deliberate snub or just thoughtlessly rude. He could easily spend the rest of the afternoon fretting about how to assert himself and make it clear that even he had his limits. Now, though, there were more important matters to worry about, such as the set of facts that Marina was waiting for, which clearly did not exist. Should he confess, while there was still time, that he had been too hasty, and there was no case to be made for St Edmund as patron of the whole United Kingdom? He pictured for a moment what that might be like. All he could see were his colleagues' faces: Karim sneering, and Giles shaking his head in disappointment. It would confirm their every prejudice about him: that he was out of his depth, a liability, not cut out for the role. No, it was unthinkable. He would have to give Marina the facts she wanted. Failure was not an option.

He glanced over his shoulder to check that Karim had gone, and looked at his watch. He knew now what he must do. What was it that Hannah had said? *You just have to make the case. The life of St Edmund is a bit of a blank canvas, which has given people licence to do their own colouring in.* Exactly so. All he needed was a box of crayons.

Hannah said the announcement of the discovery was due at around five o'clock. It was now ten to three, which meant he had a couple of hours, maximum, to get some facts of his own into play. That should be enough. It was oddly perfect, in fact. The scheme taking shape in his mind would only work within a very narrow window of opportunity. While he needed a certain amount of time to do what had to be done, too much would increase the risk of someone else undoing it. Two hours was about right. It was serendipity.

So, to business: what were the facts to be? This would take a degree of artistry, as well as imagination. Fortunately, the bar for deception was not high, because who knew anything about ninth-century history? All he had to do was make the information look plausible to the intelligent layperson. Even that was overstating it. If all went to plan, he simply needed to convince whichever ill-paid and harassed trainee was cutting and pasting from the internet on this particular shift. Most of them would not know the ninth century from the nineteenth.

Essentially, he needed three inventions. No, that was too crude a word. Three splashes of colour, that was better; one for each of the countries as yet unmentioned in Edmund's official biography.

Scotland first, because it was the biggest of the three, and the Scots were the most likely to kick off at having an English saint foisted on them. They needed something juicy.

He contemplated the options: it should be marriage or blood. Since Edmund was supposed to have been unmarried, it would have to be blood, and the best place to put that blood was obvious: he must have a Scottish mother. Any opponent of his cause would need a heart of stone not to respond to such a connection. Mark swiped back to Wikipedia. A putative mother, Siware, was mentioned, if Edmund was the son of Alkmond of Saxony. In the more likely option, that he was the son of the previous king, Ethelweard, no mother was named. Here, then, was the opportunity. King Ethelweard of the Angles deserved an aristocratic bride. Why not the daughter of the King of the Picts? It sounded like a fitting match. Could Mark find a list of Pictish sovereigns of the ninth century? Of course he could, courtesy of the ever-obliging St Wiki. He ran his eye down the column of names and dates. The most appropriate monarch, living at the right time, seemed to be a King Uurad. What an extraordinary resource this site was. He felt a stab of guilt as he contemplated what he was about to do to it. Then he reminded himself of the wrath of Marina Spencer. He had no choice. He would salve his conscience by making a donation some time.

He switched to his desktop, navigating to the same page, but this time logging in as an editor. He had done this a few times before, in more innocent circumstances, and the site let him in without asking for his password. That felt like another piece of serendipity. From there, the job was simple enough. In the sentence on Edmund's page which referred to Ethelweard, Mark added '*and his wife Blah-Blah-Blah*' – he would decide her name in a moment – '*daughter of [[Uurad]], king of the [[Picts]]*'. Those square brackets would link automatically to King Uurad's own page, where any curious amateur researcher would learn he reigned over the Picts from around 839 to his death in 842. It was a short tenure, but long enough to betroth the fair Blah-Blah-Blah to the noble king Ethelweard. Yes, that would work nicely.

It was all so plausible that Mark felt a twinge of guilt at dispatching poor Blah-Blah-Blah, who he decided should be no more than sixteen or seventeen, to marry a man she had never met in a faraway kingdom. At least she would enjoy a more comfortable life in the richer south, and the weather would be better.

Cheered by that thought, he took a moment to investigate Uurad's recorded family. He had four known sons, but no daughters were mentioned. There were bound to have been some. He just had to choose a name. Was there a list of Pictish women's names anywhere? How could he doubt it? A couple more clicks, and he was scanning a list of possibilities. Coblath, Darlugdach, Domelch, Nadbroicc… They all looked a bit frightening; the least he could do was give Edmund a pronounceable mother. Brigid, that was better, although perhaps a little obvious. Ebbe? Maybe. Ethne? Yes indeed! Ethne and Ethelweard; Ethelweard and Ethne… They sat on the page and tripped off the tongue like a couple destined to be together.

The entry looked perfect when he checked it in preview, and he was conscious that time was getting on. He was about to click on the button that would publish his amendments for anyone to see, when something held him back. Attention to detail, he told himself: that was what counted in these cases. There ought to be a source for this marriage. A book would do it: something written long enough ago that it would be hard to establish for certain that it did not exist. He thought for a moment, then keyed in:

'<ref>{{cite   book|last=McAdoo|first=Elspeth|title= Women   in   the   Pictish   Royal   Houses|date=1988| publisher=Glasgow University Press}}</ref>'

As he switched back to preview, the code arranged itself into legible text, and his new entry was now neatly footnoted with the reference 'McAdoo, Elspeth, *Women in the Pictish Royal Houses*, Glasgow University Press (1988)'. Mark imagined for a moment how grateful the fictitious Professor McAdoo would be to see her thirty-year-old work acknowledged in the twenty-first century, bringing long-overdue recognition to the role of Pictish women in Scottish Dark Ages history.

One last touch was necessary in order to do full justice to her work. Having hit 'publish' so the Edmund page was now live, he called up the page dedicated to King Uurad. It consisted of a few scant paragraphs. In the second one, which detailed the known facts of Uurad's family life, he inserted the line:

'His daughter Ethne married [[Ethelweard]], king of the Angles, and she is reputed to have been the mother of [[Edmund the Martyr]].'

He referenced it back, naturally, to Prof McAdoo. All that was left to do was hit 'publish' on this page too and then sit back and marvel at his own brilliance.

There was no room for complacency, though. Wales and Northern Ireland still called, and time was ticking on. What embellishments could he dream up to cover those bases?

It was a shame he could not marry Edmund off. He would have liked nothing better than to give him a Welsh queen. The idea was a non-starter, though, because it departed too obviously from the virginity myth. What other kinds of connection were there? Another sort of union, perhaps... such as a peace accord. Were the Angles and the Welsh ever at war? It did not seem far-fetched, given that the Picts and the

Angles had fought each other at the battle where St Andrew saved the day for the Scots. What if, forswearing further conflict between the two blameless populations, wise King Edmund had sought a treaty with his Welsh counterpart? Yes indeed, that was clever, because it would show Edmund as the pioneer of the very political union he was now meant to represent in the modern day! All Mark had to do was find out who the King of Wales was at the time... Unfortunately, a couple of minutes' checking revealed that no such monarch existed, because Wales was divided into several independent kingdoms until its conquest by the English in the thirteenth century. Powys and Gwent were the closest geographically to East Anglia, and less linguistically daunting than the ancient kingdoms of Deheubarth and Seisyllwg; thanks to his own half-Welsh heritage, Mark could just about get his tongue around those two names, but he could not imagine Marina doing so.

In next to no time, Edmund had signed two treaties, with Rhodri Mawr of Powys and Meurig ap Arthfael Hen of Gwent – both genuine historical figures. The source was cited as Dr Llewelyn Rhys-Williams' scholarly sounding *The Hand of Friendship: Welsh–English Relations in pre-Norman Britain*, published in 1931, which was not so genuine.

All that remained was Ireland.

This was harder, as his options were dwindling. He had already done a family connection and a political alliance. Repeating either would look suspicious. What else was there?

He ran his eye rapidly over the life of St Edmund once more, followed by that of St Patrick, in search of inspiration, but none came. He checked his watch: an hour until they made the announcement. He knew from experience as a journalist that an hour could drain away horribly quickly, particularly if he carried on flailing around like this. He forced himself to concentrate. Could Edmund ever have visited Ireland? The rulers of these tribal kingdoms did travel, but Ireland seemed a long way, particularly when Edmund's little kingdom of East Anglia was hemmed in by the bloodthirsty Danes who controlled all the territory up the middle of the country from Cambridge to York. Could he have had some long-distance interest in Ireland? It should not be political: that sounded too much like the Welsh embellishment. If not that, then... religious? Yes, of course! Why had he not thought of it before? King Edmund's piety was crucial to his martyrdom story and to his sainthood. Might he not have heard about and admired St Patrick's missionary work in Ireland four hundred years earlier?

It was plausible and completely in character. All Mark had to do was identify some evidence of this Hibernian homage. This time, it would be nice if it really existed, so he could point to an authentic source without having to create another fictitious academic. He sped through Edmund's biography for a third time, convinced that something would suggest itself now he knew what he was looking for. Again, he reached the end of the text without inspiration. Panic was seeping in now, lapping quietly but steadily at his confidence. It would be his undoing if he let it get the better of him. He tried his deep-breathing trick again. As he did so, he noticed the main illustration on Edmund's Wikipedia page, to which he had paid no attention so far. It was part of a medieval painting showing three bearded figures, each with a halo to show they were saints, and two of them wearing crowns, against an intricately patterned background in gold leaf. One of the bearded figures held a lamb, the second a ring, and the third an arrow with red tail fins. In front of them knelt a smooth-cheeked young man with pink lips and a pointed nose, wearing an elaborate golden robe and a crown of his own, but it was the third saint, the one with the arrow, who mattered. More importantly, the cloak he was wearing. Mark clicked on the image to magnify it. Oh yes! Now the panic ebbed completely away, for there was his inspiration. The cloak was lined with ermine, much of which was on show as it hung draped over the wearer's right shoulder. On the left-hand side, however, its velvet exterior was plain to see. It was a rich pea-green, providing a verdant splash in an image otherwise dominated by gold, brown and blue. It immediately drew the eye. How could it not be significant?

Switching to 'edit' mode, he wrote a couple of sentences which he then sourced back to the jpeg he had been viewing. He switched to 'preview' in order to scan his new text for errors, corrected the wording to improve the flow, previewed it again, then hit 'publish'.

The entry now read:

Edmund was a recorded admirer of his fellow saint from the British Isles, St Patrick. There is a clear visual allusion to this veneration in the best-known artistic image of Edmund, the National Gallery's Wilton Diptych, in which the East Anglian king, imagined at the coronation of King Richard II alongside his fellow saints Edward the Confessor and John the Baptist, is depicted in a cloak of Irish emerald green.

It was remarkable how authoritative it looked once it was live. Mark could almost swallow the claim himself. And all with a full half-hour in hand.

He glanced up and saw Karim in the doorway of Marina's

office, frowning in his direction. He was sure neither of them had any faith that he would deliver the package of water-tight political arguments they had demanded. For the moment, Mark had no intention of disabusing them: let Karim stew in his own bitter cauldron of neuroticism and mistrust. All Mark had to do was wait.

Conscious of his tormentor's eyes following him, he stood up, yawned in his most nonchalant fashion and sauntered into the lobby, where he helped himself to a watery cup of government-issue coffee from the drinks machine. Through the grimy window opposite, he could see the north face of Big Ben, showing five to five. He had grown to loathe this view of the clock. Working within sight of it was like being born with earshot of Bow bells for a proper Cockney: it was proof of residence of the Westminster village, and it generally reminded him how misguided his ambition had been, to seek to belong in this vicious, backbiting bubble. Today, however, the sight made him smile. He was engaged in a deception that could yet ruin his career if he failed to make it work but, for now, he was ahead of the game. More importantly, he had bested Karim. At least, he had confounded the latter's expectations of him, which amounted to the same thing. He scrunched his empty cup and pitched it at the swing-bin marked 'paper and plastics'. Its momentum had just enough force to knock the swing mechanism open, and the cup dropped neatly into the plastic sack below. That never happened. This was beginning to pass for an excellent day at the office.

Back at his desk, he started work on the document Marina had asked for, beginning with a brief summary of the day's events, followed by a short biography of St Edmund, a couple of paragraphs on his adoption and later abandonment as patron saint of England, then a bulleted section laying out the case for his revival not just as England's canonical champion, but as a new, unifying figure for all four nations with his English birth (thereby trumping St George), his Scottish lineage (ditto St Andrew) and his powerful Welsh and Irish sympathies.

Marina was far too suspicious by nature to go into cabinet with a case based entirely on Mark's own say-so, so it would need referencing. He added a couple of names of genuine biographers: there were several books and articles by someone called B.L.R. Bellamy (O.S.B.), plus a couple of other authors with less prolific contributions to Edmundian scholarship. To this authentic list he could now add Professor McAdoo and Dr Rhys-Williams. Those references were imperfect, however. Neither of their imaginary books had a proper ISBN number, which might alert a vigilant editor on the site to Mark's dodgy activity. If that vigilant editor put a red flag on the entry, it would telegraph his mischief to any half-critical reader checking Edmund's entry, and the game would be up. With any luck, however, he would soon have some better sources to cite. If it came off, that was where his plan became a work of art.

He had deliberately kept away from any kind of news media while drafting Maria's document, but it was nearly seven o'clock and there was no point in putting it off any longer. It was crunch-time, and he suddenly felt sick with nerves. What if, for some reason, the announcement had not been made or, worse, it had fallen flat, failing to get any media traction?

He clicked on the tab of his browser that sent him directly to Twitter, his go-to destination for breaking news. He brightened immediately to see that St Edmund was trending.

He scrolled quickly through the posts, looking for links to news stories. The BBC seemed to have been first off the blocks, with plenty of shares to dominate the traffic. There were also stories in the online editions of the *Telegraph*, the *Mail* and *The Guardian*. Opening a new tab, he did a quick Google search on news stories featuring St Edmund, just to check there were no others. Sure enough, those same four links appeared at the top of his results; everything else, including a report of the impending dig in the *East Anglian Daily Times*, predated today's announcement.

First he looked at the *Mail*. In characteristic fashion, the site had given the report a verbose, five-deck headline – *Remains of Edmund the Martyr, king and saint, found under the tennis courts of the abbey of the town named in his honour after being lost for nearly five hundred years* – and was cluttered with archive photographs: of the abbey ruins from the ground and the air; a bronze statue of a young, half-naked Edmund, hatchet-nosed and clean-shaven aside from a tiny goatee, holding a cross to his chest; and – it was like seeing an old friend – that gilded representation, with flaxen locks, forked beard, jewelled crown and luxuriant emerald cloak, from the Wilton Diptych. There was also a picture from this afternoon's announcement, of a T-shirted, deeply tanned man of around sixty, with a poodle-frizz of grey curls, speaking at a microphone. Standing in front of a rough flint wall, he was flanked by an assortment of equally tanned fellow diggers. Hannah was probably there somewhere, and he would look for her properly later, although he was not certain he would recognise her. At the moment, his priority was to skim-read the story. The text had a maddening habit of jumping down a screen as each picture loaded, but he eventually stopped it moving about and managed to read to the end. Frustratingly, the story contained none of the elements he had hoped for. There were lots of quotes from the press conference and a good deal of background, probably lifted verbatim from an official press release. In news terms, it did the job efficiently enough. Of his own embroidery, however, there was no sign. He tried to contain his disappointment.

The version in *The Guardian* was similar. The headline was more concise – *Anyone for Edmund? Long-lost remains of martyred king found beneath tennis court* – and the only illustration was the loincloth-and-goatee statue, but the text covered all the same ground, in much the same way. Again, it was a good result for the promoters of the dig, furnishing all the publicity they needed, but not so useful for Mark, because none of his embellishments were there. This really was dispiriting. He reassured himself that he could still submit his report to Marina even if none of the media had taken the bait, but there was no getting away from the fact that it would make his case harder to sustain, particularly if anyone tried to check his bogus sources.

Hope giving way to grim resignation, he opened the BBC story next. Abruptly his mood changed. As his eye scrolled down the feed, glancing over the same press conference quotes and background padding, it came to rest on a fresh and beautiful sight: a separate box headed *Ten Things You Didn't Know About St Edmund*. And there, joy of joys, were his factoids, in all their fictitious glory. At number three, Edmund's Scottish mother; at seven, his treaty with the Welsh; and, sneaking in at a barrel-scraping number ten, his medieval depiction in green because of his fondness for all things Irish.

He let out a whoop, thumping his desk for good measure, then swivelled quickly round to see if anyone had witnessed this unwise outburst. Fortunately he was in the clear. Both Karim and Marina had left for a reception at the Royal Opera House, and the only other person in the office, a researcher several desks away, was too engrossed in a conversation on her mobile to hear or care.

Gloriously enough, the *Telegraph* had taken the same approach as the BBC. Perhaps they had copied the idea directly. If so, they had made a half-hearted effort to ring the changes, with the odd different factoid of their own, and only eight in total, which meant the Irish connection failed to make the cut. The Scottish and Welsh ones were there, though, making it a superb result. For a plan born of foolhardy over-confidence and nourished by fear, it had come together extraordinarily well.

All that remained to be added was the finishing touch. It only took a few moments to go back to the doctored Edmund biography on Wikipedia and insert the BBC and *Telegraph* links as citations for the saint's non-English connections, in addition to the academic references. News was real if it came from the national broadcaster and a long-established broadsheet, and nobody checking the references would ever know that the relationship was completely circular.

He stood up and stretched. It was a warm evening and, dodgy leg or not, he would stroll home rather than getting the bus. If he was not mistaken, there were a few bottles of Belgian beer in his fridge that would go very nicely with a take-away pizza. He normally tried not to drink during the week, but it was no more than he deserved.

If there were any doubt about my mother's origins, I ought to be the one to settle it. Who would know the answer better than I?

It embarrasses me to admit I cannot.

I confess I do not even remember that fine woman's name. To me, of course, she was mamma, and in our halls she was Your Highness, but my father must have used her given name, so I surely knew it once. Despite that, I do not recall it. Worse, I scarcely remember her face. When I think of her, I see a blurred form charged with light and goodness. She was perfumed with rosemary and oak moss, I remember that too. Sometimes I sense the outline of her long, fair tresses curling over my upturned, childish face. Now, though, I wonder if my memory is at fault: were those locks tinged instead with russet, as is common among the pale-skinned Pictish folk?

It is not for lack of love or reverence that I cannot picture her or recall the key details of her life, but simply because it was so, so long ago. My mortal life of less than thirty summers could fit more than forty-fold into the time that has elapsed since it ended, on that foul day when the pagan Danes did their worst with me. More than a thousand years have passed. I doubt that any man or woman alive could grasp what feat of memory is required to span that chasm of time.

Too much of it has been spent in the cold, dark earth. I, who was honoured in this place for six centuries after my death, spent half-a-thousand years more in an unmarked pit. Those who hid me there did so with the best of intent: they hoped to retrieve me and return me to my place, amid rejoicing and hurrahing, when the right moment came. But it never did, and they too went to their graves, carrying with them the secret of my whereabouts. After that, I was forgotten. My name lived on, it is true. Bodily, though, I was abandoned. Hope of rescue dwindled and died, and my earthen prison became my eternity.

Then, at last, o blessed miracle, I heard it: the scrape and scratch of picks and spades that I had so long yearned to hear but had forgotten even to dream about. The last sod was lifted, and my long, lonely ordeal was over. So I do not complain of my lot. I am glad to be back, gladder than I know how to express.

I wish only that I could have had some inkling of how much the world had changed in all the time I was away from it. Then, perhaps, I might not have erred so badly.

ℌannah parked her ageing Mazda on Angel Hill, the Georgian square that separated the abbey from the town. To an outsider, 'hill' was a misnomer: it was more of a gentle tilt. Only a proper East Anglian would know that this was a serious gradient by Suffolk standards.

There had been an influx of outsiders of late, many of them hauling TV cameras on their shoulders, after the triumphant discovery three weeks earlier. The shady park in which the abbey ruins slumbered, normally a tranquil haven with an aura of sanctity even for a heathen like Hannah, had become much busier, since they were now a visual focus for what the tabloids called 'Edmania'. Interest had kicked off all over again tonight, in anticipation of the press conference that Vernon had called for the following day. Even now, she could see a news reporter pre-recording a background piece to camera under the portcullis of the fat, squat tower that had once been the main gateway to the abbey.

Hannah was heading in the opposite direction. She passed

the illuminated Art Deco signpost in the middle of the square, known locally as the Pillar of Salt, and set out up Abbeygate Street, leaving the Great Gate behind her. Here, in the heart of the old medieval town, jettied merchants' houses leaned across the paving towards curlicued Regency shopfronts. At the top of the street she turned right. Everyone from the dig had been invited to hear tomorrow's news, whatever it was, in advance. They were meeting in the King's Head, not because anyone especially liked it – it was, as far as Hannah was aware, a charm-free chain pub – but Magnus said the name was appropriate for what they were going to hear. It was meant to be Hannah's Pilates night in the village hall but, with a lure like that, skipping class was a no-brainer.

She now knew a good deal more about St Edmund than she had three weeks earlier. She devoured the news reports on the day of the discovery, noting the Scottish, Welsh and Irish connections highlighted in some of the coverage; she imagined they would please her cousin no end. After that, she carried on reading into the subject. Having gazed on the grinning skull with her own eyes, she had conceived a fascination for his life story.

She had learned that the King of the Eastern Angles was killed trying to resist the Great Heathen Army, the Viking force that arrived by longship on his coast in the tenth year of his reign. He struck an initial bargain with these marauding Danes, allowing them to winter on his territory in return for not attacking his people. In the spring, they duly headed north to maraud somewhere else, conquering York and then doubling back to take Nottingham. When they failed to do so, they consoled themselves by returning to East Anglia, scrapping their deal with Edmund and attacking his kingdom after all. Following a decisive battle, the twenty-eight-year-old king ended up dead.

There was nothing rare about that in ninth-century England, where lives, including royal ones, were notoriously short. But the manner of his death was central to his legend. The story was first written down by a French monk in the tenth century, who heard it from the Archbishop of Canterbury, who had been told it decades earlier by an old man who claimed to have been Edmund's armour-bearer at the time of his death, and therefore an eyewitness. According to this old man, the Viking conquerors told the defeated Edmund he could stay on as a client king, but he said he would only do that if the leader of the Vikings converted to Christianity; otherwise 'he would rather be a standard-bearer in the court of the Eternal King'. The Vikings did not take kindly to this pre-condition, and Edmund was beaten, tied to a tree and bombarded with arrows; the French monk said he looked like a hedgehog when they were done. They finished the job by cutting off his head and tossing it into the undergrowth. When his faithful followers eventually came to retrieve his remains, they could not find the head anywhere. It was only when it cried out to them 'here, here, here!' that they discovered it, nestling in the paws of a wolf, which had been keeping it safe.

In that context, it was clear why Magnus might think the King's Head was an apt venue. What remained to be seen was how any of this medieval legend matched up with their own discovery under the tennis courts.

She checked her watch as she pushed open the door of the pub. The invitation was for six, and it was already ten past. Having long ago learned that fashionable lateness was frowned upon in these parts, she hoped she had not missed anything important.

She climbed the stairs in search of the private room that had been set aside for them. When she reached the top, she was greeted by the sight of Vernon's grey curls bobbing up and down as he talked animatedly to one of the other volunteers. Magnus was there too, his man-bun neatly secured and his beard now three weeks longer, while Daisy with the blue hair was in the far corner. There were a few other faces she recognised, and she could hear the clump of several sets of feet on the stairs behind her, as more people arrived.

She ordered an Appletiser at the little bar at one end of the room. Turning to survey the gathering, she found herself next to a short, stout figure with a shock of unruly white hair around a bronzed, liver-spotted pate, holding a large glass of red wine. Unlike the other men in the room, who were mostly dressed in T-shirts and baggy shorts, this guest wore a black habit, with a leather belt at the waist and a hood hanging from his shoulders.

He caught her looking at him and smiled hello.

'Sorry, I didn't mean to stare,' said Hannah. 'I was just thinking your robe must be horribly hot in this weather.'

'Don't you believe it, my dear. We have heavy ones for winter and lighter ones for summer. This one is remarkably cool. The air circulates when one walks, you know.' He had an educated accent that spoke of a bygone age. 'Brother Bernard,' he added, holding out his hand.

She introduced herself in return.

'And what brings you here?' he asked. 'Are you one of these clever archaeologists?'

'Just a volunteer grunt, I'm afraid. Completely untrained and ignorant, merely a willing wielder of a trowel. I've got the aching back to prove it.'

'I can imagine. I do admire you all for your dedication.

And what wonderful results you have to show for it, which are about to get even better, I understand. Are you in on the secret?'

'Whatever Vernon is going to tell us, you mean? No, I'm far too lowly, but I'm very excited. I assume it's good news. They all look very happy.'

'Indeed. Young Magnus gave me to understand as much when he telephoned to invite me. So I am optimistic.' He took an enthusiastic gulp of wine.

'What's your own connection? You weren't on the dig, were you?' She would have remembered, unless he was there in civvies. Were monks allowed to do that?

Before the old man could reply, Magnus started dinging a spoon on a beer glass, prompting a general shushing, as a circle formed around Vernon. The room had filled up, and Hannah found herself behind two tall young men with broad backs who completely masked her view. She squeezed forward, excusing herself as she went, until she could see Vernon properly.

'Thank you all so much for coming at short notice,' he was saying. 'It's fantastic to see so many of our volunteers again. Please believe me when I say that your enthusiasm and hard work made a huge difference to the success of the dig.'

Hannah did not buy for a moment that her own tentative excavation of a distant trench at the wrong end of the tennis courts had made the slightest contribution to the discovery of St Edmund, but it was nice of Vernon to say so.

'We've invited you here tonight because we have some news. We'll be announcing it to the world at a press conference tomorrow lunchtime, but I wanted you to hear it first. It's good news. In fact it's very good news. To be perfectly frank, it's a discovery beyond our wildest dreams, which is why I've had this silly grin on my face all day.' He surveyed the room happily, as if to demonstrate.

'Come on then, tell us what it is,' shouted someone behind Hannah, whereupon a woman next to her, a middle-aged crusty with dreadlocks and a nose-ring, called out good-humouredly, 'Yeah, come on Vern. Put us out of our misery!'

Vernon held his hand up to restore order. 'I'm getting there, be patient. Now, as most of you know, DNA testing is no use when it comes to Edmund. We don't know for sure who his family were and, in any case, it's too many generations back to be effective. So we've always been reliant on circumstantial evidence, right?'

'Right,' nodded the crusty woman.

'Our initial assessment that this was the right body was based on the traces of iron in the soil, corresponding to the kind of box which the historical evidence suggested the coffin was buried in. We also found a gold figure near the body, showing the Archangel Michael, which matched the description of a protective amulet placed in Edmund's coffin in the eleventh century. As for the skeleton itself, we found cut marks on the bottom of the fifth cervical vertebra, and on the top of the sixth, which were consistent with decapitation. We also found damage to the ribs and scapula, corresponding to the kind of wounds that iron arrowheads might make. If we hadn't found those things, it wouldn't mean our skeleton was not Edmund. It might simply have indicated that the legend of his death was not an accurate guide to what actually happened. However, finding those wounds was extremely encouraging. Not only did they reinforce our belief that this really was the body of King Edmund, but they also implied the story of his execution was substantially correct.'

Someone cheered, echoed by a whoop from the opposite

corner of the room. Vernon held his hand up again, to indicate that he had not finished yet.

'We didn't go into all those details when we made our announcement to the media, because we didn't want to make the story too complicated for the ladies and gentlemen of the press. Nevertheless, those were the reasons that made us so confident to tell the world we had found Edmund.' He took a swig of beer, providing himself with a dramatic pause. 'Since then, we've been busy doing lots of tests, and the results are back, which is what we want to tell you about this evening.' Another pause. Nobody was heckling now, because the audience was rapt. 'Firstly, we sent the remains for radiocarbon dating which, for those of you who don't know, looks at the rate of decay of the radioactive isotope carbon-14 and can be accurate to within a few decades. I'm delighted to tell you – can we have a drumroll, Magnus? – that the skeleton we found belonged to a man who lived within the range of 820 to 900 AD.'

There were a few gasps and some excited murmuring.

'Just to be clear how good that is,' Vernon went on, 'who can tell me when King Edmund was born?'

'840!' shouted the heckler at the back.

'Close,' said Vernon. 'We think it was 841. And when did he die?'

Hannah knew this. '869!'

'Well done Heather,' said Vernon. 'Not just a whizz with a trowel! So we've got a man who lived in the ninth century, buried in the graveyard of an abbey that wasn't built until the eleventh century. Unless they somehow got the wrong ninth-century corpse, and we're dealing with someone else who was bombarded with arrows and beheaded in around 869, this really would seem to be our man.'

'Brilliant,' shouted the crusty woman, and someone started a round of applause.

'But that, my friends, is not all,' Vernon continued. 'If it were, it would be pretty bloody good, but there's more.' The whole room was dead quiet now. 'You all know the legend of St Edmund's head, don't you?'

'Here, here, here!' called the comedian from the back.

'That's the one. Edmund's men went to retrieve his body after his death but they couldn't find his head, until it called out to them, at which point they returned it to the body and it miraculously reattached itself. Perhaps you also know that an abbot of Bury, by the name of Leofstan, tried to test the legend in the eleventh century. He had the coffin opened and attempted to pull the head away from the body to see if it really was attached. It wouldn't budge. There are three possible explanations. First, the head really did reattach itself by magic. Some of you may believe that' – did he smile in Brother Bernard's direction? – 'but I'm a scientist, so I'm afraid I don't. Second, Edmund was never beheaded and the account of his death was mistaken. In that case, we have a problem and our body isn't Edmund, because this poor chap definitely did have his head chopped off. The third possibility is, I believe, the simplest solution and that's my favourite, because the simplest explanation is usually the best: the head was reattached to the body in such a way that the join seemed not to show. We know that Anglo-Saxon embalmers were talented people, because the body itself was still intact when Abbot Leofstan looked at it, and again when another abbot, Samson, opened the coffin a century later. It seems quite plausible to me that they should reattach the head with some kind of iron fastening, and then sew up the skin.

'Why am I telling you all this? Well, we didn't just do

radiocarbon dating on the body. We also had the whole skeleton analysed, to give us a more precise picture of the injuries and so forth. Among the findings…and this one really did exceed our wildest expectations, so can we have another drumroll, Magnus?' Beside him, Magnus mimed the action and trilled a percussive *brrrrrrrr*. 'Thank you so much, I think they're all agog now. Among the findings, ladies and gentlemen, were traces of rust around the fifth and sixth cervical vertebrae, consistent with wiring the bones together.'

'Amazing,' cried the crusty woman, and the whole room burst into spontaneous applause.

'Astonishing,' agreed Hannah as she joined in with the clapping. She had genuine goosebumps.

'Thank you for that response,' said Vernon. 'I'm glad to see that you're as excited by this as we were. Now, before I leave you in peace to celebrate the news, let me a say a couple of words about arrangements for tomorrow's press conference, which will take place in the Abbey Gardens at 1pm. You are all welcome to attend but, if you do want to come, please give your name to Magnus, because there will be a certain amount of security. Why will there be security? The answer, my friends, is that we have a very special visitor tomorrow, whose identity I cannot reveal, otherwise I'd have to kill you. But I don't think you'll be disappointed. On that note, do please enjoy the rest of the evening.'

He turned back to his beer.

The crusty woman turned to Hannah. 'Who do you think it is? You don't think it could be the Archbishop of Canterbury?'

'Gosh, that would be exciting. Or maybe even a royal. The Queen is head of the Church of England, and it's not often we dig up an actual saint.'

'The Queen? No!'

'Well, maybe not the Queen herself. I don't think she does many engagements nowadays. Maybe Prince Charles?'

The crusty woman's eyes lit up. 'Or William and Kate!' She turned away to spread the word of this enthralling possibility.

Hannah looked around for Magnus so she could put her name on his list. As she turned, she found Brother Bernard looking up at her, his wine glass filled to the brim once more.

'Hello again, my dear. What thrilling developments!' he said, wafting the glass vaguely in the direction of Vernon, before bringing it to his lips.

'Absolutely. That last bit was so exciting. Unless you found it sacrilegious?'

He smiled. 'Don't you worry, I'm not offended by science. Without science, I wouldn't be able to heat my room through the winter and a motor car would not have brought me here. If St Edmund's head was attached by earthly rather than divine means, it's not my place to quibble.'

'I'll drink to that.' She raised her glass.

He did the same, and then said: 'You asked me my connection, and we were interrupted before I could reply. It's simply that I have devoted many years' study to this subject, and Vernon was kind enough to acknowledge this by inviting me to attend tonight.'

'So you're an Edmund scholar?'

He shrugged. 'I've had a few papers published here and there.'

'That's very impressive. Will you be writing another one now that we've found him? You could put it all in a book, maybe?'

'Oh, I'm getting a bit old for writing now. I find I don't have the concentration. Better to leave all that to others. But

I'm happy to provide scholarly advice, if anyone should want it.'

Hannah thought back to that frantic phone call from Mark. If only she had known about this nice old monk, she could have referred her cousin to him. Not that Mark needed that expertise any longer, now that St Edmund's Celtic connections were so well attested. She wondered what had happened to the patron saint idea. It was surprising there had been no mention of it in all the news coverage. She made a mental note to text Mark to ask him about it. 'I'm sure your expertise will be in demand once this latest news breaks tomorrow. Have you done any television appearances? You'd be wonderful at it.'

'Oh, here and there, over the years. And I've been on a couple of times in the past few weeks.'

'Good for you. I'll look out for you, now that we've met.'

'And perhaps we shall meet tomorrow. Do you plan to attend the press conference?'

'You bet! I wouldn't miss it for the world. Apart from anything else, I'm dying to find out who the mystery guest is. Have you any idea? The woman over there thought it might be the Archbishop of Canterbury, or maybe royalty. It must be someone quite significant, otherwise they wouldn't be making such a fuss over security.'

Brother Bernard shrugged. 'I have no idea. And what times we live in, when the Archbishop of Canterbury needs security. A previous incumbent was hacked to death during the Peasants' Revolt, but I rather hoped the world had become more civilised since then.'

Hannah caught sight of a man-bun bobbing above the crowd. 'Look, there's Magnus. I want to get my name on his list. Shall I put yours down too?'

'Thank you, my dear, but I think it's on there already. Vernon has invited me to say a word or two.' He twinkled at her, clearly enjoying wrong-footing her with his modesty.

'Oh gosh! You really are important. In that case, I'll look forward to it even more.'

'You're too kind, but don't expect too much from my part in the proceedings. I will be brief.'

'I'm sure you'll be wonderful,' she repeated. 'It's been a pleasure to meet you now.'

'A pleasure for me too, my dear. *À demain*, I hope.'

She was on her way back down Abbeygate Street towards the car when her phone pinged. It was a text from her cousin.

Hi Hannah. Will you be at the press conference tomorrow? Would be great to see you if so. It will all be a bit mad, because I'm coming with Marina – keep it to yourself, but she's making a big announcement. You can probably guess what! I won't have much time to spare but it would be great to say hello. Mark

So there it was: not the Archbishop of Canterbury, the Queen, nor Charles or William, but the Right Honourable Marina Spencer. She hoped nobody from tonight's party would be too disappointed. As for the big announcement, she could indeed guess what it was.

Great! she texted back. *Exciting times. See you there! Hx*

The tannoy had reached the stage of its loop where it reminded customers they were not permitted, for safety reasons, to cycle, skateboard or roller-blade within the station.

Frowning as she was obliged to raise her voice above it, Marina was talking to Karim on the bench she had commandeered for their party, while Giles stood in front of them, scrolling through Twitter and screening her from the few other passengers on the platform. Mark had been dispatched to see where the train was. This was a pointless mission, because it was obvious where it was: en route to Cambridge, where they now were, and from which it would no doubt depart on schedule in ten minutes' time. Unfortunately that kind of explanation was never good enough for Marina. She did not like being made to wait and she always needed to know the reason why, even when the answer was as banal and immutable as 'the timetable'.

Most members of the cabinet used their official vehicles

when they travelled to engagements around the country, especially to destinations without direct rail connections to London. Marina, however, disapproved of cars and insisted on taking public transport in all circumstances, no matter how impractical it was. The only car ride permitted was a taxi journey at the end – provided the vehicle was electric or, if absolutely necessary, a hybrid. Mark could respect the principle, which was consistent with her long record as an eco-campaigner. That did not stop him feeling it was yet another reason he had drawn the short straw in serving this particular minister.

When their train did arrive – on time, for all Marina's sighing and tutting – he was bidden to take the seat next to her, while Karim and Giles faced them across the table. 'I want you to check my speech,' she said.

Mark glanced over at Karim, who had drafted it, and noticed him colour, clearly not pleased with this indignity.

Marina slid the script sideways along the table. Double-spaced and blown up into sixteen-point type, as she always insisted for a public address, it began with pleasantries about the beautiful and evocative location in which they would shortly find themselves, then moved on to praise the dig team for their hard physical work and tenacity, which was a credit to British archaeology. This was followed by some florid language about the importance of the country's national heritage. 'We cannot build our future if we do not treasure our past,' it declared, a sound bite that might not withstand much interrogation but could be relied upon to deliver a round of applause and maybe even a clip on the news.

Then the speech moved on to Edmund himself, acknowledging that most of the British population had known little or nothing about this obscure Anglo-Saxon king a month earlier, but noting with approval how the whole country had made up for that omission by taking him so joyously to its heart. This current enthusiasm was reminiscent of the pre-Reformation days when St Edmund's shrine attracted kings as pilgrims and he was revered as the patron saint of England.

Mark felt his heart thumping as his eyes sped over the lines. It was extraordinary to think that the historic recalibration of the nation's self-image which was about to take place was entirely his idea.

The speech lined up the arguments to support its big-reveal conclusion. First, there were effusive words about St George, to make it clear that his status as England's national saint was under no threat. Then came Mark's biographical embroidery of St Edmund. In addition to being English-born – unlike St George – he was also half-Scottish, he had concluded a vital alliance with the Welsh and was a lifelong admirer of St Patrick. He was, therefore, a uniquely qualified candidate to fill a vacancy that had existed ever since James VI of Scotland became James I of England in the year 1603: that of a patron saint to look after all four nations of the union.

It was a well-crafted speech, Mark could not deny that. However, the thought of Marina reading out that trio of fictions to a group of people with a specialist knowledge of the life of St Edmund made his palms sweat.

'It's good. Powerful and very nicely structured.' Across the table, a flicker of surprise crossed Karim's face. 'My only suggestion would be to make more of the media coverage. I mean, you should really play up the Edmania and say how great it is that our friends in the press have embraced Edmund so wholeheartedly. If you make your initiative seem like an organic product of the media's own enthusiasm, it will make the hacks feel like they own it already. May I?' He turned over one of the sheets of paper to write on the reverse. 'Like so.' He slid the paper back for Marina to see.

Karim was affecting to ignore the conversation, staring out of the window at the landscape, which had now acquired gentle contours, after the unremitting flatness of Cambridgeshire.

Marina grimaced. 'What's this word?'

'*Moved.*'

'You could have fooled me. And this?'

'*Outpouring.* Shall I read it to you?'

'I think you'd better.'

He glanced around the carriage. None of their fellow passengers had paid them any attention beyond the odd flicker of recognition, but that was no reason to drop their guard. The person studiously ignoring them was the most likely to sneak a quick photo or post an eavesdropped remark online. Keeping his voice low, he read:

I have been moved and encouraged by the enormous outpouring of enthusiasm for St Edmund in the past few weeks, across the whole spectrum of our media. This coverage has highlighted not only the exciting nature of this great discovery, but also many of the remarkable facts about Edmund's life, notably his links to Scotland, Wales and Ireland.

She nodded. 'Much as I'd like to take all the credit if it goes well, it would be much sounder politics to let the hacks think it was their idea. Good thinking, Mark. Karim, could you put that into the finished version, in writing that I can actually read?'

Karim made a show of not understanding at first, as if he had not been listening, before applying himself to the task. The look on his face as he started crossing out his own words and inserting Mark's was a joy to behold.

Giles had the details of their taxi in an email from Priya, Marina's formidably efficient diary secretary. The requirement that the vehicle must be electric was often a tall order for a country town at some remove from the main railway arteries. As a result, they often found that the car awaiting them had travelled almost as far as they had. Today was no exception. As they emerged from the modest red-brick Victorian railway station at Bury St Edmunds, the silver Hyundai that purred towards them bore the insignia 'Cambridge City Cars'.

Giles took the front seat while Marina squeezed into the back with Karim and Mark. The front would have been far more comfortable for her, but there was an unspoken understanding that it was beneath the dignity of the secretary of state to sit beside the driver.

All Mark could see of the latter was a broad neck below a blond buzz-cut, and pale blue eyes looking at Marina in the rear-view mirror.

'You're that politician, innit?' he said. His accent was East European. Polish maybe? *'Yeah, no, I really wouldn't.* That's you! I saw you on *Question Time* the other week too. You was fantastic.'

As an accomplished media communicator, Marina received compliments whenever she went out in public and seemed never to tire of them. 'Thank you so much. The one a couple of weeks ago, you mean? What was it in particular that you liked?'

'All of it! I don't remember what you said exactly, because my memory's not so good. But you was taking on that other guy, the one speaking lies about immigrants. You destroyed him, innit? It was beautiful to watch. I wish all politicians would tell it straight like you. You really nailed it, you know what I'm saying?'

Asking people to elaborate when they complimented her was one of Marina's stock gambits. The member of the public was flattered to be asked for their opinion in greater depth, which thereby enhanced her woman-of-the-people credentials. For Marina, it spun out the compliment for even longer.

'Where are you from, if you don't mind my asking?'

'Course I don't mind. From Latvia, innit?'

'And how long have you been here?'

'Seven years. The wife is here too and my kids was born here. They're proper English. They speak it perfect. No accent or nothing.'

'How many do you have?'

The pleasantries wore on, as she nudged him in the direction of housing, childcare, primary education and the convenience or otherwise of charging up the Hyundai. Every time Mark saw this routine in action, he had to concede it was a class act. To the untrained observer, she exuded empathic curiosity. Only those who knew her best could see what she was really doing: mining a voter for data which would go into her vast memory bank, to be pulled out and used whenever it came in handy. 'Only the other day I was talking to a migrant from Latvia who told me…' Not for nothing did a range of senior pundits call her the finest retail politician of her generation.

In the front seat, Giles had been texting ahead to let

their hosts know they were on their way. As they pulled up outside the Great Gate, a woman from the council public relations office was waiting to greet them, with a couple of flak-jacketed policemen positioned discreetly nearby. There was a smell of mashed grains in the air as they got out of the car. Mark noticed Marina wrinkling her nose momentarily, before rearranging her face for public view.

The PR woman, who introduced herself as Jemima, led them through the medieval arch, its façade studded with empty niches where saints had once stood, and into the gardens, where large lumps of flint pebbles and cement marked the site of the various ancillary buildings of the abbey. 'We're in the crypt, immediately adjacent to the dig site,' Jemima told Marina. Her dark hair was pulled back into a severe ponytail, leaving a pale band where her foundation had not quite reached her hairline. 'Derek Parker, the leader of the council, has already begun to say a few words. We let him start once we knew you were on your way from the station. He's going to introduce the three speakers, with yourself last, naturally, as our guest of honour. Wendy Wethers is here too, as a courtesy, but she won't be speaking. I'm sure you know her already.'

Wendy Wethers was the local MP, currently an opposition backbencher, who had occasionally harried Marina at the dispatch box. 'Wendy and I were first elected in the same year,' said Marina, 'so we do indeed know each other.' To her credit, she drew the line at pretending they were friends.

The path led them along the edge of a rose garden and around a corner, where it gave them a view of two giant phallic pillars made of the same rough flint rubble. 'It was once the biggest church in Western Europe, and that's all there is left,' said Jemima, leading them around the lower, skirting walls of the outlying ruins towards the semicircular east end of the abbey. They could hear a voice speaking through a sound system, but it was not clear where it was coming from.

'Down here,' said Jemima, and Mark realised where they were going: this end of the abbey had been dug down to a lower level, and they were descending into what had once been a basement floor, and now formed a natural amphitheatre. A makeshift stage had been set up against the phallic backdrop, from which a thin, balding man in silver-rimmed glasses addressed a small audience, ringed by a bank of TV cameras. Half the crowd were in their thirties and dressed in business wear, while the other half were older and more casually attired; journalists, on the one hand, and dig workers, he assumed, of whom Hannah should be one. She had texted him back the previous night to say she would be here. He must keep an eye open for her.

They descended a short flight of wooden steps to reach the lower level, and Jemima showed them to the side of the stage, carefully out of view of the TV cameras. A perfectly manicured, bird-like figure in pearls and powder-blue suit bobbed towards them, hand outstretched. 'Hello, Secretary of State,' she said, elaborately *sotto voce*. 'Welcome to Bury St Edmunds.'

'Wendy.' Marina took her hand and managed a wintry smile while Mark hovered, knowing the drill that was coming up. Without looking at him, Marina gave him her bag to hold. He held it open so that she could rummage inside, in search of a make-up mirror. Wendy, realising she was dismissed, turned back to face the stage.

The brush-off was not just because they sat on opposite sides of the House. Marina always needed five undisturbed minutes before any public appearance to read through her script. In his first week in the job, Mark had made the mistake of approaching her during one of these warm-up sessions and had been driven back by a look of such explosive anger that he had never come close to repeating the offence. She was as neurotic about public speeches as she was about broadcast appearances, even though she always performed on live stages as brilliantly as she did in media gigs. If reminded of that, she would retort that complacency was the shortest route to cock-up, and there was nothing any of her staff could do to calm her, so they gave up saying it. It was easier just to give her a wide berth.

Unfortunately, nobody had warned Jemima of this. Having vanished for a moment, she now reappeared. At her elbow was a tall, deeply tanned figure in baggy shorts. His hair was a mass of grey curls which he had vainly attempted to tame under a red bandana.

'Marina? Can I introduce you to...' she began in a hoarse whisper.

Marina waved her brusquely away, without even glancing at the newcomer, and turned on her heel.

Mark stepped forward. 'Sorry, don't take that personally,' he said softly to Jemima and the guy with the bandana, who was blinking in bewilderment. 'She gets very nervous and always needs some alone-time before a public appearance. My fault, I should have warned you.' He offered his hand in consolation. 'How do you do? I'm Mark Price, Marina's special adviser.'

'Vernon O'Connor, chief archaeologist,' said the other, not looking consoled.

Mark glanced over at Marina. She was pacing up and down, mouthing her speech, blithely unaware of the offence she had caused.

On the stage, the council leader was finishing up and introducing the first speaker. 'He'll never tell you this himself, because he's far too modest, but he knows more about King Edmund the Martyr, or St Edmund, than anyone else alive. Please welcome Brother Bernard Bellamy.'

The dig workers duly applauded, while the journalists checked their recording devices or looked at their watches.

A stout, elderly man in a monk's habit was helped onto the stage and approached the microphone stand. The name Bellamy sounded familiar. Where had Mark heard it recently? For a moment it would not come, then suddenly he had it: B.L.R. Bellamy (O.S.B.), who had written all those books and articles. Mark sidled into the lee of a television camera, as if disappearing from the monk's sightline would render his shameless inventions equally invisible.

At first he was too unnerved to pay any attention to what Bellamy was saying. Forcing himself to focus, he was relieved to find that it was all very bland. The monk spoke of the honour of being invited to speak, the excitement of a discovery that he never thought he would live to see, and the importance of what would happen to the sacred relics now. There was nothing polemical, or the slightest indication of disquiet at the new narrative that Mark had constructed. Not that there was any reason for him to touch on such matters. If the odd rogue fact had crept into some of the media summaries of St Edmund's life, Brother Bernard could have no reason to suspect foul play.

The old man was admirably disciplined, keeping his remarks very short before leaving the stage to applause from the dig team.

Next up was Vernon O'Connor, who got a big, loyal hand from his team. He set about building the case: detailing all the arguments that established beyond reasonable doubt that he and his colleagues really had found Edmund, the ninth-century king of the Eastern Angles, and revealing that the legendary account of Edmund's martyrdom by Danish invaders had proved remarkably accurate. This was new to Mark, and genuinely enthralling. They had used science to divine the skeleton's identity, in a kind of Anglo-Saxon crime-scene investigation. Mark glanced around at the news reporters and saw that they all looked equally hooked. If he got the chance, he would attempt to collar his old colleague, Rebecca Longden, the BBC religious affairs correspondent, who was listening attentively in the front row, and suggest a colourful expression or two. It would be gratifying if he could get the phrase 'CSI Bury St Edmunds' onto the *Six O'Clock News*.

O'Connor was drawing to a close now and cueing in Marina. 'Brother Bernard has spoken about the historical and religious importance of our find, and I hope I've conveyed some sense of its archaeological significance,' he said. 'But that's not all. In a hugely important development, I understand that St Edmund may have a renewed role to play in our national story. To explain more about that, I'm delighted to welcome that great rarity in modern life, a politician whom most people seem to like.' He had clearly written that line before meeting her in the flesh. 'I'm sure you know her very well already, so she needs no introduction from me, beyond saying that we're honoured to have her with us today. As if you hadn't guessed already, it's the secretary of state for culture, Marina Spencer.'

The dig volunteers all clapped diligently. Mark watched the hacks' faces. Marina was popular among journalists as well as the public, because she gave good value. They had been primed to expect her, so her presence was not news to them. However, the mention of a renewed national role for Edmund clearly was, and he saw them all grow markedly more alert, glancing at each other to check that their colleagues were as surprised as they were. He saw one of two of them texting, no doubt to warn their news desks there might be a stronger-than-expected story on the way.

Marina took her place at the microphone. 'Thank you, Vernon, for that wonderful explanation of what you've all been doing here.' She beamed at him as if they were the oldest of friends.

Mark listened in grudging admiration as she moved seamlessly from some off-the-cuff remarks about the speeches they had just heard – it was remarkable that she had managed to pay any attention at all – into her prepared text. She was warm, fluent and engaging, living up to her billing as the kind of politician who gave her calling a good name. It might all be an act, but it was a good one. No wonder so many people from all walks of life regularly told him how lucky he was to work for her. There was a kernel of truth in it: if he wanted his career to develop, he was better off working for the most impressive performer in the government, however glacial she was behind the scenes, than some genuinely pleasant minister – there really were one or two – who was either unknown to the public or, worse, a national embarrassment. The only flaw was that he no longer had any such ambition. His daily humiliations had long since put paid to that.

She was most of the way through her preliminary formalities now, having sung the praises of the setting, the dig, the authorities who had made it all possible and even the weather. On she moved to the substance. 'I have been moved and encouraged by the enormous outpouring of enthusiasm for St Edmund in the past few weeks...'

As she spoke, Mark surveyed the audience to try to gauge the reaction of the journalists. He noticed that Brother Bernard was standing next to a woman who looked uncannily like Mark's own mother, only about ten years younger. Dressed in a man's striped business shirt, tucked loosely into a pair of capacious jeans, she was cheerfully ungroomed, with a mess of chestnut hair cut to much the same length all the way round, so that the fringe flopped into her eyes. The resemblance to his mother was strongest around her mouth, which was wide and good-humoured. She noticed him looking and raised her hand in a discreet half-wave. It was strange how he and his cousin Hannah could recognise each other so easily, despite barely having met in adulthood.

'This coverage has highlighted not only the inspiring nature of this great discovery...'

He nodded in ostentatious acknowledgement, but was distracted by the look on Brother Bernard's face. As Marina mentioned Edmund's links to Scotland, Wales and Ireland, the monk visibly winced.

Mark glanced at the journalists. Since they, like Brother Bernard, were all facing forwards, none of them had noticed his reaction. It was only a matter of time, however, before some bright spark sought the monk out for a comment on the major announcement that Marina was now making. If that happened, Bellamy was bound to say the Scottish, Welsh and Irish links had come as news to him. Mark could not allow that to happen, so he must act fast. There was literally not a second to lose.

A few steps to his right stood Giles, arms folded, watching Marina, lost in the miasma of admiration that he and Karim reserved for their boss's public performances. He jumped, startled, to find Mark whispering in his ear.

'Giles, mate. I'm going to make sure the old monk is on board with Marina's vision. I'm sure he will be, but let's not leave anything to chance. If I'm not back by the time you're all ready to leave, go ahead without me. I'll catch you up.'

His colleague shrugged and whispered back: 'All right, buddy. If you think you need to, that's cool.'

Mark turned away and raced around the back of the press pack to the other side of the stage, positioning himself as close as he dared to Hannah and Bellamy, without drawing attention to himself.

'...and that's why I am proposing that St Edmund be adopted once more as patron saint, not to displace St George, but to sit alongside him, as well as St Andrew, St David and St Patrick, as the patron saint of the whole United Kingdom.'

The look of surprise on the monk's face made it clear he had had no forewarning of this.

Hands shot up to ask questions. Mark took advantage of this sudden burst of movement to dive into the crowd. 'Great to see you, Hannah,' he whispered. 'Brother Bernard, I work with Marina. Could I possibly ask you to step this way?'

It was clear from the look of disappointment on the monk's face that he would have much preferred to stay and listen to Marina's replies. But a summons from Mark in Marina's name was as good as one from the government itself, and Mark had learned that few members of the public were able to resist it. He waited as Hannah and Brother Bernard duly filed out of the crowd and up the wooden staircase out of the crypt. He stopped on a patch of grass adjacent to the old north aisle, at a safe distance from the press conference.

He offered his hand. 'I'm Mark Price. As well as working

with the secretary of state, I'm also Hannah's cousin. I don't know whether she mentioned it? I'm sorry to pull you out of the gathering like this, but Marina specifically asked me to have a word with you. She wanted me to convey her personal apology that you weren't informed about the content of today's announcement in advance.' Or she would have, if she ever thought about such things. 'Ordinarily, with a respected authority such as yourself, we'd aim to keep you in the loop as much as possible, as a basic courtesy. In this case, however, we anticipated quite a lot of excitement about the announcement, so it was important to keep a tight lid on it. These things have a terrible habit of getting out. Not that I'm suggesting for a moment you would have…' He was blabbering now. This was not impressive. 'It's just that, in these situations, we prefer to batten down all the hatches. Classic Whitehall mentality, I'm afraid. I'm sure you understand.'

'Yes of course,' said Brother Bernard. 'I don't have any right to know these things. I'm not so important as all that, you know. It has been an honour to be present at the announcement today, although I must confess to being a little puzzled by…'

Mark looked ostentatiously at his watch. 'Sorry to interrupt, but I have roughly twenty minutes before we have to set off back for London. Why don't we grab a quick coffee somewhere a little quieter, and continue our conversation on the way? Naturally I can fill you in on Marina's thinking. Again, she apologises that she isn't able to brief you personally, but she has asked me to do so on her behalf.' One of the things he had learned in this job was that, once you started to make things up, it soon came so naturally that you barely noticed you were doing it. 'Hannah, do join us, so we can have a quick catch-up too.' He explained to Brother Bernard: 'We haven't seen each other for…what is it? Twenty years?'

'Sorry to break this to you, but I think it may be nearer thirty,' said his cousin.

'Goodness, in that case you don't want me at your reunion,' protested the monk. 'You two should use the short time you have to reacquaint yourselves, without me getting in your way.'

'No!' said Mark, a little too urgently, earning a puzzled look from Hannah. 'I mean, it would make it all the more special to have you along. And, as I say, Marina is most anxious that I reach out to you, to make up for her not being able to do so in person. So, if that's settled, can either of you recommend somewhere nice and quiet that's not too far away?' He was already leading them towards the rose garden.

'There are various places in Abbeygate Street,' said Hannah, falling into step. 'Don't run though,' she added, with a slight frown in the direction of Brother Bernard, who was struggling to keep up.

'Sorry.'

'I thought you had a gammy leg, anyway. That's what your mum said.'

'It comes and goes.' Depending on the urgency. They had rounded the corner now, safely out of sight of the journalists, so he was happy to slacken the pace. He turned back to the monk. 'All this must be immense for you, Brother Bernard. I know you've written a huge amount about Edmund. In fact, it's a great honour to meet the great B.L.R. Bellamy in person.'

The old man looked at him in surprise. 'If you've heard of me, that puts you in a very small club, and if you're honoured to meet me, it's an even smaller one, whose membership may be limited to yourself alone. You are either a great Edmund enthusiast or a great flatterer.'

'I'm impressed too,' said Hannah. 'Did you read some of Brother Bernard's books or papers after we last spoke?'

Was that an innocent question, or was she snarking? Since he barely knew her, it was hard to tell. 'I'd have to say I'm more familiar with B.L.R. Bellamy's name than his actual *œuvre*. I did some rapid reading that brought me into contact with various bibliographies.' What was he saying? This was dangerous. He was virtually admitting to having crawled through the notes and references section of Wikipedia, which was the one subject he wanted at all costs to avoid. A change of subject was needed. 'Have you had a chance to inspect the body yourself, Brother Bernard?'

'Me? No, although I would very much like to, in due course. I imagine there will be conversations at the highest of levels about his permanent resting place. Perhaps you have been involved in them?'

'What's your own view on that subject?' He figured it was better to let the monk do as much talking as possible, to avoid making any more gaffes himself. It would also deflect attention from the fact that no, nobody had involved him in any such discussion, and they were unlikely to do so, because they enjoyed freezing him out of stuff like that.

Brother Bernard cheerfully took the bait. 'A century ago, when it was mistakenly thought St Edmund's remains were in France, there was a certain enthusiasm among the cardinals for bringing him home to a shrine at Westminster Cathedral. The Catholic one, you understand, not Westminster Abbey. I fear that would be controversial now: if he is to be our patron saint, our friends in the Church of England would never let us Catholics get our hands on him. So I think by far the best place for him is here in Bury, where he was always meant to be.'

'And if they buried him somewhere else, Bury St Edmunds would have to change its name to Not-Bury St Edmunds,' chipped in Hannah.

Brother Bernard laughed. 'Not true, of course,' he added, for Mark's benefit. 'Bury is simply the Old English word for a fortified town, like Canterbury, Salisbury, Newbury and so forth.'

Mark nodded, as if he had always known that.

They had reached the Great Gate, where they paused under the portcullis and weathered gargoyles. Hannah pointed past the striking retro signpost in the middle of the square to a pair of coffee shops straddling the entrance to Abbeygate Street. 'Both of those are nice.'

Mark squinted in the sunlight. Nice as they might be, both places had massive Dickensian picture windows, which meant all customers were visible to any journalist on his or her way out of the Abbey Gardens. 'Is there somewhere a bit further up the street?'

She pulled a face. 'There's a Caffè Nero, I think.'

He ignored her obvious distaste for a chain coffee shop. 'Perfect.'

They made their way across Angel Hill and up Abbeygate Street, where there was indeed a Caffè Nero. It was much more secluded, and therefore suitable. Reluctant to leave anything to chance, Mark settled his companions at a table as far from the front window as they could get, while he went to queue for their order.

As he stood at the counter, his phone vibrated. It was Giles. 'Hey, buddy. We're ready to go. Are you coming with us or not?'

'No, mate.' Mark dropped his voice as low as he could. 'Like I said, I'm trying to keep the old monk onside. It's important.'

'Where are you, anyway? Marina wanted to meet him. She hoped to do photos with him, because his monk's outfit was so visual, but she also wanted to say hello to him and find out what he thought of her plan.'

'Habit.'

'What?'

'It's called a habit, not an outfit. And I needed to get him away from the press as a matter of urgency. Between you and me, I think he may need some persuasion, and I didn't want the hacks picking up on that.' Sometimes the truth was the safest option.

'Really? I thought the whole thing was a no-brainer, and nobody could possibly object. Sorry, maybe I misunderstood.'

'It's, er, complicated. Theological stuff. You know what monks are like. Angels on the head of a pin and all that. But I'll sort it, trust me. Anyway, gotta go. Go on without me, and I'll see you all later.'

'No worries, buddy. I'll tell Marina.'

Giles was not so bad, Mark thought, as he ended the call, switching his phone off for good measure. Sometimes he wondered how different his life might be if there were just the two of them working for Marina, without Karim. There was no time to dwell on that though. He needed to face the more pressing issue of how the hell to bring Brother Bernard round.

Arriving back at their table with a tray of coffees, he was disappointed, if not entirely surprised, to find his cousin and the monk were already discussing the subject Mark had been most anxious to avoid.

'It's just that I'm at a loss to know where it has all come from,' Brother Bernard was saying. 'I've spent the past thirty years studying Edmund, and I've never seen any mention of it.'

'What's that?' asked Mark, in as light a tone as he could muster. It was clear his previous tactic of changing the subject would no longer do.

'Brother Bernard is puzzled by all this talk of Edmund's mother being a Pictish princess,' said Hannah, ripping open a paper tube and tipping sugar into her latte.

'That's putting it mildly,' the monk broke in. 'I'm utterly baffled. Before the find, I'd never heard anyone say it, and now it seems to be mentioned in every article.'

'Really? That does sound strange.' Mark frowned, making a show of wracking his brains. 'I'm just trying to think when I first saw it mentioned. I have to confess I didn't know anything about St Edmund until the day of the find, when I did some rapid catching up to write a briefing for Marina. And if I remember rightly…it's coming back now, because I can remember including the Scottish connection in what I wrote for her… Yes, it was definitely in the media that day.' By the end of the day, anyway, even if not at the start of it. 'I mean, as I understand it, we don't know anything for sure about Edmund's origins, so it's all based on myth and conjecture, and there are various rival theories, aren't there? So what's your worry? That the Scottish theory doesn't stand up? If that's the case, it has very serious implications and I shall naturally have to pass it on to Marina immediately.' He made a show of pulling his phone from his pocket. 'The problem is, I know from experience what she'll do. She'll insist on cancelling the whole initiative, and Edmund will never be the patron saint of the whole United Kingdom, or even of England, because she certainly doesn't want him to displace St George. Most politicians wouldn't react like that, because they'd be too bothered about losing face, but Marina's no ordinary politician. For better or for worse, she's a woman of integrity.' He wondered if they could hear his heart pounding. This was a major gamble but, with his options running out, he was not sure what alternative he had.

To his great relief, Brother Bernard shook his head.

'No, let's not be hasty. I'd hate to be responsible for that. Oh dear. What should we do for the best? I merely want you to understand the epistemological problem. It's not so much that I disbelieve the theory. On the contrary, I have no view on it, for the simple reason that I have never heard it argued, so I am necessarily agnostic. I have simply seen it referred to, by various news organisations that have now taken to recycling it *ad nauseam*, but I don't have the slightest idea what they are basing their reports upon. It's as if a rumour has appeared out of nowhere and become fact without anyone questioning it.'

Welcome to the world of fake news, Mark wanted to say. 'Are you quite sure there isn't some research paper you've missed?' he said instead. 'I can imagine it must be hard to keep up with all the scholarship that goes on in the world.'

The monk looked pained. 'I suppose it's possible. But where is it? I've searched, and I can find no reference.'

Mark had been feeling guilty for gaslighting the old man, but he found this last remark oddly hurtful, after all his efforts to credit the fictitious Professor McAdoo for her seminal work on the subject.

'It's not just the Scottish mother,' the monk went on. 'There is also the matter of the Welsh treaty. It could have happened, and I don't say it didn't. But where is the record? To read all these news reports, you would think the accord between Edmund and Rhodri Mawr – and the other fellow, Ap something – was a matter of undisputed historical fact.'

'You're saying it isn't?' Mark hoped he sounded suitably incredulous.

'It most certainly is not. It would be in the histories, and there are not many of them. Almost everything we know about the period comes from one or two chronicles.'

'One or two *Anglo-Saxon* chronicles?'

'Yes indeed. And, I assure you, I have read them in their entirety. Many times.'

'What about Welsh chronicles, though? Presumably Welsh historians made an equivalent historical record. Mightn't the treaty appear in that?'

'I didn't think of that.' The old man looked dazed, unnerved by this possibility.

'I imagine it would all be written in Welsh, so no one could blame you for not having looked,' Mark added. This was a low blow. Nevertheless, bigger considerations than the old man's feelings were at stake. It was time to press home his advantage. 'The same might be true of the Irish connection,' he said. 'If you can't find any record of Edmund's devotion to St Patrick, it may appear in some Gaelic text.'

Hannah, who had taken no part in this discussion until now, said: 'Is there a problem with the Irish connection too?'

Mark cursed his stupid, babbling mouth for bringing it up.

'I must admit, I was also surprised by the supposed Irish angle,' said the monk. 'I had never before seen that interpretation of the Wilton Diptych.'

'I honestly don't know,' said Mark. 'I agree, it's strange

that all these facts are in the media when you, as the leading expert on the subject, have never come across them. As I say, part of the story may have come from Welsh scholarship, which you mightn't know about because it's not your field and you don't, I assume, read the language. There could be other equally good explanations. However it happened, can we not just celebrate the fact that St Edmund is making himself known to us in a new way at the perfect moment, when all four nations of the union need him?'

The monk shrugged. Mark's shameless, last-ditch point had at least shut him up.

'I'd really rather focus on the good things that could come from all this,' he continued. 'And we should talk in more detail about Edmund's final resting place. If you have any specific thoughts on the nature of the shrine, do tell me, and I'll do all I can to make sure they reach the appropriate ears. We really do want to get this right, and that involves making sure we listen to those voices that ought to be heard.'

An hour later, he was on Northgate Street, heading back to the station on foot. It had been a difficult encounter, not least with Hannah shooting him so many puzzled looks, but she did not seem to be on to him, and Brother Bernard himself had perked up once they got onto the subject of the logistics of a modern-day shrine. Mark had flown through the whole thing by the seat of his pants, but he did that most days. Landing safely with no bones broken was what counted, and he appeared to have done so. Crucially, he had kept the monk far away from the press pack who would, even now, be filing their copy or preparing their packages for the evening news.

Suddenly he remembered his line about CSI Bury St Edmunds, and how nice it would be to get it into a correspondent's script. He pulled his phone out and texted as he walked:

> *Hi Rebecca. Saw you from afar earlier. Sorry I didn't get a chance to say hello. I hope you got everything you needed. Fascinating stuff, all that archaeological detective work, no? I call it 'CSI Bury St Edmunds'! Give me a call if you need anything and let's grab a drink some time. Mark x*

A minute later, his phone buzzed with her reply:

> *'CSI Bury St Edmunds'! Great line! Hope you don't mind if I steal it for the Six O'Clock? Bex xx*

He grinned to himself. No, he did not mind at all.

I have been reflecting more on memory and its limits. I am relieved to find that there are many events in my own deepest history that I *can* bring back to mind, so my recall is not quite as rotten and decayed as I had feared. Almost all of them, though, happened after my death.

I am certain that I never came to this place that bears my name when I was alive. At that time, there was no town here. It was just a monastery, founded by a forefather from my own royal house. I was brought here, after those pagan Vikings took my kingdom and my life, because it was a holy place.

From the beginning of my time here, pilgrims brought coins, jewels and other precious offerings made of copper or silver, which they left with me, to remind me of their supplication. In time, word spread among the basest of the local folk that such treasures lay unguarded in the hours of darkness. It was true: the custodian of the place was worse than useless. No matter how much noise the thieves made as they went about their rascal business, their racket was masked by the snores of that fat wastrel.

If anyone was to protect what was mine, I realised, it would have to be me. I took no action until one night when a whole gang of robbers tried to steal in, and I decided that this plunder must stop. I was aware of those scoundrels attempting to make their entry, and I conjured all my anger to direct against them. I froze each one of them where he was, rooted to the spot, and left them until the sun rose, when they could be discovered. It was one of my most famous miracles, at the time. The abbot turned the miscreants over to the Bishop of London, who had them all hanged by the neck, side by side on one long gibbet.

After that, no thief dared lay hands on my treasures, which lay undisturbed all through the night. My shrine would have been the safest place in all the kingdom without any custodian at all, although that man was now reformed in his ways, and maintained from that night on a most zealous vigil.

For half a century thereafter, my position was unchallenged. Then the Danes came attacking again. The Vikings had launched an assault on the town of Ipswich, so the sacrist of my abbey decided that the land of the Eastern Angles was no longer safe for me. Flight was an unseemly and shameful course but, in my coffined state, I had no say in the matter. I was borne away, to endure a forced exile for three summers in London. There I could at least receive my pilgrims still, which eased the nuisance of my dislocation, and at length the order came from the sacrist that it was safe for me to return to my own town. I was much lauded along the way by abbots, priests and common folk, and I, too, rejoiced.

Just as I arrived back, however, a Viking leader whose real name I have forgotten, but who was known to all as Forkbeard, invaded Mercia. He reached as far inland as

Gainsborough on the Trent river, only three days' ride from what had once been my own kingdom. By this time, all England was ruled by Ethelred, an imprudent leader who chose counsel badly. Weakened during his reign, the country now fell to the invaders, and Ethelred himself fled to the land of the Normans. Forkbeard was crowned King of England in London, but he was fonder of Gainsborough and made it his capital. From there, he turned his greedy eyes on my town.

My townsfolk had long been exempt from paying geld and all other taxes, as a mark of respect to myself. Forkbeard, in his greed, made it known that this exemption no longer stood: he wanted money, and if he did not get it, he would burn the town to the ground.

This offence was an outrage too far. I had lain passive throughout these late disruptions, but the time for inactivity was over. Having made this resolve, the enactment of it was a simpler thing than ever I had imagined. Confined within the stones of my shrine, I had thought my powers restricted to the bounds of the abbey. Howbeit, once I had fixed on my resolve, I found that this limitation was no hindrance, for my spirit was more mobile than my bones. Thus emboldened, I arose and took myself to the usurper king when he was at his mead-bench, and there I revealed myself. I warned him bluntly that I would not allow his wicked breach of custom.

I own that I expected Forkbeard to fall down in fright and show immediate penitence. Not he. Swollen in his pomp, or in his cups, the old Dane did not care to take my counsel nor even to acknowledge my arrival. I returned to my own place downhearted, thinking that the task was not so simple as I had first believed. I pondered on what next to do, and eventually I knew my mind. Acting on this new resolve, I had my sacrist go to Forkbeard and bid him heed my warning, else the affair would end for him in the most dire way. Alas, I sent the poor fellow into danger. Forkbeard had my man beaten with sticks so hard that he was near to death, then threw him roughly from his court.

At this, my full wrath was roused. First this trespassing Dane had menaced my town, then he had ignored my own presence and now he had used my brave sacrist most ill. I rose up from my place again, this time with vengeance, not persuasion, in my heart. I paid a second visit to Forkbeard, entering his private chamber while he was at his rest. I did not ask him to rethink his threat against my townsfolk; the time for that was past. Instead, I woke him from his slumber and allowed him to look full on my face, as I said to him, 'Do you want to have a tribute, O King, from the land of St Edmund? Rise up, behold, take it.'

His gnarled features were wreathed with sudden terror as he knew too late the identity of the visitor he had spurned. He was right to fear me. As he sat up in his bed, I plunged my lance into his chest with all my might, breaking his breastbone. Gore spilled from that wound, and from his mouth. The deed gave me much satisfaction, and I stood watching the life drain out of him, until his guards came running, alerted by his death-cry, and I made my clean escape.

My people loved me already, but after this great feat I was held in boundless esteem. I had saved them in the hour of their need and slain their foe, and I was proud of it. I was proving a better defender of my people in death than I had been in life. I was a protector again, and what protector would not have done the same, in the name of Almighty God? It was my role.

That is who I was when last I was in this shrine. Now that I am back, I assumed it should be so again, if ever my help was required. Why would I not?

It was on the radio news headlines at the top of every hour: the Archbishop of Canterbury was due to attend a service later that morning to mark the re-enshrinement of St Edmund, on his holy day, in the cathedral that now stood within the grounds of the old abbey at Bury St Edmunds.

The day seemed to glow with the excitement of it: cold and crisp, but without a breath of wind, under a piercing blue sky. Winter in these parts, when it eventually arrived, was not for the faint-hearted, as the wind raced down from the Arctic or the Urals with nothing to halt its icy progress. That was still a month or so off, however, and this was the kind of radiant November day when the landscape was a place of heart-skipping enchantment as far as the eye could see. How nice that it should be like this, for St Edmund and his congregation of well-wishers.

It would have been lovely to be one of them, but Hannah had not been invited. Not that she had expected to be: it was a grand occasion, and she was a grunt not a grandee. However, it was hard to not to feel a stab of envy when her cousin texted her the night before to say he would be there with Marina Spencer and to ask if she was going. She was relieved when Frances, an elderly friend who lived a couple of villages away, called to say she had sprained her ankle and to ask if Hannah could walk Ringo, her springer spaniel. While this felt slightly disloyal to her own three-legged companion Arnold, who was no fan of dogs, it would be a good distraction from the ceremony.

She picked up her charge – who owed his name to his habit, even at rest, of thumping his tail percussively on the ground – and let him sit beside her in the front seat of the car. Frances had recommended her normal walking route, starting at her village church and then across farmland, where Ringo could safely be let off his lead. The village was the sort that had become separated from its church, perhaps in time of plague to put distance between surviving inhabitants and the graveyard, or because some squire of old wanted to free up the land around the church and made the village up sticks. Whatever the reason, the ancient building, with its stumpy tower, low eaves and small, round-arched windows set in flint-cobbled walls, stood in peaceful seclusion at the end of a narrow, pot-holed track about half a mile from the village proper.

There were a couple of other cars in the rough-gravelled parking area. An overflowing poo-bin beneath the fingerpost at the start of the footpath was testament to the popularity of the place with dog walkers. The path itself led along a ploughed field towards a copse. Jagged shards of flint gleamed in the fresh-turned soil, and Hannah had visions of Ringo slicing a paw if he were allowed to scamper at will, so she resolved to keep him on lead until they reached the trees, where the path veered north and the ploughed land gave way to grassy meadow. Her charge registered his protest at this arrangement by tugging hard, pulling her along behind him, except when he found something to sniff or dig at, when the lead became a rein to hold her back. It was a relief for both of them to reach the grassy part. He tore about, ears bouncing joyfully, as he celebrated his liberation.

Slinging the leather cord around her neck, she was free to look around and enjoy the morning. Behind her, the tower of the church marked where she had come from. In front, the landscape rolled gently away, then rose again on the other side of the broad, shallow valley. When she first came to live with her mother, she tried to photograph this sort of view, but the camera flattened the undulations, rendering the countryside featureless, and the distant towers of other village churches – from her current spot she could see one, two, three of them – shrank to pin-pricks. That, she eventually realised, was the real charm of this countryside: it defied technology and evaded easy capture, so you had to look at it with your own eyes to appreciate it. That was a quality to treasure in a remorselessly point-and-click world which assumed an experience had only happened if it was photographed.

Up ahead, she saw another walker approaching. It was a woman, younger than herself, in yellow wellingtons with a woollen hat pulled tight around her ears. She had a golden retriever on lead, and Hannah called to Ringo to put him back on his. He chose this moment to chase after a pigeon, jumping and snapping at its tail-feathers before it managed to gain height. 'Ringo! Come here now!' she shouted, more to show the other woman she was making an effort than in any expectation he would obey.

'Don't worry,' said the woman, coming closer now. 'You

don't need to bother on our account.' The retriever, on an extendible cord, now came nosing around Hannah's pocket in the hope of one of the treats with which Frances had armed her.

'Is he allowed a biscuit?'

'Go for it. Say thank you, Monty.'

Monty was too busy crunching to take any notice.

The woman peered at Hannah. 'Don't we know each other?'

Hannah was good with faces and disliked being caught out. She looked back at the young woman, who had a nose ring and wide, pale cheeks. It was a striking face, and she was sure she would remember if... Then she noticed a strand of blue hair that had escaped from beneath the woollen hat. 'Of course we do! You're Daisy, aren't you, from the dig? I'm sorry, I didn't recognise you with your hat on.'

'Don't worry. I'm used to it. The blue hair is the only thing anyone ever remembers. If I cover it, people are completely thrown. I'm sorry, I don't actually know your name. I just recognise you from that party we had in the King's Head. You were with Brother Bernard, weren't you?'

Hannah introduced herself, then said: 'I would have thought you'd be at the service this morning, instead of out here.'

Daisy pulled a face. 'I'm not big on organised religion. I'm an archaeologist with a passion for history, and I love the spiritual feel of the abbey ruins. But when it comes to God and hymns and all that, I'm not so keen. Each to their own. It just doesn't do it for me. How about you? Did you not fancy it either?'

'I wasn't invited.'

'You're joking? Now I feel really bad! If only I'd known,

you could have had my ticket.'

'Oh, don't worry. In any case, how could you possibly have known? We've only just properly met.'

'I still feel bad.'

Ringo had decided to rejoin them and was now pouncing playfully at Monty, oblivious to the restrictions of the other dog's lead. 'Stop that, Ringo!' said Hannah, conscious of how ineffectual she sounded.

'He's fine. Look, I'll let Monty off, then they can run together. That's better. Go on, the pair of you. Wear yourselves out!'

The two animals were mismatched in size but seemed happy to chase each other around the meadow.

Daisy beamed as she watched them go. 'How old is Ringo?'

'To be honest, I'm not quite sure. Three or four, I think. He's not mine, you see. I'm walking him for a friend who's temporarily out of action.'

'That explains why I haven't seen you out here before. Come to think of it, I do recognise Ringo. What does his owner look like?'

'Frances? She's in her seventies. Very fine white hair, cut short. Nice Scottish accent, even though she's lived down here for years. Posh Edinburgh, I think. You know, a bit Miss Jean Brodie.'

Daisy said she thought she knew her. 'Anyway, how do you know Brother B?'

'I don't really. I met him for the first time that evening, at the party. Then we sat together the next day at the press conference, which was nice, and we ended up going for coffee with my important cousin, which was a bit weird.'

'Your "important" cousin? How so?'

'He works for Marina Spencer. He's one of the smart

young men in her entourage.'

'No way? I think maybe I saw him with her, in that case. As I remember, there was an Asian one, a ginger one and another one, quite good-looking.'

'He's the other one. I suppose he is, vaguely.'

'It must be a brilliant job.'

'I guess so. I don't know him very well. I'm much closer to his mother than to him. He'll be there today, of course, with Marina.'

'That's quite a coincidence, isn't it? I mean, to have two members of the family so closely associated with St Edmund.'

Hannah reddened. 'Not entirely.'

'How do you mean?'

'It's kind of a long story.'

'I don't need to be anywhere, and the dogs seem to be getting on like a house on fire, so why don't I turn round and join you for the rest of your walk? Unless you'd rather be on your own?'

'No, of course not. It would be lovely to have the company.'

They fell into step.

'So,' said Daisy. 'You were going to tell me why it's not a coincidence.'

'I know I shouldn't worry about it, because the outcome seems to have been good for everyone, but I do wonder if I perhaps spoke out of turn, and now it's becoming a national policy...'

'Slow down! You're not making sense. Rewind. Start at the beginning.'

'Sorry.' As they reached the end of the meadow and turned to follow the line of the hedge on the wide loop that would bring them back towards the church, Hannah recounted her first, excited call to the aunt who was more like a big sister, who in turn had passed the news to Mark, with his important job in Whitehall. With the benefit of hindsight, she explained, she should have told Pauline not to mention it to her cousin, or she ought not to have told Pauline, full stop. In her own defence, how was she to know Mark would see the discovery of the skeleton of an Anglo-Saxon king as a political opportunity for his boss? Then came his own call, which had taken her completely unawares, given that they had not spoken directly in years. At first she thought it was just her long-lost young relative catching up, but then she realised he had an agenda – and she was it. 'He said they wanted to make Edmund the patron saint again, not just of England this time, but of the whole United Kingdom.'

'Yes, I read about it. But that's brilliant, isn't it? What are you worried about?'

'Well, just that I blabbed before the news was properly out. Before I knew it, I had cabinet ministers making policy about it. It's scary. If it goes wrong, I'll feel it's my responsibility.'

'How can it go wrong, though?'

'If the Scots and the Welsh and the Irish all hate the idea. I did say that to Mark when he first mentioned it.'

'I thought they all love the idea because Edmund was half-Scottish and a big fan of the Welsh and Irish. I keep reading that in the papers.'

'Yes, so do I.'

'So what's the problem?'

'Nothing, I suppose, if you put it like that.' They climbed a stile and descended into the next field, which had been left to go to weed after harvest. The dogs cavorted ahead.

'You still don't sound very happy.'

Hannah was indeed worried about something else, but she could not put her finger on what it was. There had been something peculiar, that day in the Abbey Gardens, about the way Mark appeared at their side to hustle herself and Brother Bernard away. He had behaved oddly the whole time, and it was like he had some kind of ulterior motive. Perhaps she was just imagining it. She barely knew him, after all, so that edgy, slightly manic manner could just be his normal way. In any case, he was family, and it was not right to bad-mouth him to a virtual stranger.

'No, honestly,' she said. 'There isn't a problem. I'm just being silly. Call it sour grapes for not being invited to the service.'

The church tower was in sight now, and Hannah called Ringo back to put him on lead.

'Like I say, I'm so sorry they didn't invite you,' said Daisy. 'At least they managed to ask Brother Bernard. I know he's been really looking forward to it. This whole thing has been wonderful for him. Just think: he has devoted his life to the study of St Edmund, and now, on St Edmund's Day itself, he's seeing his body restored to a new shrine in the cathedral. I bet he'll be in the guest-of-honour seats, along with the Archbishop of Canterbury and Marina Spencer. Isn't there meant to be a member of the royal family there too?'

This had been mentioned in one of the news bulletins: the Duke of Gloucester. Or was it Kent?

'I expect it will be on the lunchtime news,' said Hannah.

'It better had be.'

'Will do you me a favour, though? I know you think I'm being silly, but please don't tell anyone else I tipped off my cousin before they made the formal announcement. Not Vernon, not Magnus, not anyone. If anything does go wrong with this patron saint idea, I'd be mortified if people thought it all came from my speaking out of turn.'

'You're worrying about nothing, but I can see it's important to you, so I promise I won't breathe a word. It'll be our little secret, among the four of us.'

'Four?'

'Me, you, Monty and Ringo. I'll make sure Monty doesn't blab, if you do the same for Ringo.'

Hannah smiled. 'Deal. And thanks for your company. It's been almost as nice as it would have been to go to the service.'

'My pleasure. And stop beating yourself up, that's what I say. Your cousin is flying the flag for St Edmund, which is a wonderful thing. If it's all your doing, you should be proud of the part you played in it.'

As they looked down on the bishop at the nave altar from their limestone eyrie in the raised north transept, Mark could hear Marina's rage rushing in and out of her nose. Peering up at the brightly painted ceiling of the tower crossing – a riot of red, blue and gold, in modern homage to the gaudiness of the pre-Reformation English Church – he mouthed a silent prayer of thanks that it had been Giles' job to liaise with the cathedral authorities, not his.

The day had begun so promisingly. There had been editorials about St Edmund in *The Times* and the *Mail*, both treating him as the *de facto* patron saint of the United Kingdom and celebrating the re-establishment of his shrine. There had been a similar win on the *Today* programme, which devoted Thought for the Day to the issue, as well as a discussion slot. Buoyed up by this coverage, Marina had been less tense than usual on the journey. It helped that she had no speech to deliver today, so there was nothing for her to fret about. She engaged cheerfully with selfie-hunters on the platform at Cambridge, and there were no gripes about timetabling. Even her choice of outfit, a tailored blue coat and matching pill-box hat, with a gold silk scarf at the neck, was a triumph. She never normally wore blue, for obvious political reasons, and Mark was surprised by her choice when he first saw her on the platform at King's Cross. When they reached the cathedral, however, he saw the point. Flags of St Edmund hung at intervals all the way down the nave: three gold crowns on a field of the exact same blue as Marina's coat. She was asserting her new allegiance as proudly as a football supporter in team colours, and she had done it with panache. Any photograph of her today would convey the clear message that this crowd-pleasing event was her political baby.

It was only when they were shown their seats that the mood plunged. Mark knew from advance briefings that the new shrine was in the gated St Edmund Chapel, to the north of the chancel. This was clearly the plum spot for the most important guests. As their usher escorted them down the nave towards the tower crossing, Mark naturally assumed that was where they were going. They could see the wrought-iron railings of this holy of holies ahead of them. Before they reached it, however, their guide stopped and indicated a steep, narrow staircase beside them. It appeared to lead to a raised side gallery of private pews, which would afford a bird's eye view of the great pulpit and nave altar, but was completely detached from everything that was going on.

'Up here?' said Marina. 'You're joking!'

'This is the seating plan I've been given, madam,' mumbled the usher, a spotty young man barely out of his teens, reddening at this whiff of oncoming trouble. 'If you wouldn't mind taking your seats…'

Marina's demeanour made it clear she was going nowhere.

Realising he could not actually force the secretary of state to climb the staircase, the hapless youth hastened off in search of reinforcements, leaving Marina tapping her foot and snorting dangerously. With a faster instinct for self-preservation than Mark possessed, Giles and Karim also shot off, in opposite directions, each muttering about looking for someone to sort it.

'I haven't come all this way to sit in the blasted gods,' Marina hissed at Mark. 'I'm the secretary of state, for Christ's sake. This should all have been arranged in advance. Who was responsible for advance prep with the cathedral?'

'That was Giles.' It was every man for himself at the court of Marina Spencer, and Mark had no doubt Giles would finger him no less promptly if the roles were reversed.

She pursed her lips, and he took the opportunity to stare at his phone screen.

'Secretary of State, welcome to St Edmundsbury!' A cleric of about Mark's own age, with a lanyard announcing he was the sub-dean, was smiling bravely, with the usher lurking nervously in the slipstream of his robes. 'I understand there's some difficulty?'

'There certainly is. I can't possibly sit up there. I won't see a thing. Why on earth aren't I in the chapel with the archbishop?'

'Space there is extremely limited, Secretary of State, and the dean has taken the decision, in consultation with the police, to seat the ecclesiastical dignitaries in the chapel and our distinguished secular guests in the transept gallery. I assure you, it's a wonderful vantage point. Think of it as the royal box at the theatre. And you're in exalted company. The Lord Lieutenant is already up there, I believe, with Mr Parker, the leader of the council, and of course Wendy Wethers, whom you will know…'

If Mark could have given the sub-dean one piece of advice, it would have been to avoid suggesting it was a privilege for Marina to share a confined space with Wendy Wethers. The cleric seemed to reach that conclusion of his own accord when he saw the look on Marina's face. 'The main consideration is the security, though. The police insisted that you should be seated here. It's by far the safest location.'

'And the Duke of Gloucester?' she snapped. 'Is he up here too?'

Mark thought it was Kent, but perhaps he was wrong.

'No, His Royal Highness will be in the St Edmund Chapel, because he's here to represent the Queen in her capacity as head of the Church of England.'

As Marina opened her mouth to reply, Mark spotted a familiar figure – gaunt and vulpine, weighed down on one side by a heavy leather shoulder bag – lurking behind the nearest pillar. Cupping his hand around his mouth, he leant in close and whispered: '*Daily Mail*, three o'clock.'

Crispin Knott was the *Mail*'s chief colour-writer for grand occasions. He also had a hotline to every gossip columnist who counted and was no fan of Marina. A slight widening of her eyes was enough to indicate that she had grasped the problem. 'Thank you very much for your help,' she told the surprised sub-dean in a suddenly friendly tone, loud and clear enough to carry as far as Knott's pillar, and proceeded to climb the steps to the gallery with a glacial smile, with Karim, who had rejoined them, trotting behind. Now Giles arrived back too, looking distinctly sweaty.

'Are we not being moved?' he said to Mark.

'Crispin Knott's hanging around, so she's decided not to make a scene.'

Giles followed Mark's gaze, nodded his understanding, and wiped his forehead with the sleeve of his suit as he followed the party up the narrow staircase into the gallery.

Mark hung back, ready to deflect Knott if he came sniffing around to seek out the source of friction. 'Sorry about that,' he said to the sub-dean. 'Highly strung, politicians, eh?'

The cleric lowered his voice. 'If you think I don't know about petty jealousies and fragile egos, you're clearly unfamiliar with the inner workings of the Church of England.' He winked and hurried away.

Smothering a smile, Mark climbed the steps up to the gallery. There he found the rest of his party hastily reordering themselves so that Marina did not have to sit next to Wendy Wethers.

'Morning Marina,' the latter called. 'I love your outfit. You know, blue really suits you. You should wear it more often! What a shame no one can see it, hidden away up here.'

'I'm simply here to witness St Edmund's return to his proper place, Wendy. That's all that matters,' said Marina, but the look that went with her words could have refrozen the polar ice cap.

With Wendy still smirking, Marina had no choice but to take her seat as if nothing was wrong. Only the gale-force fury coming out of her nose spoke otherwise. Wedged between her and Giles, Mark took refuge in his phone once more. Ordinarily he would resist the temptation because they were all on show. Up here, however, it did not matter. Or it would not have mattered if it had been possible.

'Forget it, mate,' said Wendy, on the other side of Giles. 'No reception up here. Trust me, I've already tried. It's like being in a cave.'

He sighed and slid his phone back into his pocket.

118

As the service began, it was bizarre not to be able to see the hundreds of other people in the congregation. In compensation, the choral singing swirled high into the air and wrapped them in its music. Had Mark been on his own, he might have allowed himself to relax into the majestic, holy atmosphere, but of course there was no chance of that, with the ever-present ministerial pressure cooker steaming away to his left.

He had been wondering whether any of his own biographical embroidery would feature in the service and, if so, how he would feel about it. Bare-faced deceit in the rough-and-tumble world of Westminster might be fair game, but would his conscience get the better of him when his fictions were repeated under his maker's roof?

If there was to be any reference, it would come in the bishop's address. When this part of the service arrived, a lean figure, made even taller by his gold mitre, climbed into his pulpit and proceeded to tell the story of St Edmund's martyrdom and then his journey in death: from initial burial near the site of his violent execution; his transfer to Bury; his hasty removal from harm's way during yet another Danish incursion; his return to the abbey; and finally his disappearance when the abbey was reduced to rubble by Henry VIII's zealous enforcers. For nearly five centuries he had been lost, thought perhaps to have been spirited away by loyal monks to France or some more discreet part of Suffolk, but now it turned out he had been within the ruined abbey precincts all along. This, the final part of his journey, was all about restoring the dignity that had been rudely denied him this past half-millennium.

'We do not know much about Edmund's life,' he continued. Mark tensed: if there was to be any mention of Pictish blood, Welsh allegiance or Irish affinity, now was the moment.

'But we do know that, before he was killed for being a Christian, he was bound by the Vikings. That violent event took place eleven centuries ago, in a period of history about which we know so little that we call it the Dark Ages, but there is nothing archaic or obscure about being bound. Many people in our world are held captive by poverty, conflict, anxiety and fear. Our Lord himself described his work setting captives free. As the Gospel of St Luke tells us…'

On he went in similar vein, and Mark realised there was no danger of his own version of the story making an appearance. As the prospect dwindled, the anxiety it had provoked gave way to a perverse disappointment that his efforts would not be recognised after all.

The final part of the service took place in the St Edmund Chapel. It was frustrating not to be able to see any of the proceedings, although it was some consolation that the congregation in the nave could not do so either. The gale-force snorting resumed for a short while, but Marina appeared in better humour when it was all over and she could get up and receive the attentions of the Lord Lieutenant and the council leader, who were eager to pay court. Her mood improved further when the sub-dean appeared at the top of the steps, asking if he might escort the secretary of state to the St Edmund Chapel, where His Royal Highness and the Archbishop of Canterbury were anxious to greet her.

'You know what to do,' she hissed at Mark as she turned to follow the cleric.

Of Marina's many foibles, her assumption that her aides knew by osmosis her every wish and requirement was the one Mark found hardest to get used to. It always created a dilemma. Coming right out and asking what she meant would be an open confession of his own inadequacy, by her impossible standards, and was therefore best avoided. On the other hand, guessing wrongly could lead to far more grief and possible public carpeting, such as on the occasion when he thought she wanted him to fetch her coat at a turgid civic reception and she actually wanted another glass of wine. The best option was a middle course: take a stab but seek clarification in case he had misunderstood. This was the path he now followed. 'Snappers?' he muttered, directing his head away from the sub-dean and the prying ears of Wendy Wethers.

'Just one will do,' she said, equally *sotto voce*. 'Let's not go over the top.'

'Got it.' Excusing himself as he squeezed ahead of the party, he hastened down the steps and set off in search of the press pack. He imagined there would be a posse of photographers outside the south door, waiting to catch the great and the good emerging into the churchyard. For a set of exclusive shots, it was better to find a loner operating independently of his rivals. As he crossed the front of the nave, he saw just the candidate: a paunchy old-timer with a mullet and low-slung jeans, who was taking long-distance shots of the congregation through a heavy-duty pap lens.

'Psst, Steve!'

Steve looked up and Mark beckoned him over.

'Yes, boss?'

'Steve, mate, I don't know if you've seen Marina Spencer this morning. She's looking stunning, but she was tucked away during the service, very discreet, because she's keen to take a back seat. Let the Church take all the limelight, and all that. But I do know she's on her way to meet the Archbishop of Canterbury and the Duke of Kent…'

'Gloucester, isn't it?'

'Whatever. If you hurry, you'll catch the three of them now in the St Edmund Chapel. Do me a favour, though, and don't let Marina see you. She'll have my balls on toast if she thinks I tipped you off.'

Steve's eyes shone at the prospect of shooting something he was not meant to see. 'Cheers, boss. I owe you one.' He shuffled off in the direction of the chapel, lens poised.

Congratulating himself on a job well done, Mark followed at a safe distance. He arrived at the wrought-iron gates of the chapel just in time to see Marina dropping a respectful curtsey to the royal visitor – not dipping so far, fortunately, as to lose all dignity – while the archbishop smiled on them both. Steve had managed to position himself in the sanctuary, which was divided from the chapel by a row of pillars, and offered a perfect view into it. He was now capturing this 'private' meeting for tomorrow's papers. With the trio positioned in front of the shrine – a polished limestone box draped with the blue-and-gold flag of St Edmund – the shot would show Marina's carefully chosen ensemble to its best possible advantage. This ought to make up for her humiliation of spending the service up in the gods.

He took the opportunity to check his phone to see whether the *Times* and *Mail* pieces had opened up any discussion on Twitter. He was pleased to see that St Edmund was trending once again. One of *The Guardian*'s Roedean communist columnists was trying to whip up controversy by saying it was racist to replace the foreign-born St George with a home-grown saint. Her article had become the butt of Twitter hilarity because someone had found a tweet from the same Guardianista a couple of years earlier, in which she maintained that the cross of St George was a fundamentally racist emblem. The fuss would no doubt blow itself out in a few hours, but it would be enjoyable while it lasted.

Aside from that, there was nothing else he needed to bring to Marina's attention. There had been an announcement about preliminary trade talks with the Chinese, which had no impact on her department. The prime minister was touring a pilchard-canning factory in Cornwall, an engagement much less glamorous than her own, and there were flood warnings in the North-east, but nowhere near her own Midlands constituency; so there was nothing pressing.

He looked up to see the archbishop and the duke walking towards him, deep in conversation. Marina seemed to have disappeared. He had a moment of panic, like a parent losing a toddler. Then he glimpsed a tell-tale patch of blue behind the men: it was Marina's hat, which was all he could see beyond a row of chairs, and it seemed to be at waist height. Puzzled, he took a step into the chapel as the two men passed, and now he could see his boss properly. To his surprise, she was kneeling on a blue-and-gold cushion beside the tomb, apparently deep in prayer.

Mark had never before seen her make an open religious display. During the service, she had joined in with the Lord's Prayer and muttered 'amen' in all the appropriate places, suggesting she was a believer, but Mark had never known her go to church of her own volition or engage in any other kind of piety, public or private. He had assumed her faith was roughly equivalent to his own: somewhere in the background, shyly acquiescent. But there was nothing shy about her present genuflection, eyes tight shut and lips silently moving. Her positively Catholic posture brought to mind illuminated images of medieval kings at prayer beside St Edmund's original shrine. He wondered if that comparison had also occurred to Marina, and glanced over to see if Steve was still discreetly snapping. He was indeed, and yes, he realised, of course it had occurred to her. This, not her encounter with the archbishop and the minor royal, was the shot Marina wanted the world to see.

She was getting to her feet. He moved towards her as she smoothed her coat, to show her he was there. 'I found a snapper,' he murmured as he drew closer, pointing with his eyes towards Steve's pillar. 'Unfortunately he may also have intruded on your private moment.'

'That can't be helped.' She marched briskly ahead of him, head high, with no trace of a smile that might allow them to share the joke of this staged photo-op. Of course not. That would require her to treat him with some kind of camaraderie.

Leading the way out of the chapel and towards the nave altar, she lingered at the front of the central aisle, where the archbishop was still in conversation with the duke. She allowed herself to be waylaid by admiring members of the congregation, agreeing that it had been a beautiful service, smiling for selfies and signing someone's order of service. When the duke was ushered away by a couple of royal protection officers, leaving via the south door to a smattering of uncertain cheers from the crowd outside, she broke off abruptly. With sure-footed skill, she managed to fall into step with the archbishop as he too headed for the door, so that the pair of them emerged into the autumn sunlight side by side. It was a masterful performance, at the cost only of the hurt feelings of the few admirers who had been denied their selfies. Mopping up from the rear, Mark did his best to assure them that the secretary of state had urgent matters to discuss with His Grace and that, such were the pressures of office, she could not always pass the time of day in as relaxed a fashion as she might like. It would be nice to get thanks or some kind of credit for this regular, unbidden work, but it was pointless even to think about it. Expecting gratitude from Marina was like expecting not to be squeezed to death by a boa constrictor: it was an unreasonable hope that went against nature.

He caught up with her in the churchyard, where Karim was checking his phone and Giles was sucking on his vape. Their hybrid taxi was idling on Crown Street, ready to take them to the station. It was a relief to get into it and shut the door on the outside world, safe in the knowledge that the engagement had finished on a high note.

All four of them had their faces in their phones for most of the train journey: Marina reading briefing papers from her civil servants, the other three checking for reports of the service. Both the Duke of Gloucester and the Duke of Kent were trending on Twitter, amid continuing confusion as to which of the two had been present, but there was no such doubt concerning Marina's identity. A couple of bystanders had posted snaps of her and the archbishop in the cathedral doorway. One had caught Marina in mid-gurn, eyes closed and mouth open, which Mark saw no need to bring to her attention, but the other was a decent enough shot, and she nodded approval when he showed it to her.

They had just pulled out of Cambridge when the first full news report dropped. Steve had done a great job. He had lost no time in getting his exclusive shots on the wires, and the BBC had chosen Marina kneeling beside the tomb of St Edmund as the main image to illustrate its web story.

'It's fantastic, Marina,' cooed Karim.

She frowned at the screen. 'I hope people won't think it's too…' She paused, searching for the word.

Staged? Cynical? Mark bit his tongue.

'…overtly religious,' she said.

'I don't think so,' said Giles. 'It was a private moment. If there's any negative comeback, we can always brief that it was unwarranted intrusion by the photographer.'

'And the photographer would say he was specifically asked…' began Mark, then remembered he had told Steve he was acting without Marina's knowledge, so if there was to be any retribution, he had placed himself squarely in the firing line. He left his sentence unfinished. Fortunately no one was listening. 'There won't be any criticism,' he said instead, more assertively. 'It's a sincere, deeply personal image, showing Marina's commitment to the cause of uniting our divided nations as well as giving us a glimpse of her intimate values. The way her outfit matches the colours of the flag on the tomb also makes it look as if she and St Edmund were meant for each other. That's an iconic photograph.'

'I think Mark's right, in this instance,' said Marina. She might have added that Mark had made a smart choice of snapper, who had got just the right shot and then distributed it promptly and efficiently, but just saying he was right was rare praise, and Mark would settle for that.

He was still reading the full BBC report when his phone pinged. So, at almost exactly the same moment, did Marina's, Karim's and Giles'. All of them were used to such notifications throughout the day and night, but it was rare for a chorus of messages to chirp in such perfect unison. Each of them checked their alert.

'Shit,' said Mark.

'God,' said Karim.

'Holy crap,' said Giles.

It was a text from Number 10. *PM has had heart attack in Cornwall*, it said. *Condition serious. More as we get it.*

Marina was already on her phone, twisting away from their table into the window, in an attempt at discretion. Whoever she was calling was clearly engaged, so she tried another name from her directory, and then another, before she finally got through to someone.

'What's going on?' Mark heard her say. 'Right… Jesus… And when did it…? Uh-huh… So where is he now? … Right, will do. And you'll let me know? … Thanks.'

She turned back to them. 'That was Rex, from the PM's office,' she whispered, with a glance around them at the other passengers, some of whom were now picking up news alerts on their own phones. 'It sounds bad. Morton collapsed at the end of his tour of the pilchard factory, and they've rushed him to hospital in Truro, but they're saying it's touch and go.'

They all sat in stunned silence, processing the bombshell. Then, as instinct kicked in, they sought more information from their phones. Since the incident had happened during an official visit, with the media in attendance, the news was breaking everywhere. There was footage of the prime minister, still in his white coat and protective hairnet, stumbling and falling, whereupon his security detail formed a protective wall around him, and other minders screamed at the media to back off. The immediate assumption was that this was some kind of terrorist attack, but it had soon become clear the prime minister was having a heart attack and needed air. The media had been cleared from the area, but the cameras had managed to record his prone figure being stretchered into an ambulance, after which the press all piled into their own vehicles and raced after the blue lights. They were now camped outside the hospital, with the broadcasters doing live pieces to camera for the rolling news stations.

After an agonising ten minutes, Marina's phone went and she snatched it up at half-ring, once again twisting into the window for privacy. The news had gone right round the carriage now, prompting strangers to open conversations with each other. Many of the passengers were openly staring at their party, looking for insider clues with the mesmerised blatancy of motorway rubberneckers.

Mark could not hear Marina's conversation this time because she was speaking more quietly than ever, but the call did not last long. She turned back to them, opened her mouth to speak, then seemed to think better of it and set about writing a text message. She pressed send, and a couple of seconds later it pinged into all their devices at once.

Mark looked at his message. It read, *Don't react to this. The whole carriage is watching. It hasn't been announced yet, but he didn't make it. DOA at hospital.* He felt the need to swallow, and tried to suppress it, because it felt like an obvious giveaway. He failed. His colleagues nodded agreement at Marina. Both their faces were ashen. He assumed his own was too.

Marina's phone rang again. Mark could just about hear, this time, as she said, 'Yes, I have... I know, appalling. Stunned, absolutely stunned... Such a shock and... No, of course I haven't. It's far too early and I couldn't possibly... The man has only been... Look, I'm not having this conversation. Later, maybe, but not now. Bye.'

She snapped her phone shut.

He wondered who it had been, and how much time would need to pass before the conversation was permissible.

It was extraordinary to receive such shattering news, with

all manner of possible implications, and not to be able to show any emotion, let alone discuss it. Marina was right, though: until it was officially announced, it was up to them to maintain an inscrutable façade. There would be time enough for reaction later. So, for the rest of the journey, they each buried themselves in their phones once more. Mark noticed Karim sending discreet texts, and he could imagine the news fanning out across Whitehall. Living alone, and with no close friends inside the Westminster loop, he did not feel the same urge to confide. Marina, meanwhile, was sending and receiving a flurry of texts.

His own phone pinged when they were ten minutes away from King's Cross. It was an editor from the BBC newsroom. They knew the prime minister was dead, and their political editor was already tweeting the announcement. They wanted to know what time Marina's train was due in, so they could get a reaction from her. Mark showed Marina the text. 'Is this all right, or do you want me to fend them off?'

'It'll have to be,' she said, reaching for her bag and pulling out a make-up mirror.

As they stepped off the train, they could see the phalanx of cameras waiting behind the ticket barrier. After Marina's prominent engagement in the morning, it had been easy for the whole pack to trace her. By the time she reached the barrier they were calling out to her, in the unnecessary charade that was part of the media ritual. It was not as if she was going to pass them by.

Passing through the gates and moving to one side to let other passengers go past, she allowed the lenses to cluster around her. A couple of journalists started firing questions at her, and she held up her hand to quieten them. It was important, on occasions such as this, for the politician to show they were in control of their own statement.

'Like the rest of the country,' she began, 'I have only just heard the tragic news about the prime minister. As you can imagine, it has not yet fully sunk in. The country has lost a great leader, still at the height of his powers, and I have lost a friend. Morton Alexander came to office in one of the most extraordinary election victories in modern times, and he had so much to offer this country. I'm sure I speak for everyone when I say we are not yet ready to speak of him in the past tense. This has been an immense shock for me, as it has for the whole country. My heart goes out to Morton's wife, Linda, and their two daughters. Inadequate as it may be, I hope it will bring them comfort to know we are all thinking of them, and that we are all grieving with them, because this truly is a loss for the nation as a whole. Now, if you'll excuse me…'

It was dignified, warm and well-judged – the consummate Marina Spencer – but of course it was not enough for the hacks. 'What will happen now, Secretary of State?' one of them called out. 'Who's in charge at Number 10?'

She turned back, jaw clenched. 'Look, the prime minister passed away less than an hour ago. I've been on a train and I've had very little chance to discuss the situation with anyone at Number 10. I'm sure they'll be able to answer any procedural questions you may have. For the moment, let us please show some proper respect.'

Mark could see she meant that. While few politicians played the media game better than Marina, he was pretty sure her anger was genuine.

The hacks had to up the ante. It was what everyone expected of them. 'Any thoughts about the succession, Secretary of State, or is it too early?' shouted a distinctive voice. It was Geraldine Jones from ITN.

Marina glared at her. 'I think you know the answer to that already, Geraldine. It's far too early. I know you're all just doing your jobs, but please bear in mind that all of us in government, and many people in Parliament, have lost a friend as well as a leader.'

Not to be outdone by ITN, the political editor of *The Sun*, a notorious weasel called Nick Major, pushed a tape recorder into Marina's face and said, 'Might you be a candidate yourself, Secretary of State?'

'I repeat, now is not the time. Thank you all very much.' She turned away and strode towards the exit of the station. Mark hoped, for Giles' sake, that there was a car waiting for them outside.

Falling into step behind her, he heard Major say to a colleague, 'That's not a no, then.'

I supposed that the lady sporting my colours was the present queen. Why would I not? I am accustomed to being paid court by leaders of the highest rank and the bluest blood, so it was natural to expect the sovereign to come in person.

I remember that William the Norman used to come often when I was last in my shrine, although he used the French tongue, so I understood but little of what he said to me. His great-grandson, the second Henry, did not come at first, but when discord broke out in his reign, and rebel forces came within sight of my abbey, along with three thousand Flemish mercenaries, my abbot sent his knights out under my banner to help the king's men. The rebels were ambushed and most of those three thousand Flemings were hunted down and slaughtered. After that, King Henry was no longer a stranger. Twice he came to give thanks, kneeling by my side, as well he might.

The first King Edward was also in attendance very often.

One time he could not come in person so he sent his personal standard to be touched by the clothes I had worn in life, which were conserved by the monks of the abbey as holy relics. He believed I brought good fortune to him in battle, and how could he doubt it?

I remember too, much later, another Henry, the sixth, I think: a boy king who had inherited the crown when still a babe in arms. He had uncles to rule in his name, which allowed him great leisure. He used it to tarry at my side and stayed half a year. It all ended when another Henry, the eighth king to bear that name, pulled down the holy cloisters of this place. Down the abbey came, stone by stone, and the deed was done before I had the chance to muster a response. To save me from this Henry's baleful clutches, I was taken from my gold-trimmed shrine and laid without ceremony in the darkest of pits. And there it was my fate to languish for half-a-thousand years, until my recent sweet rescue.

I had, then, known all the greatest monarchs until that time, so my expectation that the present queen might come to see me restored to my shrine was not, I think, unreasonable. It transpired that she had not done so and had sent instead a son of her father's younger brother. This royal cousin did not speak to me directly so I could not form any impression of him. In the past, I have learned to be suspicious of those who are close to the crown but do not wear it. They either wish to wear it and are prepared to scheme most wickedly in the hope of winning it, or they have that indolent form of greed that afflicts those who are high-born but do not bear the burden of responsibility.

One such was Prince Eustace, another great-grandson of William the Norman. He was both a wicked schemer and an indolent brat, an unlovely combination which would cost him dear. England was torn asunder in those years by civil war between feuding royal cousins. It was a conflict that affected the common folk grievously. Their suffering was so bad that it was said the saints slept – although I did not. At length, to bring peace to the land, it was agreed that the crown would pass not to Eustace, as the rules of heredity dictated, but to his kinsman Henry (the one on whose behalf I fought the Flemings). This was a happy solution for all save Eustace himself, who took it sore amiss. In his rage, he plundered lands and levied heavy taxes wherever he could. He came to my abbey, where he was welcomed with good heart by the monks and entertained royally at a feast, but our generosity was not enough for him. Having eaten his fill and seen all his men eat their fill too, he demanded money to pay his soldiers. My monks told him no funds could be provided, whereupon the haughty prince became tyrannical. He gave the order to loot the abbey and lay waste to its lands, which his men did with much zeal, in spite of all our hospitality.

Perhaps he thought my abbey was an easy target that would offer scant defence. If so, he reckoned without my own wrath, which was more than a match for his ill-temper. When this preening young ingrate returned to his own castle at Cambridge and sat down to dine on food he had stolen from my monks, he took sick after the first bite. Spitting and choking, he broke off from his meal and tried to find remedy by putting his fingers down his gullet to fetch up the morsel he had consumed, but he was too late to save himself, and those who came to his aid were powerless to undo what had already been done. He writhed in agony and cried out for God to save him, but our Father in Heaven either did not hear his pleas or chose not to heed them, and Eustace died a painful death.

When the news of the prince's fate began to spread, the people took it as my vengeance, and I was glad they quaked. For those who had forgotten my fatal blow to Forkbeard, it sent a sign that no one could raid my abbey with impunity.

This cousin of the present queen did not, as I say, come to speak to me. But in his stead it was pleasing to have a respectful supplicant kneeling by my side once more. Even though she was not the sovereign and merely a fine gentlewoman, I sensed that great changes had been wrought in this kingdom, so that those who wear the crown have little power, and far greater authority is vested in those who wear it not. This supplicant who wore my colours so proudly and so loyally was, I believed, a commanding figure, despite her sex, and it was natural that I should treat her homage with fitting respect.

Therein, I know now, were the roots of my mistake.

Hannah had a spare key so she could let herself into Frances' cottage, to save her friend hobbling to the door. 'It's only me,' she called, wondering if she ought to try to get the mud off Ringo's paws, then giving up on the idea as he ran off in search of his water bowl, trailing his lead behind him.

'Have you heard the news?' came Frances' voice from the sitting room.

With Ringo for company in the car, Hannah had not bothered to put the radio on.

'I haven't been listening, no. What is it? About the service? I expect it will be all over the TV tonight, won't it?'

'Not the service, the prime minister.'

'What about him?'

'He's dead!'

'No!'

'Come and watch.'

Hannah entered the room, where Frances lay sprawled on

the sofa with one foot bandaged up, remote in hand.

'What happened? It's not terrorism, is it?'

On the screen was Marina Spencer, in French blue coat and hat, with a gold scarf at her throat, trying to fend off reporters' questions. 'I've had very little chance to discuss the situation with anyone at Number 10. I'm sure they'll be able to answer any procedural questions you may have. For the moment, let us please show some proper respect...' She looked dazed.

Hannah could see Mark at Marina's elbow, but this was not the time to brag about her connections in high places. Along the bottom of the screen, the ticker-tape headlines set out the key elements of the shock development: *Prime minister collapsed on visit to Cornish pilchard factory... Taken to hospital but pronounced dead on arrival... Initial fears of terror attack unfounded... Morton Alexander believed to have suffered massive heart attack...*

Mesmerised, the pair of them sat and watched the harassed-looking anchor attempt to coax meaningful commentary out of a series of correspondents and pundits, most of whom could only repeat the same platitudes about how shocked they all were, which was clearly true, but uninformative. Someone mentioned that Alexander was the first prime minister to die in office since Lord Palmerston, a fact that was duly repeated at regular intervals.

'And of course it's far too early to think about the succession, I'm sure,' the anchor flailed, 'but what are you hearing at your end, Charlotte? What's the word, if any, in Whitehall and the corridors of Westminster?'

Charlotte agreed it was far too early, and nobody was even whispering any names, not least for fear of prejudicing the chances of a preferred candidate who might be tarnished by any suggestion of unseemly haste.

That line held throughout the day and for most of the next. By the following evening, when plans were announced for a state funeral – a perk of dying in office – and the deputy prime minister had stepped temporarily into the breach, names were being muttered into the ears of lobby correspondents, who duly relayed them to the public. Of these mooted candidates, two immediately ruled themselves out. By the weekend, it was clear there was only one serious contender. That person was, by common consent, the best communicator in government, frequently triumphing against all-comers on *Question Time* and managing to combine a strong sense of principle and authenticity with pragmatic effectiveness. A vast chunk of the electorate, across the spectrum, believed this was a politician who bucked every norm and was a genuinely likeable person. Up against a favourite with such rare gifts, any other hopefuls back-pedalled, not relishing immortality as a pub-quiz answer, which was the most they were likely to achieve if they stayed in the contest. One by one they fell away and pledged their loyalty to the frontrunner, who was, soon enough, the only runner.

Political coronations had a sketchy history: although memories were cruelly short, nobody had quite forgotten the ill-fated Theresa May. However, the consensus was that a no-contest arrangement would be respectful in present circumstances, because it would avoid the indignity of an internal battle. The fact that it was nearly December was also a consideration. Politicians and the commentariat agreed it would be better to have the new hand on the wheel as the New Year began, to deal with forthcoming challenges at home (the state of the economy, the ever-growing pressure on the NHS, the future of the union) and abroad (new trading and political relationships to be forged, not least with the burgeoning superpower, China).

There were formalities to be observed, even for a coronation, but it proved surprisingly easy, in a general spirit of positivity and can-do, to fast-forward the normal procedures. So it was that Christmas arrived in Downing Street with Marina Spencer installed as the new prime minister.

In few places was her popularity greater than in East Anglia, which had taken her enthusiastic embrace of the cause of St Edmund as an immense compliment. The local press endlessly recycled the pictures of her wearing Edmund's colours, particularly the prayer shot beside the shrine. It was not clear what, if any, practical benefit the region would gain from this iconic show of devotion, but the image flattered the Eastern counties' vanity, tickling them behind the ears in a way that no one in authority had bothered to do for centuries.

Hannah was by no means immune to this emotional blandishment. It addressed some atavistic tribal need that she had not previously been aware of harbouring. She had never cared in the slightest about the fortunes of Norwich City or Ipswich Town, relative to each other or the rest of the country, but this was a deeper, older tribalism that reached back to the glory days of the Iceni and the Trinovantes, when a tribe really was a tribe. On one level it was nonsense, but it was a novel experience to feel pride in an ancient culture, a kind of primal romantic attachment that she had assumed to be the exclusive preserve of the Cornish, or the Scots. In a flight of romantic whimsy, she imagined herself and her neighbours woading their faces in St Edmund's shade of blue, standing on their modest hilltop and shouting in their best brogue: 'They moight tick away ower loives, but them'll never tick ower freed'm!' Maybe she could invite Daisy, whom she had met a few more times while walking Ringo and who had now become a friend. She already had the right colour hair.

She also knew it was absurd, this yearning for connection with a long-dead culture that had no bearing on her actual life. Taking the whole thing too seriously was all the more daft given the random way in which Edmund had been adopted as a government talisman. Her new-found knowledge of the political process had taught her how capriciously these things were taken up, which meant they could be equally capriciously set down.

Furthermore, she found herself in the lonely position of not believing the hype about the new prime minister. While her cousin had never voiced explicit criticism, he had said enough to get the message across. If Marina Spencer really was as wonderful as the whole country seemed to believe, how come her staff were so cowed by her? Not that Hannah really knew Mark; perhaps wary and downtrodden were his default settings. If so, the prime minister's fabled charisma and sunny attitude had failed to lift him out of them.

She came right out and asked Pauline about it on the phone one evening. 'Does Mark like Marina? I got the impression that she might be a bit of a...'

'Tyrant? Witch from hell?'

'I was actually going to say slave-driver, but your versions will do just as well.'

'How much has he told you?'

'Nothing really. It was more what he didn't say. I got the impression there was no love lost. Is that fair?'

Mark did not seem to have told his mother much either,

but no, there was definitely no love lost. 'Whatever he does is wrong, and he never gets any praise, even though he works all the hours God sends. It beats me, but everyone tells me how nice she is, how pleasant, not like other politicians, etcetera etcetera, and he's so lucky to work for her. It's like she's cast a spell over the whole country. I don't say anything, because I don't want it to reflect badly on Mark, but it makes me see red.'

'It's certainly true that everyone seems to love her. And I know what you mean: you don't want to be the lone grump saying you're not so sure. It would make you sound graceless and horrible, particularly after everything that's just happened.'

'It's all in the eyebrows, you know.'

'The eyebrows?'

Pauline explained what Mark had told her about the artificial height of Marina's brows giving her a joviality at odds with her actual demeanour. 'Just you watch them, next time she's on television. The eyebrows smile but the eyes and mouth don't. Once you've spotted it, you'll wonder how you ever missed it.'

Hannah promised she would.

'Mind you, it won't last,' Pauline added. 'Character will out, and the country will realise soon enough what a sour-puss she is. The trouble is, that won't help Mark. If people turn against her, she could lose her job, and then where would he be? I liked it at first, him working for all those powerful people, but I don't any more. I don't like what I've learned about them and I feel for him, having to spend his life in that bear pit.'

'He could always leave.'

'He says nobody leaves, because it makes you look like you

can't hack it. And he does love walking through those gates in the morning, carrying his coffee past the television cameras. He has his picture taken all the time. Only yesterday, he was on the front page of the *Telegraph*.'

'Really? Amazing!'

'Not just him, obviously. He was getting into a car with She Who Must Be Obeyed. But you could clearly see his head and his sleeve behind her.'

As it happened, Marina's political honeymoon did not last long.

The trouble had clearly been brewing for a few weeks, but the first Hannah heard of it was one evening in February. It had sleeted solidly for three days and she had barely left the house, getting by on food supplies from the freezer. She treated herself to all-day fires, rather than just in the evening. With half an acre of garden to keep her occupied by day, and a hectic village social calendar in the evening, she did not normally watch much television. In this weather, however, it made a decadent change, and she took the opportunity to catch up with a couple of iPlayer box sets, binge-watching snow-covered Norwegian noir from the afternoon to the late evening. After one of these marathon sessions, she happened to switch over to find shots of Bury St Edmunds all over *Newsnight*.

'Has the prime minister blundered in her embrace of St Edmund?' intoned Kirsty Wark over the introductory footage. 'She championed the ninth-century East Anglian king and martyr as a patron saint for the whole United Kingdom, but now angry voices in Scotland, Wales and Northern Ireland are pointing out that St Edmund has long been a symbol of English oppression and conquest. In a special report tonight, we ask: how could Marina Spencer, who owes her hitherto stellar career to her astute political instincts, have been so tin-eared when it came to the feelings of the non-English nations? And can her coalition with the Scottish National Party, Plaid Cymru and the SDLP survive the strain?'

Hannah groaned. This was precisely the possibility she had warned her cousin about. It gave her no satisfaction to be proved right. How could it have happened, though? What about those wonderful Scottish, Welsh and Irish connections that everyone had been talking about?

The report proper was starting. It began with archive footage of the first press conference, on the day of their discovery, with champagne corks popping in the Abbey Gardens. There was a quick recap of what little was known about King Edmund's life and martyrdom, followed by his veneration at Bury and the disappearance of his body when the abbey was shut down and demolished by Henry VIII. Then came a clip from Marina's speech in the Gardens, the part where she announced her patron saint plan, plus the now-famous image of her, resplendent in St Edmund's blue and gold as she prayed at his shrine. So far, so uncontroversial.

'The culture secretary, as she then was, listed a number of reasons why Edmund would make a good patron saint for Scotland, Wales and Northern Ireland, as well as for England,' said the reporter's voiceover, in an ominous tone that presaged some terrible take-down. The three key facts on which the argument rested – the Scottish connection, the Welsh connection and the Irish connection – now came up in bullet points on the screen. 'But do those reasons stand up to scrutiny? Despite our best efforts, we've been unable to independently confirm any of these claims.'

The film cut back to the reporter himself, talking directly to camera. Far from being in Bury, as Hannah had expected, he was standing beneath the crag of Edinburgh Castle. 'Does any of this matter?' he was saying. 'Well, it certainly does here in Scotland. A couple of weeks ago, a leading historian wrote an article in *The Scotsman* pouring scorn on the idea that Edmund was half-Scottish, for which he said there was no evidence. And that's not the half of it. In a blistering critique of the prime minister's policy, he also noted that St Edmund was a powerful symbol of the subjugation of Scotland to the English.'

A goateed, bow-tied talking head now appeared, with shelves of leather-bound books behind him. A caption identified him as Campbell Murray, professor of Scottish military history at Stirling University. 'In the year 1300, Edward I sent his personal standard to Bury to be touched by Edmund's relics,' he said. 'He declared he had no doubt the saint would be on his side when he arrived in Scotland to conquer the enemy. He was dubbed the Hammer of the Scots, but I prefer to think of him as the butcher of Berwick-upon-Tweed, who led annual campaigns to subdue Scotland, captured and brutally executed William Wallace, stole the Stone of Destiny from Scone and burned the royal cemetery at Dunfermline to the ground. He did all this under the banner of St Edmund, which makes the prime minister's current campaign a profound insult, and I'm surprised her SNP coalition partners have gone along with it so far. I don't know who is advising Marina Spencer on this subject, but they are either an opposition agent trying to bring her coalition government down, or a numpty of colossal proportions.'

Ouch. Hannah wondered if Mark was watching this in his own flat, and whether she ought to call him. But no: if he was watching it, he would have far more important things to worry about than talking to her. She thought of calling Pauline instead, but that would not do either. 'Are you watching your son being called a numpty of colossal proportions on national television?' was not a question any mother wanted to hear.

Now the reporter was back, in front of a different landmark. 'It's not just in Scotland that the revival of St Edmund has gone down like a lead balloon, although that would be troublesome enough for the prime minister. Here in Cardiff Bay, there has also been controversy after this historian wrote an article in the *Western Mail*.'

Cue another academic, this time a woman with jet-black hair and matching eye make-up, liberally applied, who was captioned as Dr Carys Thomas. She was highly animated, and not in a supportive way. 'Edmund is an obviously problematic saint from a Welsh point of view. Edward I, the imperial English warlord who conquered Wales, ringed it with military fortresses modelled on crusader castles and put our princes to death in the most barbaric and humiliating way, strongly believed he had St Edmund on his side. There is a triumphant report in the thirteenth-century *Chronicle of Bury St Edmunds* of a Welsh prince coming to the abbey there on St Edmund's Day and' – she made air-quotes with her fingers – '*bowing his neck in dutiful subjection* to the king. That's not just a one-off. When the future Richard II was made Prince of Wales – an ancient Welsh title that the English kings stole to give to their eldest sons – the ceremony took place on St Edmund's Day. If that's not a calculated insult, I don't know what is.'

Off-camera, the reporter asked: 'So you don't support the idea of St Edmund becoming the patron saint of the whole United Kingdom?'

It seemed a redundant question, but the interviewee had clearly rehearsed her answer. 'Honestly, short of tying the first minister to the back of a horse and dragging him to England to be publicly hanged, drawn and quartered, like they did to our last independent ruler, Dafydd ap Gruffudd, it's hard to think of a greater insult to the people of Wales. If the Plaid Cymru members of the cabinet are not prepared to resign over this, they really have sold their souls for the sake of their ministerial cars.'

This was gruesome.

A text pinged into her phone. It was from Daisy: *Are you watching Newsnight?*

Yes. It's a catastrophe, Hannah texted back.

The reporter was on screen again, in yet another location: a set of medieval ruins in a soft green landscape. 'And if *that* weren't trouble enough, a third row has broken out here in Ireland.' This package clearly came with a lavish travel budget. 'Behind me is Athassel Priory in County Tipperary. It's the largest medieval abbey in Ireland, and dates back to the late twelfth century, when it was founded by William de Burgh, an English knight who defeated the local Irish kings. It's thought he founded the priory to celebrate this conquest. And which saint did he dedicate it to? No prizes for guessing...'

Hannah could hardly bear to watch as yet another talking head explained that St Edmund was so closely associated with the English conquest of Ireland that his three gold crowns on a blue background were adopted as the coat of arms of the Lordship of Ireland, a title given by the monarch to favoured English aristocrats and courtiers.

As the package ended and cut to Kirsty Wark leading a studio discussion, her phone rang.

'Did you watch all of it?' said Daisy.

'Unfortunately, yes.'

'I didn't know about any of that stuff. Did you?'

'No, of course not. I had no idea. I'm shocked.'

It was not just the impact on her cousin, she realised, or her own tangential involvement in the political embarrassment. Having felt stirrings of unaccustomed cultural pride over their local saint, she was upset to find Edmund identified with such belligerent and unsavoury causes. 'As far as I knew, Edmund never hurt a fly. When he was king of East Anglia, he preferred to do a deal with the Danes rather than fight them, so he wasn't much of a warrior, and then he lost his kingdom when the Vikings went back on their agreement. After that, he was brutally executed when he refused to bow down to anyone but God. That makes him sound like a thoroughly decent, peace-loving soul. Yet they're saying he's a symbol of invasion and brutal conquest. It doesn't make sense.'

'It really doesn't. I wonder what Brother B makes of it. Do you think he's seen it?'

'I'm surprised he's not part of the discussion.' Hannah had muted the volume but the picture was still playing. She squinted at the screen to double-check but no, the elderly monk was not there.

'He's quite hard to contact,' said Daisy. 'He's got an email address, but he lives under strict rules in his monastery and he only logs on occasionally.'

'Have you got it? His email address, I mean.'

'Yes. Shall I drop him a line now?'

'Go for it. See if he watched the programme and ask him if it's really true that St Edmund was a symbol of all these horrible things. I'd love to know what he thinks.'

'I'd also love to be a fly on the wall in Downing Street.'

'Don't. It doesn't bear thinking about. I feel so bad for Mark. Marina will do her absolute nut.'

'I can imagine. Sorry, I was being insensitive.'

'Don't worry about it. I'm sure we'll hear soon enough what the reaction is. And I'm as curious as you.'

'In that case, you let me know if you hear from your cousin, and I'll let you know if I hear anything back from Brother B. Deal?'

'Deal.'

'Good. Anyhow, it's getting late, so I'll let you go. Good night, and sleep well.'

'And you. 'Night.'

The *Newsnight* discussion had ended at last, and Hannah flicked the TV off, put the grate in front of the fire and climbed her steep, uneven staircase to get ready for bed.

Running the tap as she cleaned her teeth, she did not hear her phone ringing again. She only saw the missed call from Daisy when she came back down to fetch a glass of water.

Her friend picked up immediately when she called back. 'Sorry, I know it's late, but I've had an idea. I've got to go to Cambridge tomorrow. There's something I need to pick up from the archaeology department, and I was thinking of popping into the university library while I'm there, to check a few things in this Edmund story. Do you fancy coming along?'

For Mark, arriving at Number 10 was a double surprise: partly, as for everyone else involved, because of the suddenness of the events that brought Marina there; but also, on a personal level, because he fully expected her to ditch him in the move.

The immediate aftermath of Morton Alexander's death was remarkably easy for him, by the normal standards of his job. Once it became clear that Marina was in pole position, it was equally obvious that fortune would favour the candidate with the least apparent desire to fill the vacancy. It was not quite the Vatican principle that he who least wants to be pope is, by definition, the best-qualified. In this case, everyone knew Marina wanted it really; it was more that appearances mattered and the selectorate required a degree of face-saving pretence for the sake of good taste. Seeming not to want the job had the additional virtue of requiring very little effort on the part of Marina and her staff. All they had to do was carry on as normal and refrain from any comment or active involvement in the race. Formal candidacy had, with ostentatious reluctance, to be declared, but there was no need to build lists of supporters or whisper promises in the tea rooms, in the normal way of leadership battles. All this was a great relief to Mark, because an active campaign would put Marina under stress, and Marina under stress was a miserable experience for everyone around her.

Nevertheless, he remained convinced she would sack him once she got the top job.

'Why are you so sure she's going to get rid of you?' asked his mother.

'Because she hates me. Or, at least, she shouts at me all the time, and I can't do anything right for her.'

'I thought you said she shouts at everyone and no one can do anything right for her.'

'Me more than most.'

As ever, Karim and Giles seemed to enjoy far greater trust from their boss, and Karim lost no opportunity to remind him of it. Doors closed in his face and conversations stopped when he approached, as though they thought he was not just a liability, but some kind of hostile agent. If Marina did sack him when she became prime minister, perhaps she would be doing him a favour.

Yet still he clung on, frightened both by the prospect of the public humiliation and the uncertainty of his post-Whitehall future. And, in the event, his mother was proved right. Whether it was because Marina maintained a tiny morsel of esteem for him after all, or because she had simply not got round to firing him yet, Mark remained a member of the inner circle that decamped to Downing Street.

It was an undeniable thrill to pass every morning through the gates at the bottom of the street, with early-rising tourists peering through the railings after him, and to saunter past the yawning camera crews to the world's most famous door, which swung silently open to admit him, then shut silently again in the faces of the media.

At first the building seemed huge inside, and so plush, with its thick carpets, its grand staircase, its smell of wood-polish and its network of Tardis corridors reaching all the way back up the street, behind the black-bricked façade, to Whitehall. That impression quickly wore off as he was shown his own windowless cubby-hole and he realised quite how many people were supposed to work in this crumbling Georgian terrace. There was, at least, safety in numbers. The fact that Marina now had a much larger team around her meant there were more people in the firing line, and Mark's statistical chances of going a whole day without being screamed at improved substantially. If that came at the price of being a less important courtier in a larger court, he was more than happy to pay it.

Life at the heart of the machine was bewildering at first, but the Spencer administration enjoyed, by general agreement, a soft landing. The media was in benign mood, its usual spikiness blunted by the tragedy of Alexander's death. The general bonhomie of the coronation was further lubricated by the round of Christmas parties and a football-in-the-trenches suspension of normal Westminster hostilities, both between government and opposition and between politicians and press. This atmosphere of calm endured through most of January, and Mark was beginning to think it was easier to work for a prime minister than a secretary of state, when his complacency was rudely overturned and he saw the depth of the Edmund-shaped pit he had dug for Marina and himself.

He first had wind of it a fortnight before *Newsnight* joined the dots, and he was only spared the horror of bringing it to Marina's attention because she brought it to his first.

'She wants to see you urgently,' said Karim first thing one morning, bearing down on Mark's cubby-hole in a cloud of Eau de Beckham.

He could usually read what kind of mood Marina was in from the way Karim delivered these messages. If she was calm and there was no trouble in store, the summons would be relayed with disdain, which was a cover for Karim's resentment that Marina wanted to talk to Mark rather than him. If, however, the messenger looked pleased with himself, it was a sure sign the prime minister was in a rage and about to take it out on Mark.

Today was different. Karim seemed agitated and avoided looking Mark in the eye. This was unusual. Since there were no nice surprises in this job, it must be unusually bad. As he was marched through the hall, Mark wondered whether it might not be better to make a run for it now, to save time and some vestige of dignity. Then the moment passed and he found himself outside Marina's door.

She seemed to be reading a newspaper cutting as they entered her study. She did not look up, nor did he hear her invite him to sit down, as she normally did. Feeling awkward standing over her, and assuming that she must have asked him to sit and he had simply not heard it, he began to lower himself onto the corner of the nearest leather armchair.

'Don't sit!' she snapped, still not looking up. 'No, Karim, don't go.' This was in a lighter tone, accompanied by a glance in Karim's direction. 'You can sit.'

Mark snuck a glance at his colleague, who was still not smirking, despite being so blatantly favoured. This really was bad. What the hell had he done?

Finally she lifted her head. 'You told me Edmund would make a "brilliant patron saint" for the whole United Kingdom.' She imitated his voice as she quoted his words at him, in an unflattering, dull drone. Did he really speak like that? 'The Scots would love him because he was "virtually one of their own". It would "bring the whole nation together". That was what you told me, wasn't it?'

'Er, yes, pretty much,' said Mark. His mouth was dry and he was conscious of croaking like a teenager. 'Is there some problem with that?' His fakery over Edmund's mother must somehow have come to light. That was bad, but did it really deserve this level of fury? He had done a bit of embroidery in a good cause, that was all. Was it the end of the world?

'I assume you haven't seen this?' She held up the cutting. It looked to be an opinion piece from a broadsheet, but not one whose typeface or design he recognised. *The Herald*, perhaps, or *The Scotsman*? Next to the byline 'Campbell Murray' was a line-drawn cartoon of a goateed face above a bow tie. The headline read: *The imposition of imperialist Edmund is England's greatest insult to Scotland since the theft of the Stone of Scone.*

Mark gulped. 'No. Not seen that.'

'When you suggested I effectively promote a new patron saint of Scotland, it didn't seem relevant to you that…let me read to you precisely what it says… "King Edward I, who vanquished the Welsh and then spent the rest of his life trying and very nearly succeeding to subjugate Scotland, waged all these bloodthirsty campaigns under the banner of St Edmund"?'

Everything in his mouth had clenched up and it was physically hard to speak. 'I didn't know that.'

'Speak up, I can't hear you.'

He said it louder.

'You didn't know that? I see. Did you know it, Karim?'

'No, Marina,' came his colleague's subdued voice from behind him. On their first day at Number 10, one of them had called her 'prime minister' and she had laughed it off with a 'Please! It's still Marina', so that was how they tended to address her.

'I didn't know it either, so that makes three of us. The difference, Mark, is that Karim and I, not being in possession of the full facts, didn't go round arguing that St Edmund would be a brilliant patron saint of the United Kingdom, healing old wounds and bringing us all together.' She smacked her hand on her desk, making Mark jump. 'Did you not think to check the facts?'

'I did. I mean, I thought I had. Sorry, Marina.'

'It's *Prime Minister!*'

'Sorry, Prime Minister. If I'd had any idea, then obviously I never would have...'

'Being sorry is all very well, but it won't get me out of the giant cesspit you've dumped me in. Shall I read you what *The Scotsman* says? "How can someone with the sensitive political antennae of Marina Spencer be so tone-deaf where Scotland is concerned? Sad to say, however progressive a face she may present to the rest of the world, she has defaulted to chauvinistic Sassenach factory settings when it comes to England's dominance of the United Kingdom." Your being sorry won't fix that, will it?'

'It's only one writer saying that, not the official line of the paper.'

'It's one writer too many, speaking to tens of thousands of readers, whose worst prejudices about the English I now confirm. And one of those readers, need I remind you, is the foreign secretary.' Ailsa Danieli, the secretary of state for foreign affairs, was the Westminster leader of the Scottish National Party, the Alliance's biggest coalition partner.

Now that he had found his tongue, Mark was beginning to think more clearly. 'I don't think we need worry too much about the foreign secretary, do we? She knows that being in government with you is the only way she can get another independence referendum, so she's not going to bring the coalition down.'

'A referendum that we will then lose, meaning I go down in history as the prime minister who destroyed the union.'

She had a strong point. 'Well, let's not get ahead of ourselves. The first thing to do is rebut that article.'

'Rebut it? How are you going to do that? Do you think it's not true?'

'There's always a way of rebutting everything. Let me see what I can do. The alternative, of course, is to apologise and renounce the policy but...'

'That would make me look even more ridiculous, and the Nats won't ever stop rubbing it in. At the independence referendum – which, I need hardly remind you, we are committed to holding under the formal terms of the coalition agreement – they'll plaster the whole of Scotland with pictures of me kneeling beside that blasted tomb.'

'Exactly. That's why we don't want to go down that route. So will you let me see what I can come up with?'

'I don't seem to have much choice, do I? Take it' – she held out the offending article – 'and get out of my sight.'

His hand was shaking as he took the cutting. Closing her door behind him, leaving her alone with Karim, he had to pass Giles' desk. His colleague had his head down, making eye contact impossible. Mark's disgrace was known.

Back in his cubby-hole, he tried to concentrate on the article, but the words swam before his eyes. He knew he had messed up by faking evidence, but to discover he had messed up in ways he had not yet considered was truly alarming. This was worse than some minor and harmless deception. He had made his boss into a hate-figure north of the border or, at best, a laughing-stock. Maybe it was the other way round: for a politician, to be a laughing-stock might well be worse than a hate-figure. Either way, with another independence referendum looming, it was a catastrophe.

Gradually the words came into focus. Now he read the piece properly, he could see that the case it made was actually fairly flimsy. It was chiefly a rehearsal of the crimes of Edward I, who was indeed a deeply unappealing figure from a Scottish point of view. Murdering the entire population of Berwick-upon-Tweed in order to show who was boss was savage, even by the standards of the thirteenth century, and the king seemed to have taken psychopathic pleasure in ordering the most barbaric possible executions of vanquished leaders. But the connection with St Edmund was tenuous, to put it mildly. It was guilt by the most limited association. The king went to the saint's shrine occasionally. Presumably he also prayed to God and Jesus Christ. Did that make them symbols of English brutality against the Scots?

As these thoughts began to flow, his confidence revived. Caving in at the first sign of dissent would be a disaster, and rebuttal was definitely the answer. He spent a further hour or two reading into the subject, following leads in this or that direction and giving himself a crash course on the end of the Canmore dynasty of Scottish kings, which left the vacancy that triggered Edward I's expansionist ambitions. These were the real stories of characters hitherto familiar only through the swords-and-sporranery of Hollywood.

He then placed a call to the lobby correspondent of *The Herald*, inviting her for coffee at the nearest Starbucks, and another to one of the loudest tabloid polemicists in Scotland, a former firebrand Labour MP called Stewie Hunter, who had always been friendly towards Marina and loved nothing more than a scrap in defence of the union.

By the time he got home that evening, he was able to congratulate himself that he was still strapped into the rollercoaster, and had not been flung out of his seat during an upside-down corkscrew twist and dashed to his death on the tarmac below. Given how bad everything had looked when he was standing trembling in Marina's office a few hours earlier, this was progress.

At times like this, he felt the absence of close friends to confide in. In his BBC days, most of his social life had revolved around the office, which seemed to be the natural order of things. Gradually, colleagues of his own age paired off and had children, which meant they were less available for drinks after work, and Mark grew less reliant not just on their friendship, but on social life in general. A legacy from his grandparents, shortly after his graduation from the LSE, had enabled him to buy a one-bedroom conversion flat on the first floor of an unloved Victorian house just off the four-lane gyratory on the south side of Vauxhall Bridge, an area abandoned by everyone save gays and spies. Since then, a lot of the area had come up, but his street remained determinedly shabby. His front window gave him a ringside view of the crack-dealing on the walkway of the council block opposite – a source of occasional alarm, but more often just fascination, as he watched the comings and goings. Having his own place had spared him the kind of flat-share hell that most of his peers moaned about. Having no design flair, he furnished the place with all the imagination of a buy-to-let landlord; even the pictures on the walls came from Ikea. Nevertheless, the flat was his bachelor refuge. Only rarely, on nights such as this, did he find himself thinking how good it would be to be able to go down the pub with a friend or neighbour and pour out his woes. He consoled himself by cracking open some bottled beer in front of Netflix.

The next morning, his mood brightened. A sympathetic news story in *The Herald* quoted Downing Street sources who explained that the prime minister would not be diverted from one of her proudest and most unifying cultural politics by hyperbolic hysteria. Professor Murray, they said, had conflated the aggression of a medieval English king with a Christian martyr who had been dead for four centuries by the time of the events he was talking about. There was also a rousing column by Stewie Hunter in the *Daily Record*, ridiculing what it called the 'McSnowflakery' of certain ultra-sensitive journalists and academics who seemed to have learned all their history from Mel Gibson. Did they know, Hunter asked, that Edward I was the brother-in-law of the king of Scotland and also his step-cousin? Were they aware that John Balliol, the Scottish king whom Edward locked in the Tower of London, was the son of the Sheriff of Nottingham, of Robin Hood notoriety? Did they realise that Robert the Bruce spoke French much better than he did Gaelic and was as likely to have supported Spurs as Celtic or Rangers, because his vast property holdings included estates in Tottenham? If they did not know all that, Hunter concluded with a flourish, they should pipe down, because the turbulent history of the Middle Ages was about competitive, intermarried dynasties who comfortably straddled the border, rather than glorious

Scottish heroes and wicked English villains.

The columnist had not written much about St Edmund himself, but Mark was still pleased with the result. His aim, in drip-feeding these factoids to Hunter, had been to change the subject, by throwing some unexpected material into the mix and hoping it would cause a distraction. He was especially proud of the Spurs line, which would surely get people talking. When he arrived in the office, he, set about drafting a memo, highlighting his successful rebuttal. He sent an email to Marina, attaching both articles and expressing the hope that they could now regain control of the narrative. He received no reply, but calm seemed to have been restored.

Three days later, he looked up to find Karim at his desk again. He sighed and got wearily to his feet.

The prime minister was staring out of the window into the Number 10 rose garden. She turned to face him and, wordlessly, held out a new piece of paper. She did not seem quite so nakedly furious as she had done on the previous occasion, but the look on her face was more unnerving. It was one of disgust, and its unambiguous object was Mark.

The paper was another cutting from the government clippings service, stamped with the current day's date and marked *Western Mail. Marina's "pet saint" Edmund is a symbol of Welsh submission, historian claims*, read the headline.

No, no, no. This could not be happening. It really was not fair.

'Open your eyes and read the damn thing,' growled the prime minister.

There were times when shutting the world out was the only possible thing to do. He blinked his eyes open and attempted to digest the article, but it was difficult with Marina standing over him.

'Shall I save you the bother?' she asked. 'You told me Edmund would go down a treat with the Welsh because he was so nice to them. You said you knew about all this because you're half-Welsh yourself. It turns out he was actually synonymous with the national humiliation of Wales. When Welsh princes were summoned to grovel to the English king who had conquered them, they went on a particular saint's day. Guess which. Go on, take a shot at it, Mark. And when the English king made his eldest son the Prince of Wales, as a big up-yours to the Welsh, after the actual Prince of Wales had been slaughtered and beheaded in battle, he invested him with the title on a very specific saint's day. Any idea which?' She had started speaking in a menacing whisper, but her volume had steadily increased and Mark was fairly sure that the entire Downing Street staff, if not the journalists on doorstep rota outside, could hear that last part.

He opened his mouth to speak but she cut him off. 'Whatever it is, I don't want to hear it. Just do something about it. Kill this. And don't let me see you again until it's sorted.'

Do something? He had spent a whole day neutralising the first instalment of this nightmare, he reflected miserably as he found his way back to his desk, avoiding eye contact with colleagues and hoping his face was not as red as it felt. She had not even acknowledged those efforts, which were impressive by any yardstick. Instead, it was Groundhog Day. He now had to try and pull off the same trick with the Welsh press.

The trouble was, he grudgingly acknowledged as he slumped into his chair and attempted to read this new cutting properly, he had only himself to blame for advocating this half-baked, unresearched idea in the first place. She had every right to be livid, and the only surprise was that she had not sacked him already. Perhaps she was waiting for him to try and clear up the mess, and then he would be out. For the moment, he had no choice but to get on with it.

Once the outrage and the background detail were weeded out, the argument of today's offending piece of journalism rested on two events, each involving humiliation for the Welsh, which were supposed to have taken place on St Edmund's Day, the twentieth of November. The first was the submission of a prince called Rhys ap Rhys to Edward I in Bury St Edmunds in 1296, and the second was the investiture of the future Richard II, at nine years old, as Prince of Wales in 1376.

Trying not to think about the prime minister's fury and his own disgrace, and forcing himself to focus on the matter in hand, he set about looking up Rhys ap Rhys. He expected the name to be prominent in the lists of Welsh princelings, but was surprised to draw a blank. All the great Welsh leaders were dead by 1296, defeated by Edward's forces, and there was no mention of any Rhys ap Rhys. Eventually, he managed to track down the original source that the historian, Carys Thomas, had clearly used. The *Chronicle of Bury St Edmunds* for 1296 recorded that Edward I was attending high mass in the abbey to celebrate the feast of St Edmund when the Welsh rebel, Rhys son of Rhys, submitted, 'bowing his head in dutiful subjection to the king'. He read the passage several times. While Thomas had taken it to mean that Rhys had come to Bury to submit to the king, it was not clear the original actually said that. The prince might simply have surrendered in battle somewhere in Wales and the news reached the king on that day. The thirteenth-century chronicler wrote that Edward himself thought it was no coincidence Rhys' submission had come on St Edmund's Day; but that very statement implied there was no formal connection between the two events. And the question remained: who was this prince?

The name Rhys appeared in one royal family in particular, in the realm of Deheubarth, in south-west Wales. Its last great prince was the Lord Rhys, Prince of South Wales. His great-grandson, Rhys ap Maredudd, led a revolt in 1287–88, after his country had already fallen to the English. He was eventually captured and executed in York in 1292, which was where most accounts of the revolt ended. But they did mention he had a son called Rhys, who would therefore be Rhys son of Rhys, or Rhys ap Rhys. Far from being a figure of political or military importance, he seemed chiefly to be a historical footnote, having been arrested after his father's death and imprisoned in Norwich for the rest of his long life, spending some sixty years in captivity. Was this really the great rebel whose submission was the ultimate humiliation for the shattered Welsh nation?

After a further half-hour searching for further details, Mark finally stumbled across the reference he needed. In the accounts of the constables of Bristol Castle for the last decades of the thirteenth century, it was recorded that three Welshmen – one of them named Rhys ap Rhys – were held there from the beginning of January to the beginning of March 1297, after being captured in West Wales. They were then delivered to the sheriff of Norfolk, when Rhys' long imprisonment presumably began. He could conceivably have been captured on or around St Edmund's Day, at the end of November, but it was clearly a coincidence, and Carys Thomas was wrong to say he had submitted in Bury.

So what of Richard II? Mark pressed on with his crash

course in medieval Welsh history. Grandson of Edward III, the young Richard became heir to the throne on the death of his father, the Black Prince, in June 1376. Because his uncle, John of Gaunt, had his own designs on the crown, it was deemed prudent to invest the nine-year-old Richard as Prince of Wales – and thus heir to the throne – as soon as possible after his father's funeral. That ceremony did not take place until the end of September, so it was not unreasonable for his investiture to happen six and a half weeks later, on a day in late November that happened to be the feast of St Edmund. The available sources differed on the location of the investiture: some put it in a royal palace in Essex, others at Westminster Abbey. There was no suggestion from anyone that it took place at Bury St Edmunds, which reinforced the impression that there was nothing significant about the date. It was another coincidence being spun out of all proportion by a mendacious historian.

After jotting down a few extra facts that caught his eye, Mark clicked off all the open windows on his desktop and picked up the phone to two of his friendliest contacts in the Welsh media, inviting them for coffee later in the afternoon. He would not get any thanks for this from Marina, but he could at least feel proud that he was fighting these fires with exceptional skill.

The next morning he was pleased to see, once again, that his contacts had delivered. As it happened, Carys Thomas was a notorious rent-a-quote who had form when it came to jumping to headline-grabbing conclusions, and both Mark's contacts' editors had been more than happy to run rebuttal stories that made her look an idiot.

One of the papers had quoted a Downing Street spokesman

saying: 'It's not hard to cherry-pick random events and make the date look significant if you're trying to reach a pre-ordained conclusion. That doesn't mean it's real. Do you know two other things that happened on 20 November? Windsor Castle burned down and Princess Diana went on *Panorama* to talk about her adultery, a media event which nearly brought the royal family down. Should the Queen have blamed St Edmund for her *anni horribilis*?' The quote was not completely verbatim – a helpful subeditor had clearly found the correct plural of *annus horribilis* – but Mark was delighted with it. Was it too much to hope that Marina would be too?

He knew the answer to that already. Sure enough, not a word came from her office. At least silence was better than rage. For a few days, therefore, he thought he was through the worst.

In the middle of the next week, Karim appeared.

'What the hell have I done now?' Mark snapped. He had done hair-shirted penance for long enough.

'I'll let her tell you that?' Again, there was no detectable triumph, which was a worry.

This time she was pacing. She did not break her stride as he came in.

'You know, Mark, I was stupid enough to think that this mess couldn't get any worse, but I underestimated your capacity for cock-up. You've made the Scots hate me, you've made the Welsh hate me, so why wouldn't you make the Irish hate me too?'

Mark had resolved to stick up for himself this time, to fight back and assert how skilfully he had reacted to neutralise these crises. Not all the Scots, not all the Welsh, he wanted to say. Anyone who wanted to be loved by everyone should have gone into light entertainment, not politics, he would tell her. Now it came to it, he lost his nerve.

'Nothing to say?' she demanded.

He opened his mouth to show willing, but she saved him the bother of thinking of something.

'Today, since you ask, it's the turn of *Irish News*. Apparently the flag of St Edmund was also the flag of the British Crown in Ireland. A symbol of the colonial project, no less. At least the unionists will love us, and we have to take all the support we can get, now you've alienated half the United Kingdom.'

'I'm sorry, Prime Minister. I really had no idea. But it may not be as bad...' It might not be as bad as this article made out, he was going to say, given that the Scottish and Welsh stories were based on wild exaggeration, conjecture and wilful distortion, but she did not give him the chance to finish.

'Save it for someone who believes you, Mark. That will be all. Karim will give you the cutting.'

Once again, he was dismissed. As he was crossing the hall to return to his desk, the main door of Number 10 opened to admit a visitor. The fleeting glimpse of the outside world was tantalising, as when a prisoner manages to see a tiny patch of sky from their cell. If he could only...

On the spur of the moment, he turned abruptly back in the direction he had come and knocked on Marina's door.

'Come,' she called, then froze when she saw who it was.

'Prime Minister, I won't take up any of your time. I just wanted to give you my resignation. With immediate effect. It's all a mess and I've caused it, so I'll take responsibility. Blame me, tell the world it's all my cock-up. Don't worry about a reference. I'll go now.'

'No you bloody won't! You'll sort out this blasted mess.

Now get out of here and get on with it.'

It had been worth a try, he sighed, as he closed the door behind him once more. He had no choice but to slope back to his desk to look for ways of rebutting the latest material about the English conquering Ireland under Edmund's banner, wondering if his life could possibly get any worse.

Two days later, when the switchboard put through a call from a *Newsnight* researcher, he realised that yes, it certainly could. With Scotland, Wales and half of Northern Ireland up in arms, the researcher said, the programme was putting together a package on the Great Edmund Revolt, to be followed by a studio discussion. Did Number 10 want to send a representative? Perhaps Mark himself would like to come? The researcher was reliably informed the patron saint policy was his baby.

Mark put up the best fight he could. Most of those arguments had been squarely debunked within twenty-four hours of the original articles appearing, so why was *Newsnight* wasting its time and misleading its viewers with a non-debate that would give a completely distorted impression of the strength of feeling in the three countries concerned? The researcher responded just as he would have in her position: the package had already been filmed, so it was going to be broadcast whether Mark liked it or not; if he had such powerful counter-arguments, why not come to the studio and present them in the panel discussion?

Aside from the fact that he had no desire to be eaten alive by a panel of baying nationalists, Mark felt sure there was no way that Marina, in her present mood, would allow him to go out and represent her views to the public. 'Downing Street aides don't do *Newsnight*. You know that.'

'Can you suggest someone else who might be able to defend your policy, then?'

'I'm not going to do your job for you. You have an obligation to provide balance, so it's up to you to find the right voices.' The contempt was all bravado. Inside, he was sick with dread, but it was important never to show vulnerability with the media. Making it seem like an exasperated afterthought before he hung up, he added: 'There were follow-up pieces with a string of very strong arguments debunking those claptrap academics in both the Scottish and the Welsh media. If you're serious about providing balance, invite the journalists who wrote them onto your programme.'

From the series of texts he received over the next half-hour, it was clear the researcher had indeed followed his suggestion. Mark's friendly contacts were now weighing up whether they wanted to appear. Eventually, to his immense relief, Stewie Hunter volunteered and came back seeking a further background briefing. This was the best result he could have hoped for in such otherwise unfavourable circumstances. Armed with this meagre snippet of good news, he steeled himself to tell Marina what *Newsnight* had in store. She had a stream of visitors all afternoon, which meant he could not get in to see her in person. It felt safer breaking the news via email, which he now proceeded to do, playing down the probable hatchet element of the forthcoming film and playing up their firebrand defence. He knew from Priya, who had accompanied Marina to Downing Street from the Department of Culture, that the prime minister had a dinner with a trade delegation in the evening. He hoped it would delay her sufficiently to miss the broadcast.

He himself watched the programme with a bottle of vodka at his elbow. The package was a horror show, focusing entirely on the negative, without so much as a nod at the subsequent press coverage with the rebuttal stories. The studio discussion was better – a seasoned television performer, Hunter was witty as well as articulate – but it was the film that would stay in people's minds. Mark wondered who else was watching it. He wished he could text a friend to ask if they were tuned in, but he was not really sure who that would be. He simply needed to discuss it with someone with a grasp of the situation – even his cousin. She was unlikely to be watching it either, though, and it would be embarrassing to draw her attention to it.

The next morning he kept his head down, not least because he was groggy after too much vodka. Plates would fly sooner or later and he had no desire to put his head in their way before it was strictly necessary. For the moment, the place was ominously quiet. Finally, just before lunchtime, he received a calendar alert for a meeting, subject '*Newsnight*', at two o'clock. Attendance was clearly mandatory.

At two minutes to two, he knocked on Marina's door. Everyone else on the meeting list was there already: Karim, Giles, Jack O'Callaghan, the new culture secretary, and Rachel Rose, Marina's parliamentary private secretary. Mark nodded a general hello, but nobody seemed to notice.

'Shall we begin?' said Marina. 'By now, you've all caught up with *Newsnight*. I think you'll agree it was a brutal and potentially very damaging attack. We can probably also all agree' – here her eyes did briefly alight on Mark – 'that we should never have got ourselves into this ludicrous position. However, we are where we are, and the key question now is what we do about it. Thoughts?'

'If I may, Prime Minister,' said O'Callaghan, a fast-tracking millennial with a West London seat who had become the youngest member of the cabinet when he replaced Marina. 'Obviously, as you say, we should never have got into this situation. One clear route out of the whole mess would be to shut it down completely. Hold your hands up, say new information has now come to light that makes the policy unsustainable and, on that basis, you're withdrawing it immediately. It's basically going, hey, we messed up, but we're owning it. Nobody will expect that and it will boost your image as a different kind of politician, someone who isn't afraid to say they've made a mistake. Voters will respect you for it, and it would also pull the rug out from under the Nats, so it could be a big win for you in the long term.'

And would save O'Callaghan himself being lumbered with this unpopular, inherited policy at his new department, thought Mark. He wondered if that was as obvious to everyone else in the room as it was to him.

It clearly was to Giles, who was pulling a face. 'There's a good reason why politicians don't back down and apologise at the first sign of dissent. It would make Marina look weak and inconsistent. To capitulate this early into her premiership would give the green light to every opponent of every other policy. It would send the message that whingeing works and this government gives in at the first sign of trouble.'

The culture secretary shrugged. 'It doesn't have to mean weakness. This policy was only window-dressing, anyway. It's easily dispensable. If Marina drops this, it will allow her to be even tougher on her core agenda.'

'The problem, Jack,' said Marina, 'is that it may be window-dressing, but I'm in the window with it, draped in blue and gold. Those photographs from the cathedral are everywhere. If I back down now, they'll be used against me forever more. No, like it or not, we've got to brazen this out.'

Mark was conscious he had not yet spoken. Initially, he had thought his role at the meeting was as whipping-boy, but Marina had been clear this was about looking forward, not handing out blame for past mistakes. When it came to rebutting the charges against their policy, he had plenty to contribute. 'We do have the truth on our side,' he began. 'I've already refuted...'

'When I want input from you, Mark, I'll ask for it,' snapped Marina.

He felt his cheeks burn.

Karim filled the silence. 'I don't know if you all watched the full discussion last night, but that Hunter guy was very sharp? He made a lot of very powerful points, suggesting that most of the arguments advanced by these nationalist historians are actually wildly exaggerated. I can get on to him, if you want. You know, tell him how much the prime minister valued his spirited defence and see if I can get more of those rebuttal points out of him? He's a very useful ally to have.'

'Good spot, Karim,' said Marina. 'Here's what we'll do. I'll make a speech where I come out fighting. You draft it, Karim. Get Stewie Hunter to share some of his material. Rachel, can you look through the diary for a suitable occasion? It needs to be soon.'

'Good plan, Prime Minister,' said O'Callaghan.

'Yes, excellent idea,' nodded Giles.

Mark said nothing, hoping the disgust he felt for them all registered adequately on his face. Unfortunately, it did not matter if it showed or not, because they all continued steadfastly to avoid looking at him.

Back in his cubby-hole, he wished he had something to kick

or punch. It was true, he had messed up initially, but he had done a superb fire-fighting job. Now the world and its dog would get the credit, rather than him. How he loathed them all.

He was feeling only marginally less murderous a couple of hours later when his extension rang.

'Is that Mark Price?' said an elderly Scottish voice.

'Yes.'

'Oh good. My name is McAdoo. Professor Elspeth McAdoo. I understand you may be familiar with some of my work. I'm sorry to see that my area of scholarship has become the subject of some controversy, down south as well as here in Scotland, with yourself and your poor prime minister in the firing line. So I was wondering... Could I perhaps offer you some assistance?'

The first King Edward was a great warrior. Very strong and very tall – they called him Longshanks – he was a man of action as well as ambition.

As I have said, he came to me often. One time, he summoned his barons, knights and burgesses to a parliament within my town. He believed he might draw strength from me in his battle with the Archbishop of Canterbury over the question of taxation for the clergy, although on that score he was mistaken: my own abbey had never paid money to the Crown and I was not about to make it start. In all other matters, however, I was glad to give him succour, most especially in his military campaigns. I had shown already that I was a better defender of my kingdom in death than in life, and now it pleased me to aid one of my successors not just to secure his borders, but to expand them most gloriously.

He used to whisper by my side about the mighty fortresses he was building to crush the Welsh, and his campaign to bring the Scots under English rule. He craved my support in these endeavours, and why would I deny it him? If his prowess were the greater for it and his victory more complete, I rejoiced to play my part. And if my mother were herself a Scot? As I have said, I cannot know for certain if she was or not, but what matter if she were?

For Longshanks, it was normal to wage war on his own kin. The last of the Canmore kings of Scotland wed Edward's own sister, so those crowns were closely linked. That did not restrain him. On the contrary, it only increased his wish to have Scotland for his own once the Canmores had expired. Nor did kinship curtail his ambition in Wales, whose princes were his cousins. Not in God's eyes, it is true, since the Welsh line came down from old King John's bastard daughter, but Nature would not mistake the bloodline. Llewelyn, the last prince, was slain in battle by an English soldier who mistook him for an ordinary swordsman, else he would have taken him prisoner. That deed robbed Longshanks of the chance to drag Llewelyn in chains to England, where he would have cut his guts from his chest and burned them in front of him, before putting him to the noose. How do I know? Because that was what he did to his other Welsh cousin, Llewelyn's brother Dafydd. Such was the lot of kings and princes in those days, and Longshanks would have expected it for his own fate if the scales were reversed and he fell into his victorious cousins' hands.

It was my lot too, of course, and I have not complained of it unduly.

That was the way back then. It seems it no longer is. Alas, I learned it only recently. I wish I had known it sooner.

Hannah was not clear what Daisy hoped to achieve by their spur-of-the-moment dash to the university library, but she was happy to show willing. A day out for just the two of them would be fun.

The weather had finally cleared by the time they set out, in the late morning. High Suffolk rolled away ahead of them as they took the back lanes westward, dropping down into sheltered villages then climbing onto the higher grasslands again, before finally plunging down the long, arrow-straight road into Cambridgeshire.

'So, tell me properly why we're doing this,' Hannah said, as they entered the outskirts of the city. 'You didn't make a lot of sense on the phone last night.'

'I know. Sorry. I wasn't explaining it very well. Maybe it's a wild-goose chase, but I was hoping we might be able to dig your cousin out of the hole he's in.'

'I get that bit. What I don't understand is how you think we can do it.'

'Well, you know those Scottish, Welsh and Irish connections?'

'How could I forget them?'

'Exactly. They've been all over the media from virtually the moment we found the body, haven't they? I thought it would be interesting to go back and look for the sources. So after *Newsnight* ended last night, I tried to check out the references, and I discovered something strange. My first port of call was Wikipedia, obviously, to look up St Edmund's biography. Sure enough, there's stuff on there about him having a Pictish mother, and at first sight it looks like it's properly sourced.'

'Only at first sight?'

'One of the references is a BBC online story called *Ten Things You Didn't Know About St Edmund,* and another is a similar piece in the *Daily Telegraph.* Both of them constitute proper, approved media organisations, which means no Wikipedia editor would ever question them.'

'So what's the problem?'

'The problem is the date. Both of those articles were published on the exact day of our discovery. Isn't that weird?'

'Yes, I guess so. And the articles themselves, the BBC and *Telegraph* ones, don't offer any other source?'

'No, but you wouldn't expect them to, because the news media don't reference every piece of information they publish.'

'I suppose not.'

'Anyway, I then had a look at the Welsh connection – the peace treaty, or whatever it was. Again, it was mentioned on Wikipedia and it was sourced to a couple of news articles. Do I need to tell you which ones?'

'The same two?'

'That's right. So I googled some more, and I couldn't find any reference to either of those claims that went back any earlier than the day we found the body. Strange, no?'

'Maybe. But the fact that you couldn't find it doesn't mean there isn't some literature somewhere. Maybe a Welsh chronicle or something? That's what my cousin said.'

'As it happens, there are a couple of books cited in the Wikipedia references, one by an Elspeth McSomething, about Pictish royalty, and the other about English–Welsh relations in pre-Norman Britain, by someone Welsh and double-barrelled. I couldn't find any mention of either of those books anywhere else, so that's why I thought of the university library, where they have a copy of every book ever published.'

'I see. And when we find them?'

'We can look up the mentions of St Edmund in the index, make photocopies of the relevant passages and send them to your cousin, to help him fend off some of this onslaught. It may help poor St Edmund too. I don't like to see him trashed, after everything we did to find him. Are you with me now? Not regretting agreeing to come?'

'No, not at all. It sounds like a good idea. I can't wait to find them.'

When they arrived outside the Department of Archaeology, Hannah sat in the car on a double-yellow line, ready to move it if she saw a traffic warden, while Daisy ran inside. Then they drove across the Backs to the library, its uncompromising redbrick tower offering a brutal response across the Cam to the exquisite Gothic jewel-box of King's College Chapel.

They entered through the revolving doors in the portcullis gate at the bottom of the tower. At the rotunda reception,

Hannah was allowed to sign in as a visitor. Having checked her belongings into a locker, she was keen to explore the stacks in the tower itself, but Daisy insisted they had a job to do. Hannah hurried to keep up as her friend took the stairs to the first floor two at a time and headed for a row of computer terminals. Clearly very much at home in this environment, she sat down at one of the screens and started inputting her reader number and password on the welcome page.

'Have you got the precise names of the books?' said Hannah, panting slightly, at her shoulder.

'Yep.' Daisy pulled a scrap of paper from the pocket of her jeans. 'Elspeth McAdoo, *Women in the Pictish Royal Houses*, and Llewelyn Rhys-Williams, *The Hand of Friendship: Welsh–English Relations in Pre-Norman Britain*. Let's try with the first author's surname and see if anything jumps out at us. So that's 'McAdoo'...' She input the name and hit search, whereupon a screen of titles appeared.

'Who knew so many people called McAdoo wrote books?' said Hannah. 'Try with Elspeth too.'

Daisy input the full name, but the system replied that there were no entries.

'That's odd. Try with just her initial, maybe.'

'Good idea. 'McAdoo, E'... And now we've got an Edward, an Edgar and an Eric.'

'No Elspeth, though.'

'No. Let's try with book title instead of the author. *Women in the Pictish Royal Houses*... And enter...'

'Still nothing. Are you sure you're in the right section of the catalogue?'

'Yes. This is the main catalogue, so everything ought to be here.'

'Is there someone we can ask to help us?'

'I know how to search. Trust me, I use this system all the time.'

'Sorry, I know you do. Why don't we try the other book then?'

'What was his name again? Rhys-Williams... I bet there'll be loads of those. Ha! Told you.'

'Try it with 'L'...'

'There you go. That narrows it down. I can't see *The Hand of Friendship*, though, can you?'

'Try searching directly on the title rather than the author. With double-barrelled names you can sometimes mess it up by putting a hyphen where there isn't meant to be one, or vice versa.'

'Very true. Let's try.' Daisy tapped in the title, then the subtitle and, for good measure, the author's full name, with and without hyphen. Still nothing came up. 'This is seriously weird. Sometimes a book is in use, or it's stored off-site and will take ages to call in, but I've never had this before, where the system can't find a book that we know exists.'

'Are you sure we shouldn't ask someone?'

'All right, if it will stop you going on about it. There's an information desk over there. Come on. Let's see what they say.'

The librarian, a middle-aged blonde woman with a Slavic-sounding accent, shrugged when Daisy explained the problem. 'If the book exists, it should of course be in the catalogue you've just looked at. Are you sure you have the correct title and author name?'

'I'm sure I copied them down right, but I can double-check if you like. Bear with me.' Daisy pulled out her phone and logged onto St Edmund's Wikipedia page. 'Here we go. Yes, Elspeth McAdoo, *Women in the Pictish Royal Houses*, and

Llewelyn Rhys-Williams, *The Hand of Friendship: Welsh–English Relations in Pre-Norman Britain*. See?' She turned her phone so the librarian could see the screen.

'Let me try it myself,' said the woman, copying one of the names into her own terminal. 'No, nothing there. You don't have the ISBN number?'

'There isn't one here. I can't locate any other reference to either book, so I can't find it anywhere else either.'

'There isn't any way that, when you were digitising the catalogue, some books got, you know, overlooked?' said Hannah.

The librarian raised an eyebrow. 'It's theoretically possible, but I've never heard of it happening before. The chances of it now happening with both the books on your reading list are, to be honest, so tiny as to be non-existent. It's far more likely that whoever put those titles there simply made them up, perhaps as some kind of prank. It happens, trust me. If that's what happened here, you should get those references removed.'

'But who would…?' Daisy left the question hanging, as the librarian turned away.

She and Hannah remained silent as they walked back to the car. Hannah could sense how deflated her companion was over their wasted trip, but there was something on her own mind that she needed to get out in the open. She took a deep breath. 'There's something I haven't told you.'

'What?' said Daisy, beeping the doors open.

Hannah got into the car and clicked her seatbelt into place. She sighed. 'It was very strange at the time, and I didn't know what to make of it. Then I put it out of my mind. Now it feels horribly relevant all of a sudden.'

'Go on.' Daisy started to reverse out of their space.

'That day of the press conference, the one with Marina Spencer in the crypt of the abbey, Mark behaved really strangely. He came over to Brother Bernard and me and pulled us out of the crowd, as if he didn't want us to be there. He said Marina had sent him to give her apologies to Brother Bernard for not telling him about her initiative in advance, which was fair enough. I was expecting him to take us over to meet her, though. That would have been the natural thing, and it would have cost her nothing to shake Brother Bernard's hand. But he didn't do that. Instead, he wanted to take us for coffee, and it was like he couldn't wait to get us away from the press conference. He marched us off, looking over his shoulder really shiftily until we were out of the Gardens. He refused to go to one of those nice coffee places right on Angel Hill, but insisted on going further up Abbeygate Street and hiding away in the back of Caffè Nero. Even there, he was really antsy the whole time, gabbling away about nonsense and always glancing at the door.'

'That does sound a bit odd, but I don't really see why…'

'Hang on, I haven't told you the main point yet.'

'Sorry. Go on.'

'Well, while Mark was getting our coffees, Brother Bernard started talking about St Edmund's Scottish blood, which Marina had just been talking about in her speech, of course.'

'Oh yes? And what was his view?'

'He said he didn't know where the story had come from.'

'Really?'

'I know. It was quite a surprise. He said he was really puzzled, because he'd spent half his life studying St Edmund and he'd never heard of any of it, and suddenly everyone was talking about it as if it was definitely true. Then Mark came back with our drinks. When he heard what we were talking about, he started acting more strangely than ever. He said that, if Brother Bernard really wanted him to, he could tell Marina that Edmund might not have been half-Scottish after all but, if he did that, she would drop the patron-saint policy like a hot brick. It was basically a threat. You know, emotional blackmail. Of course Brother Bernard backed right down. But then he started saying he'd never heard of the Welsh connection either, so Mark told him it was his own fault for not bothering to check the Welsh-language sources. He said it more politely than that, but that was what he meant. And I felt really bad for Brother Bernard, because my cousin was putting him down quite insensitively, and I just thought, you know, maybe Mark wasn't a very nice guy. Then I told myself not to be judgy, and after a while I forgot all about it, but now it seems like it may matter after all.'

'So what are you thinking?'

'I'm thinking my cousin got very jumpy and defensive, to the point of being quite rude to that nice old monk, when St Edmund's connections to Scotland and Wales were called into question. And now we've discovered there's something very dodgy about the supposed sources for those connections, as if someone made them up. What if it was Mark?'

'Wow. That's quite an accusation.'

'I know it is, but there's something else I haven't told you.'

'There's more? You've been harbouring so many secrets!'

'I didn't realise any of it was important until today.'

'So what else have you been holding back?'

'Way back when this all started, on the afternoon we found the body, my cousin rang me up out of the blue. It was the first time we'd spoken on the phone in our entire adult lives, so it was quite a surprise. At first I thought something must have happened to my aunt. It hadn't, but there was obviously something on his mind. He was trying to sound calm, but it was clear he was in a complete panic. Then he told me he'd sold Marina this policy about St Edmund becoming a new patron saint for the whole United Kingdom, she was dead keen on it, and he desperately needed some Scottish, Welsh and Irish connections to make it work. He wanted to know if I knew any.'

'Bloody hell. And a few hours later, the BBC and the *Telegraph* are magically reporting just those connections, apparently on the basis of books that don't actually exist?'

'They probably just looked on Wikipedia and didn't even check the other sources.'

'Devious devil.' Without warning, Daisy burst out laughing. 'Do you fancy making him suffer a little?'

'I think he's suffering quite a lot already, isn't he?'

'The suffering we inflict won't go on for too long. After that we could help him. But we can't help him unless we know for sure he really did it, and he knows we know.'

'What have you got in mind?'

'I'm just wondering... Your friend Frances, with that lovely Edinburgh accent. Is she a good sport?'

'It depends what the game is,' said Hannah cautiously.

Daisy grinned. 'Do you think she might be up for making a phone call?'

They drew up outside Frances' cottage just before three o'clock. They had stopped for a sandwich in a village pub en route, where Hannah had tried to talk Daisy out of an idea that seemed to her as hare-brained as Mark's own scheme. Her friend would not be dissuaded, however, and had made her call Frances just to ask. To Hannah's surprise, Frances had agreed to help, and now here they were.

'Tell me again what you want me to do,' their hostess said, when they were settled in front of the fire with cups of tea and plates of home-made tea bread. 'To be honest, I couldn't quite hear you when you called. It was a very bad line.'

Hannah stared pointedly at Daisy who ignored her, equally pointedly.

'All we want you to do is make one phone call. It's only to Hannah's cousin. It's kind of a prank call, really, and it's partly to pay him back for a prank he played on...' She faltered, and Hannah could see she had been going to say 'on the whole country' but thought better of it. Quite right too. That would frighten Frances off.

'...well, for a prank he played, but also, we want to make absolutely sure that it really was him, and this is the best way of doing it.'

'I don't understand why I have to make this call. Why can't you do it?'

'You've got the perfect accent. The caller has to sound Scottish. I could try and do the accent, but I'd mess it up and he'd see through it immediately. Also my voice is a bit, er, young.'

'Oh, it's like that, is it? You don't just need a Scottish accent, you need an old lady with a Scottish accent?'

Hannah licked her finger and proceeded with great care to gather cake crumbs from her plate. She was not going to help Daisy dig herself out of that one.

Her friend pressed on, undaunted. 'You'd be perfect for it, Frances. We'd like you to pretend to be a pioneering feminist historian who did ground-breaking work on the role of women in Pictish society.'

Frances hooted. 'And how in God's name am I going to do

that? I don't know a thing about the Picts.'

'Don't worry, you don't need to. We'll write you a script so you know what to say…'

Hannah looked up from her plate and raised an eyebrow. We?

'…and we can put the phone on speaker so we can all hear what he says and we can tell you exactly how to respond. Honestly, it's simple. And, I promise you, it will be great fun!'

She was persuasive, Hannah had to give her that.

'Oh, go on then,' said Frances. 'If a prank is all it is, I can't see the harm. So, tell me, what's her name, this pioneering feminist historian?'

'Professor Elspeth McAdoo.'

She shrugged. 'Never heard of her.'

'Don't worry, nor had anyone else. She's a figment of Mark's – that's Hannah's cousin's – imagination. He made her up, as a kind of scam, and he thinks no one has noticed. So he's going to get the shock of his life when he hears her on the other end of the phone.'

For all her initial scepticism, Hannah had to acknowledge there was merit in this, if only to show Mark they had rumbled him. She warmed to the task as they debated what to put in Frances' script.

'Don't say, "I think you've heard of me",' she objected, as she and Daisy huddled on the sofa over a notebook. 'I don't think Elspeth would say that. I think she'd put it more modestly. Something like, "You might be familiar with my work," no?'

'Don't I get a say in this?' said Frances. 'I'm meant to be saying the lines, and I'm also apparently the same vintage as this old dear, so I know her turn of phrase, and I can tell you for a fact that she would rather die than say "might" when she means "may".'

By the time they had agreed on their draft, they were all thoroughly giggly.

'I think we're ready,' said Daisy. 'Have you got his number in your phone, Hannah?'

'I have, but I think we should go through the switchboard. It's more plausible if the call comes through on a landline at his end.'

'Fair enough. How do we get that number?'

'I think Google can probably help us. Hang on. Yes, here it is.'

She read out the number, and Daisy keyed it into her own phone. When the dialling tone started, she put the phone on speaker then passed it to Frances.

'*Downing Street switchboard,*' said a woman's voice at the other end, after a few moments.

Frances' eyes widened in horror. 'Sorry, wrong number,' she blurted, as she cut the call.

'What's the matter?' said Hannah. 'It was the right number.'

'But…she said "Downing Street".'

Daisy laughed. 'Did we forget to tell you that Mark works at Number 10?'

Now Hannah was laughing too at the absurdity of the situation. 'Honestly, it doesn't change anything. There's certainly no reason to be intimidated. He's still just my baby cousin who's been a very silly boy.'

After a good deal more coaxing, a reluctant Frances was eventually induced to redial. 'What's his surname, anyway? I can't just ask for Hannah's cousin Mark,' she said, as the dialling tone sounded once more.

Hannah told her, and this time, when the receptionist picked up, Frances asked to be put through.

Hannah bit her lip with nerves when they heard a male voice over the speaker.

'Is that Mark Price?' said Frances. Her accent seemed to have become a fraction quainter.

'Yes?'

'Oh good. My name is McAdoo. Professor Elspeth McAdoo. I understand you may be familiar with some of my work. I'm sorry to see that my area of scholarship has become the subject of some controversy, down south as well as here in Scotland, with yourself and your poor prime minister in the firing line. So I was wondering… Could I perhaps offer you some assistance?'

There was a long pause. Daisy and Hannah each strained to hear his response.

'Hello?' said Frances.

'Er, yes. I'm here. I'm sorry, I'm afraid your name doesn't ring any bells.'

Frances gestured helplessly as she looked to Daisy and Hannah for guidance. Daisy started scribbling in the notebook.

'Hello?' This time it was Mark's turn to interrupt the pause.

'Yes, I'm still here,' said Frances, squinting at Daisy's handwriting, then reciting, a touch woodenly, 'I think you know my book, *Women in the Pictish Royal Houses*.'

'I honestly don't. Now, I don't mean to be rude, but…'

Hannah had not expected her cousin to deny all knowledge quite so brazenly. Was it possible he was innocent of this part of the deception after all?

Daisy was scribbling again.

'My work was central to the claim that St Edmund had a Scottish mother, so I'm surprised you haven't heard of it,' read Frances. There was a long pause, and Daisy carried on writing. 'You do believe, don't you,' continued Frances, 'that St Edmund's mother was Scottish?'

'Yes, of course I do.'

'So, even if you don't know my work, I'd imagine you have an interest in finding out about it.' She was freestyling now.

'I do.'

'So what's the problem?'

There was another, even longer pause. 'I think you know the problem. I know for a fact that you cannot be Professor Elspeth McAdoo.'

Silently, Daisy punched the air. There it was: he had incriminated himself.

'Why can't I?' said Frances. 'Am I not permitted to know my own name?' It was impressive to see how much she was warming to her task.

'All right, you've had your fun, but joke's over. Who are you and where are you calling from?'

'From my front room, dear.' Frances winked at them, and Daisy let out an audible cackle, then clapped her hand over her mouth.

'Who else is there? Never mind, I'm going to hang up now.'

Hannah decided it was time to intervene. 'Don't do that, Mark,' she called. 'It's only me, Hannah.' She took the phone from Frances and turned the speaker off. 'Don't worry, you haven't been rumbled by the media. We just needed to be sure it was you that made her up, and now we are. Believe it or not, we're on your side.'

'We? Who else is there with you?'

'Just Frances, who you've already spoken to, and Daisy, who was one of the leaders of the dig team. It was she who established beyond doubt that the McAdoo and Rhys-Williams books were made up. We were on speaker before, but we're not now.'

'What are you planning on doing?' His voice was cold and suspicious, putting paid to any hope that he would enjoy the joke.

'Nothing. We don't want you to get found out, partly because I do have family loyalty, but also because it will be even worse for poor old Edmund, who is getting a bad enough press as it is. I'm sorry if we frightened you but maybe, now it's all out in the open, we can have an honest discussion about how we can help you.'

'Thank you for the sentiment, but you really can't do anything. Just leave it.' There was a slight thaw in his voice.

'Are you sure? Because while I was sitting here listening to Frances, I was thinking we could put her on *Newsnight* or something.' Across the room, a panic-stricken Frances shook her head and waved her arms to say 'no way'. 'On second thoughts, that wouldn't work because anyone who actually knows Frances would know that she isn't really Elspeth McAdoo. Also, she's not very keen.' Frances rolled her eyes. 'But we could write a letter to *The Times*, from Elspeth, saying she has followed all this debate and it reminds her of the work she did in her seminal book. No?'

To her surprise, Daisy was pulling a face.

'Honestly, Hannah, leave it,' said Mark. 'That would just draw attention. At the moment, it sounds like you're the only people who checked out those books and noticed that there's, erm, anything unusual about them, so let's leave it that way, shall we?'

'All right, if you're sure. How's Marina taking it all?'

'You don't want to know. Don't worry, though, she's not going to back down on the patron saint policy. I can't tell you very much, but she's going to come out fighting. Look, I've got to go now. And do me a favour? Don't ever do anything like that to me again?' It sounded as if he was smiling, at least.

Hannah ended the call and told them what he had said about Marina coming out fighting.

'Interesting,' said Daisy. 'And well done, Frances. You were amazing!'

Frances blushed. 'I hate to admit it, but I did quite enjoy it.' She turned to Hannah. 'But don't you ever entertain the idea that I'd do it on television. Not in a million years!'

Hannah laughed. 'Sorry. It wasn't really a serious idea. It would never have worked.'

'Nor would writing to *The Times*,' said Daisy. 'I'm a professional archaeologist, don't forget. Everything I do centres on evidence. I may be prepared to turn a blind eye to your idiot cousin fabricating academic sources about Edmund's biography, but I can't be a party to fabricating them myself, which is what a letter from Elspeth would amount to.'

Hannah sighed. 'I suppose you're right. It's just that I've really grown to like Elspeth. It feels a shame to abandon her.'

'Let's just say she'll always have a special place in our hearts,' said Frances, getting to her feet. 'And it sounds, from what your cousin said, as if the prime minister has a plan, so we should all just sit tight and wait till we see what it is, shouldn't we? Now, who's for some more tea?'

The prime ministerial team was on its way to Scotland, but the prime minister herself had yet to join it.

Mark, Karim and Giles had come to Cambridge, where their instructions were to wait outside the station for Marina to arrive from some unspecified location. 'It's confidential,' sniffed Karim, when Mark asked if he knew where she had gone. That was clearly meant to imply Karim did know, but was not authorised to tell. Mark heard him and Giles discussing it later, though, and it was obvious they were no more in the loop than he was.

The hostility of his colleagues had gone up several notches since the Edmund issue turned toxic. Inured to it, he was not bothered whether he had their approval or not, but being trapped in their company at the station was less than ideal, and it was a relief when he saw the flashing convoy that meant the prime minister was approaching.

Travelling had become a more formal business since the move to Number 10. There was now a mandatory security detail, plus police outriders whenever Marina travelled by road, which she was increasingly obliged to do. The blue-light escort got them through traffic astonishingly quickly. If this was power, Mark could see the attraction. However, it also made it extremely difficult to move around unobserved. She must have been highly visible, wherever she had just been, so why the secrecy?

She did not break her step as she drew level with them, forcing the three of them to match her stride. Giles pointed her in the direction of their platform, while Karim, at her other flank, briefed her on whatever had come into his inbox for her attention. The security detail consisted of Josh (tall, broad and dark-haired) and Tom (smaller, broader and buzz-cut). 'Everything go all right this morning?' said Mark, falling into step beside the latter, whose eyes darted busily around the station.

'Yes, mate. Thanks.'

'Remind me: where were you again?'

'That's confidential, mate.'

'To the outside world, of course. But not to her team, surely?'

'I'm sorry, mate, but you're not meant to know.' Tom chuckled. 'You know I used to be Special Forces, right? If you think you can get it out of me in some sneaky way, you'll have to try a lot harder than that.'

It was a fair cop. Still, it was strange that none of them was allowed to know. It might be something security-related, or a high-level meeting with the leader of a hostile power. But why in the Cambridge area? There was one other possibility, but it was so unlikely, given the circumstances, that it was barely worth giving voice to, even within his own head. For the moment, he would continue to keep his ear to the ground.

Their train rolled into the station just as they reached the platform. Marina could afford to cut things finer nowadays: it was another perk of the job that the train companies, however much they fretted about their punctuality targets, would rather hold departure by a few minutes than leave the station without the prime minister, if they knew she was supposed to be on board.

They were heading for Perthshire, to a 200-year-old, family-run whisky distillery that had managed to tap adroitly into the vast Chinese market and had doubled the size of its production facility. The local MP, an ambitious young member of the Alliance, had floated the possibility some months earlier that a senior member of her own party might like to open the new plant, rather than let the Scottish government take all the credit. The request had languished in a Whitehall pending tray for several weeks before Rachel, Marina's PPS, dug it out. Having hoped for a minister of state at best, the MP and the distillery owners were delighted to be told the prime minister herself would snip the ribbon.

It gave Marina the chance to make a speech that might begin by praising the thriving whisky sector, but would move on to other policy areas. Her own personal condition was not to have to taste or even smell a drop of whisky, which she loathed. Her team had agreed not to trouble their hosts with this detail. The fewer people who knew about it, the less likely it was to leak to the media, who would make merciless mischief with it.

The speech had been drafted by Karim, no doubt using material gathered by Mark, only it was pointless expecting anyone to acknowledge that. Mark had not even been allowed to read it. His role during the visit was to handle the press, so he would need sight of the text at some stage. For the moment, he was clearly expected to know his place, and he had neither the energy nor the inclination to argue.

It was gone ten o'clock when they arrived at an elegantly proportioned, baronial Gothic hunting lodge, repurposed as a boutique hotel, all soft leather sofas, tasteful tartan and roaring log fires, along with obligatory stags' heads. There was an array of serious-looking malt whisky bottles on a tray in the lounge, with an honesty book next to it. No connoisseur, but more than willing to learn, Mark would have loved to sample two or three of them as a convivial nightcap with a friendly colleague. That not being an option, he poured a generous measure from the nearest bottle, signed his name in the book and carried the glass up to his room.

In the morning he woke early, breakfasted alone, then returned to his room, where he powered up his laptop and set about dropping messages into selected inboxes to make sure the national media, as well as the Scottish wing of it, was paying attention as Marina launched her fightback against the Great Edmund Revolt. Karim had finally sent him a copy of the speech. Sure enough, the text rested heavily on Mark's own rebuttal points, which Karim had clearly harvested from the various response pieces in the Scottish and Welsh media. It was a good speech. It flowed well and there were one or two memorable lines that would sit perfectly in the evening bulletins. The art, as ever, was to whet the TV news editors' appetites by telling them something important was coming, then allowing them to decide which were the best lines, thereby preserving the illusion that they were thinking for themselves. Mark liked to think of it as fork-feeding, which was slightly more grown-up than spoon-feeding, but achieved the same result.

There was also a terse email from Marina. 'Study this

193

before we go to the distillery,' it said. 'You'll need to brief on it.'

'This' was a link to the website of the Order of the Fleur de Lys, which appeared to have been established in the fifteenth century for the Scottish nobility who were siding with the French king against the English. It went into a dizzying amount of detail, which was unhelpful when Mark had no idea why he was meant to be reading it and what aspect he would be required to brief upon. Of course it was unthinkable to ask her to clarify.

They had all been told to assemble downstairs at eleven, when their cars and escort were due to collect them. Unusually, Marina was the last to appear. Normally, she was pacing and fretting at their appointed meeting-place five minutes before she needed to be. Finding she was the only one there tended to wind her up even tighter, so they had all acquired the habit of turning up ten minutes early. Accordingly, Mark, Karim and Giles arrived in the baronial lobby, with its unbaronial scents of lavender, rose and cedarwood, at ten to eleven, but there was no sign of the prime minister.

At five to, she had still not appeared.

'Do you think she's all right?' said Giles. 'Shall I go and check?'

Karim pulled a face. 'I wouldn't. Josh is up there, so we know she hasn't come to any harm. She'll be here.'

At one minute to the hour, there was a creak on the top tread of the staircase. Mark's mouth fell open when he saw the prime minister, while Karim clapped his hands excitedly. 'It's fabulous, Marina!'

She arrived at the bottom of stairs. 'Do you think it works?'

She was wearing the blue hat and gold scarf from St Edmund's re-enshrinement. Today, however, they were matched with a long, tailored, tartan coat, cinched tightly at the waist. It was daring, but it worked, mainly because the tartan was in the same blue and gold as her hat and scarf.

'Does it belong to a real clan?' asked Mark cautiously. He could imagine the uproar in the Scottish media if they thought she had faked a tartan, which was a tacky English *faux pas* at the best of times. To have faked it in St Edmund's colours would be a foolish provocation.

'It's the official tartan of the Order of the Fleur de Lys. Did you read the link I sent you?'

'I did.'

'Then you know all about it, don't you? Make sure you draw their attention to all those patriotic Scottish earls. And, before you ask, yes, I do have official permission from the Order to wear it. Priya took care of that.'

Since one of the protection officers had to be in the car with Marina, there was not room for all the rest of them, so they split into two groups: the prime minister, Karim, and Tom up ahead and Josh, Giles and Mark in the car behind. As he watched Marina get into her own vehicle, Mark noted how canny her choice of outfit was. By wearing a tartan in Edmund's colours, and looking dazzling in it, she was neutralising the pictures from the abbey. Those images would no longer say 'arrogant English oppressor' to Scottish voters. Instead they would provide a feel-good visual association with her current outfit. Now, if she had to, she could quietly drop the patron saint policy without forever being haunted by the shrine images. It was smart politics, and he sincerely hoped the idea was Marina's own. It would be irritating if it were Karim's.

Their convoy moved off. By daylight, he could take more of an interest in their surroundings. The hotel was set in a birchwood valley. The trees were still leafless but their silver bark gleamed in the sunlight. Leaving the private drive, they joined a winding road that followed the course of a narrow, rocky river. It was frustrating not to be able to stop and breathe the air. Still, it was good to be out of Number 10, and even better to be in a different car to Marina.

After ten minutes the road veered away from the river and climbed up onto higher ground, where the tree cover gradually thinned and the view opened out into rocky outcrops, heather-clad hilltops and distant, darker belts of tight-knit pine plantations. A mile or two further was the sign for the distillery, which proved to be a cluster of neatly whitewashed, stone buildings with small cottage windows under grey slate roofs, with clouds of steam emerging from ventilators along the top and a tall, slim chimney at one end. At the centre of the main building, the roofs abandoned the sober discipline of their pitch and morphed into copper-topped pagodas.

A crowd of some two dozen reporters and camera crews were waiting outside the entrance of the main building, and they now surged towards Marina's car as it pulled up. They were headed off by a smaller but not insignificant number of police officers. This defence was reinforced as the outriders from the prime ministerial convoy parked on either side of Marina's car, creating a shield to allow her to enter the building.

Mark was out of his own car before Marina emerged from hers, greeting those of the pack he knew by sight. 'Good to see you all, guys. I hope you haven't been waiting too long in the cold.' It really was cold: he turned his collar up and wished he had brought gloves. He did not in the least care how long they had been waiting, and they knew it, but the pretence was part of the banter. 'Thank you all for making the trip. If I can just quickly run through the order of events…'

One moment he had their attention, but in another instant he had lost it. Marina, behind him, had finally got out of her car to meet the waiting dignitaries on the doorstep, and it was clear from the journalists' faces, as well as the urgency with which the snappers and film crews lifted their cameras, that her coat was having an impact. Mark only hoped it was the one she wanted.

Reaching the main reception area, Marina fell into conversation with a silver-haired gent in club tie and pin stripes and a younger man in a sharper suit, whom Mark recognised from the company website as the father-and-son chairman and chief executive. Also in the group was the local MP, a pale young woman barely out of university, one of a group of new backbenchers whose own election had taken them, as well as everyone else, completely by surprise; this one, at least, seemed to have a good head on her shoulders. It was smart of her to have asked for today's visit, even if she could never have anticipated the top level at which her request would be taken up.

There would not be room for all the press to tag along on the tour, so it had been agreed that one of the film crews would pool footage for their broadcasting colleagues, while a select party of journalists would be allowed to accompany the prime minister. 'I promise you, at the end of the visit, everyone will have full access to the PM's speech and there'll be an opportunity for questions,' Mark told them, having herded them inside and regained their attention. 'You may want to ask about the tartan in her coat: she'll have a story to tell you. After that, you'll also have plenty of time to buy yourselves a souvenir of your visit in the shop.' He hoped to goodness the distillery's own PR team had had the sense to lay on some decent goodie-bags. That would make the hacks much more likely to write warmly about the label, and it would put them in a better frame of mind about Marina's whole Scottish mission.

There was some predictable moaning from those who were not being allowed on the tour, but Mark had made his selection carefully, so no one who mattered was left out. The chosen group now followed Marina and her hosts onto the traditional malting floor. Wearing a white warehouse coat over her tartan one, the prime minister cautiously accepted a shovel, to be taught how to turn over the germinating barley. She normally hated doing unfamiliar practical activities in front of the cameras, since there was always a risk of doing it badly – which was precisely why the media liked these photo opportunities so much. Today's task looked simple enough, however, and the visit was all about her looking comfortable in Scottish surroundings, so she had little choice but to get stuck in. She turned over one shovel-load, repeated the action in slow motion at the request of the photographers, then moved on to see the malted barley being dried in a peat kiln, ground into grist and mixed with hot water before going into vats to be fermented. Mark had been dreading that she might grimace on camera at the smell of whisky, but these vats would be noxious even to a full-on alcoholic, and it was actually the hard-bitten press hacks who covered their noses. Marina peered through a porthole into one of the five copper stills, each of them shaped like a giant hubble-bubble, from which pure, colourless alcohol emerged. Finally, they inspected row upon row of barrels in the long, low warehouse, where the colourless liquid was left to age into whisky.

Had they been tourists, or journalists on a jolly, they could now expect their true reward for paying attention and asking interested questions during the tour, in the shape of sample tots of eighteen-year-old single malt. Fortunately for Marina, but not for everyone else, no such treat was on offer. Instead, the prime ministerial party headed to the new facility, a pristine set of buildings constructed and whitewashed to look exactly like the old ones, containing a replicated version of the same set-up. This was where the prime minister was to snip her ribbon and deliver her speech. Karim was already making sure she removed her white coat, to give her tartan outfit maximum exposure, while Mark corralled the media into place. 'You'll get the full text emailed to you as soon as the speech is over,' he told them. That reinforced the fact that they were about to hear something significant, rather than just polite waffle about the success of the distillery.

She began with precisely that. What a privilege it had been to see whisky made in the way it had been produced for centuries, a time-honoured method that had won worldwide recognition for Scotland and, by extension, the whole United Kingdom. It was truly wonderful that, when this production needed to expand, as a result of smart and agile positioning in an ever-changing global marketplace, there had been no question of compromising on the production process itself, and the new part of the distillery was as faithful to the traditional whisky-making craft as the old. Her voice rose with passion as she said, 'This morning I have been privileged to see our future.' It sounded absurdly grandiose in front of two dozen cynical hacks, but it would play much better on the evening news. 'Finding new opportunities to do what we do best is the way for this great country of ours to thrive in a turbulent and bewildering world. That's what we're celebrating with the expansion of this iconic family business today.' The staff, who had all been herded in to listen to the speech, applauded politely.

Next, she spoke enthusiastically of China. Whisky was a minority taste in that country, but since the Chinese population was so colossal, even a minority taste meant a massive business opportunity if that taste favoured a traditional Scottish product. The key demographic was Chinese millennials. They currently preferred Japanese whisky to Scotch. But how else had whisky reached Japan in the first place, if not via a Japanese businessman, living in Strathspey, who returned to Japan with a Scottish wife and an apprenticeship in Scotch whisky-making? The task, as her hosts had so ably demonstrated, was to find a way into the Chinese market, gain a toehold and re-educate those drinkers' palates. 'It's all about confidence in the product and, if there is one thing no Scot is short of, it's confidence that Scotch whisky is the best drink in the world.'

She turned to Karim, who was waiting with a dram of something pale and golden, which was almost certainly apple juice, although Mark had not been party to the precise details of this bit of stagecraft. She knocked it back in one, with just enough of a wince to convince the crowd it really was the hard stuff, plus a well-rehearsed cry of *'slàinte mhath!'* The staff applauded more heartily this time, and the moment would certainly make a good clip. Mark prayed even harder that there would be goodie-bags. It was bad enough not giving journalists a drink in a distillery; not giving them a drink and then forcing them to watch a politician knocking back the finest malt – even if it was fake – might push them beyond the limits of endurance.

In normal circumstances, the speech would have ended on that rousing note, but Marina was not yet done. This was her segue into the material she had come to Scotland specifically to deliver. 'However important Scotch whisky may be as an export, it is so much more than a box on the national spreadsheet,' she continued. 'In Scotland, it is a symbol, a key element of national identity, whether you drink it or not, and to deny the place of whisky in the Scottish national psyche would be as foolish as denying your flag or your patron saint. Yes, *your* patron saint, St Andrew, whose relics are in the fine, ancient town that bears his name and whose cross in the sky at the Battle of Athelstaneford is as important a part of your national story as Stirling Bridge or Bannockburn. Believe me, I understand that these things matter.'

The room had gone very quiet now. The journalists held their voice recorders up a fraction higher, the better to catch this key part of the speech.

'However, for as long as we are a United Kingdom – which I, unlike some of my friends around the cabinet table, hope will be for a very long time indeed – then telling a story about our wider country matters too. Once upon a time, we knew the narrative about Britain. Britannia ruled the waves, and the whole world knew it, not least because so much of it was pink on the map. But that world has now changed. Nowadays, very many of us understand that colonialism was a cruel and brutal process whose passing is to be celebrated not mourned. What then for our national story? For a while, one of my predecessors in this great office tried to replace that old-fashioned sense of Britishness with Cool Britannia. For all its good intentions, it smacked of a certain superficiality, as if it were a passing phase. That's why, when I heard about the rediscovery of the bones of St Edmund in the ruins of what was once the greatest church in Christendom, my imagination was fired up.

'King Edmund lived two centuries before the Normans arrived, at a time when the ancient people of these islands were finding ways of coexisting: Angles next to Saxons next to Celts, with the ruling families intermarrying and forging treaties, as well as developing a new common culture through the spread of the Christian religion. Edmund chose to die rather than bow to a leader of a different faith, and he was venerated for it as a saint, not just in England, but throughout Europe. That commitment is something we can all still respect and identify with, whether we are Christian, Muslim, Jewish, Hindu, Buddhist, Sikh or of no religion at all. It was the principle that mattered. Edmund knew the Vikings could take away his life, but they couldn't take away his freedom to believe.' That, of course, was her big line – the one she hoped would catch fire in the media. The pack were nudging each other, so they had certainly noticed the shameless *Braveheart* allusion. It remained to be seen whether they would run with it or ridicule it.

Now she pressed home what she hoped was her advantage. 'That's why St Edmund was venerated far beyond East Anglia. In Italy. In Spain. In France. If you've been reading the papers lately, it may surprise you to learn that there are churches dedicated to St Edmund in Wales. Facts like that are inconvenient for some of my critics. It's why you had a King Edmund in Scotland, son of the great Malcolm Canmore. He was named partly after his great-grandfather, the English king Edmund Ironside, but also because it was a good saint's name, recognised as such on both sides of the border. Again, if you've been reading some commentators lately, you probably wouldn't know that. It doesn't fit with the particular black-and-white view of history that they prefer to promote. That's up to them, and it's not my role to tell them how to be better historians.'

That was, of course, exactly what she was doing. It was a big, televised slap in the face for Campbell Murray and Carys Thomas – which would not be lost on them, if they watched the speech in full.

'Let me conclude by saying this. It may seem strange to spend time delving into medieval history when we're talking about building a better country for all our inhabitants, whether their ancestors were born here or they are more recent arrivals on our shores. But I believe passionately that we cannot know where we are going unless we also know where we have come from. So I welcome the debate, and I welcome the enthusiasm to know more about a long-forgotten past that has sprung up throughout the country since the discovery of St Edmund's body, which our friends in the media have dubbed 'Edmania'. That's why I hope we can come together on this journey into the past, the better and the stronger to travel into the future. And I toast it, once again, with this wonderful water of life that is helping us take your traditions – *our* traditions – out into the modern world. *Slàinte!'*

If Mark had been allowed to work on the speech, he would have pointed out that it was customary, where toasts were concerned, only to raise a glass if everyone else in the room was holding one too. Hopefully that would not be as obvious in a news clip for audiences at home as it was for the assembled hacks. On the upside, to his huge relief, he saw that the in-house PR team had been piling up elegant cardboard carrier-bags emblazoned with the distillery logo. The scribblers would, after all, be in a good mood when they filed their copy.

In the meantime, there was an opportunity for questions,

which Marina handled deftly. There was one about forthcoming trade talks with China, and rumours of a state visit from President Wu, and another, slightly tougher one about the practicalities of her patron saint policy, which she dealt with competently enough, by making it clear, without saying so explicitly, that it would make no difference to anything at all. Then one of the friendlier hacks lobbed her the inquiry she wanted about her coat, which enabled her to tell a short history of the Order of the Fleur de Lys and to rattle off names of the various Scottish earls who had been its founder members. Clearly realising it would be sensible to get out while the going was good, Karim appeared at her elbow to indicate they had run out of time, and all that remained for Mark was to whisper in a few ears to make sure the hacks had all got the *Braveheart* allusion, before it was time to get back in their cars and sweep away under their blue-light escort.

He was relieved to see, as he got into the rear vehicle, that Karim was clutching Marina's empty glass. However distracted the hacks were by their goodie-bags, one of them might always be suspicious enough to sniff around in the dregs, if the glass had been left at the podium, and her apple-juice fraud would be exposed. That was the last thing they needed.

A couple of hours later, once they were on the train heading back for London, the headlines started coming through. There was plenty of upbeat chatter about Marina's tartan coat, which fashion editors had judged a success, but the main focus was the speech itself, and it was clear the most important line had hit home.

The *Daily Record* set the tone. 'The prime minister channelled Mel Gibson in a rousing speech during her visit to

Perthshire this morning, in which she said the Vikings might have taken St Edmund's life, but they could never take his freedom to believe. Her defiant, rousing tone was designed to check recent criticism of her scheme to make the English martyr a patron saint for the whole United Kingdom. In response to those criticisms, she offered a crash course in Scottish royal history, citing Edmund of Scotland, ruler of the lands below the Forth, who was named after the saint.' That could scarcely be more positive. Twitter, on both sides of the border, also seemed to approve of Marina coming out fighting.

The real confirmation that their visit had been a success came once Mark was back in his flat, settling down to the curry he had picked up on the way home, and opened a briefing from the Number 10 press office showing the next day's front pages. The Scottish *Sun* had excelled itself, mocking up a picture with Marina's face, painted blue and white, on Mel Gibson's kilted body, beside the headline 'IT'S THE PRIME MEL-ISTER'.

Just as he was admiring this artwork, a text pinged into his phone. It was from Stewie Hunter. *Good stage management today*, it read. *Looks like you're turning it around. Weird about Murray, though, eh? Today of all days.*

Mark had no idea who he was talking about. *Murray?* he texted back.

It took a couple of minutes for the reply to come. *Campbell Murray, the guy from Stirling. Haven't you heard? He got knocked off his bike this afternoon, not so far from where you were yourselves.*

This was indeed news to Mark. Before replying, he googled Murray's name, but there was nothing about an accident. *Sorry to hear that*, he texted. *I hope he's OK.*

Again, there was a two-minute wait, and then: *Not really. He's dead. It's a shame. He could be a bit of a prat, but he was a nice enough guy at heart. Maybe get your boss to send a message of condolence?*

Campbell Murray had called Mark a numpty of colossal proportions on national television. Nevertheless, this was a gruesome fate. *Shocking news*, he replied. *Yes, mate, good idea. Thanks for the heads-up. Talk soon.*

The advice to send a message was sound, and he would make sure Marina did so. It would make her look caring and magnanimous, and head off any backlash that Murray's death might trigger.

And Stewie was right about the timing too: it was a bizarre coincidence that it should happen today, of all days, when they were so close by.

ow it gladdened me to receive attention again, once I was back in my shrine. As I have explained, those centuries in the dark, without so much as a marker above my head, were lonely ones. I rejoiced to receive visitors.

Most of them were very different to the pilgrims of old. In previous times, they knelt and prayed, addressing me directly. In this, my new shrine, few of them behaved so. They began to come in great numbers, but to look, not to pray. They stared and pointed objects made of some new-fangled metal in my direction. (This puzzled me at first, but I have since deduced that these devices have the magic property of recording the look of the scene.) They seldom knelt, nor even crossed themselves, and they never asked me to intercede on their behalf. Did they no longer have problems, the people of your wondrous modern age?

The fine lady who wore my colours was a rare exception. She knelt, at least, although she did not voice her wishes in the form of prayers. That first time she came, she made no sound and did not ask for aught directly, but I could sense the desires of her heart. It pleased me to satisfy her wishes and, when she advanced soon after to the highest station in the land, second only to your queen, I rejoiced. It was a sign my powers had not completely waned through long disuse.

Then she came to me again, as I hoped she would. The second time was in the utmost secret. The custodians of this place had forbidden entry on that day to the common folk, so the cloister and the nave were silent. The only sounds were the whispers of the lady's attendants as they took up watch outside my chapel, before she herself arrived. She wore my colours once more, but now arranged in a different style upon her cloak, in a pattern of lines and squares. Her face was hidden behind a dark veil, which she lifted when she was alone with me, revealing that fair visage with its high, noble brow.

I expected her to thank me for my intercession, but she did not, so perhaps she was unaware of the part I had played in her advancement. Instead, her heart spoke of her forthcoming journey to the land of the Scots, a prospect that perturbed her greatly. When last I was in this shrine, that land was a foreign country. Now, I realised, it is part of this great kingdom, a discovery that heartened me much. She, though, was full of dread. Although the Scots were now her subjects, she feared their hostility, because their chroniclers had written most rudely about her.

At first I did not understand what irked these moaning critics. Then, as I listened keener to the turmoil of her heart, I learned their grievance was aimed not just at my fair lady, but at myself, for I was deemed to have done their people some great wrong. I asked myself how that could be, when I had been confined in the darkness of the earth these past half-thousand years. Then I understood: a long memory for stories from centuries past was not my preserve alone; these proud Scots had one too. They were smarting still from the time of Longshanks, when I took his side against their people. That was without question my duty, so I did not rue my actions then and I do not rue them now. Howbeit, I was impressed by their refusal to forget.

Once again, she did not make any direct request to tell me what she wanted. This surprised me, I own, but I surmised it must be your modern way not to speak so openly. No matter: I saw what my part must be, namely to silence those who were griping against her.

It was my duty. What help would I be to her else?

ʜannah was at the self-checkout in Sainsbury's when her phone rang. She pulled it out of her bag to see if it was anyone important. It was only Daisy, but she answered anyway.

'Hello there,' she said, trying to tuck the phone under her chin so she could carry on scanning. 'Can I call you back? I'm just at the supermarket and…'

'Let me quickly tell you now, unless you really can't talk. It's important.'

Giving up on the neck-hold, she took the phone back in her hand. 'Go on then. Very quickly.'

'You remember I emailed Brother B? The night of *Newsnight*? Well, I've finally heard back from him.'

Was that all? 'I see.'

Do you wish to continue with this transaction?

'Yes, I do, thank you.'

'What?'

'Sorry, not you, the machine. She's so impatient. What

does Brother Bernard say?'

'He says he needs to see us. Urgently.'

'He must have figured out Mark's scam.'

'He says it's a matter of life and death.'

'Life and death? Seriously?'

Do you wish to continue with this transaction?

'I said yes! Look, sorry, Daisy. I'm getting really flustered. This machine is hassling me and there's a queue of people glowering at me.'

'All right, sorry, I can hear it's a bad time. Just tell me one thing now, because I need to get back to him. He wants to know if we can go and see him tomorrow. Both of us: he specifically asked for you. Are you free?'

'I suppose I'll have to be. Tell him yes, and I'll call you to arrange the details when I get home.' *Do you wish to continue with this transaction?* 'Yes I do…!'

As she drove back to the village, she wondered what the old monk could mean. She could understand he might be angry if he had rumbled Mark's deception, but the way he had phrased it was strange. However upset he was, it was hard to see how anyone could describe the situation as one of life or death.

Daisy could shed little light when Hannah called her back. 'His email was really brief. I'm forwarding it now so you can see for yourself. It's weirdly punctuated, with full stops where there should be spaces, which makes it quite hard to read. But you'll see how dramatic it is.'

Hannah had her laptop open. 'Hang on a sec. Just let me refresh my inbox. Yes, here it is.' She clicked on the email. 'Ah, I see what you mean.'

Presented in a twenty-four-point, bright blue font, the email read:

Dear.Daisy.   We.must.speak. V.urgent.Can.u.come.here?.
Lives.may.depend.on.it.Bring.ur.friend.Hanna(?).if.poss.
It's.important.that.I.see.her.Sorry.2.b.cryptic.but.it's.
better.face.2. face.Yrs.truly.Br.Bernard.O.S.B. †

'It must be something to do with Mark, otherwise he wouldn't have mentioned me.'

'I guess so. To be honest, I don't know what to think. We'll just have to go and find out, no?'

'I've no idea where he lives. Do you? Is it a monastery?'

'Yes. I got back to him and asked, and he sent me directions. It's a Benedictine house somewhere in Thetford Forest, so it's about half an hour away. I've never visited a monk at home in a monastery before. If nothing else, it'll be an adventure.'

It sounded as if it would indeed. Hannah enjoyed her adventures with Daisy. They made her feel more alive than she had for years, and they raised the kind of possibility in her mind that she had thought she no longer entertained. More than once, she had found herself wondering whether Monty and Arnold would ever manage to co-habit. When her mind wandered down that route, she told herself not to be so daft and made it turn round and go back the way it had come. But once the idea had suggested itself, it was not so easy to dislodge.

She volunteered to drive this time. She picked Daisy up at nine the next morning. They skirted Bury St Edmunds, avoiding the remains of the rush-hour traffic, and headed out on the road to Norfolk. As they travelled north, the undulating pastures of Suffolk gave way to pine forest, punctuated with stretches of sandy, gorse-strewn heathland.

'This is the heart of Edmund's kingdom,' said Daisy, looking out of the passenger window at the ancient wilderness. 'You'd never know it now.'

'I expect you're dying to dig it all up, aren't you?'

'Ha! I'm an archaeologist, not a metal detectorist. Believe me, I'm happy with a simple dig site. And we've got enough on our plate from the last one.'

Brother Bernard had told them to look out for a crossroads in the forest, which they presently reached. From there, his directions took them off to the right, and then along an unmade road signposted Breckland Priory. This continued dead straight for almost a mile, emerging out of the forest and onto a patch of heath, then into another copse, where it ended abruptly at a flint-studded wall. Through a pair of tall, wrought-iron gates, they could see a rambling, pink-washed house. A hand-painted sign advised that this was a private community, but that visitors were welcome to visit the church and shrine, and they should enter through the low, latched wooden door to the right of the gates.

Leaving the car, they pushed open this door, an ancient contraption which needed to be lifted before it would move and then squeaked on its hinges when it did. Beyond lay a gravel drive bordered with neat box hedges. To one side, in the shelter of the boundary wall, was a small collection of gravestones, some of them weathered, others much newer. All the inscriptions bore the suffix 'O.S.B.' after the name of the deceased.

The buildings of the priory sat behind lawns ablaze with daffodils. As they drew closer, the path divided and a fingerpost pointed three ways, to the church, the shrine and the house. A rabbit ran across the lawn and a thrush sang in the treetops above them, but there was no sign of human life.

'Do we just ring the front-door bell?' asked Hannah softly.

'I guess so. Why are you whispering?'

'Aren't you meant to whisper in monasteries?'

'Only if they're Trappist, I think. And in that case, whispering would still be cheating.' Daisy pressed the bell. It rang with an ordinary electronic chime, which seemed somehow incongruous: they could have been anywhere in suburbia. They waited a couple of minutes, and she was about to press the bell again when the door opened. A tall, bearded monk, dressed in the same black robes that Bernard wore, looked down at them inquiringly.

'Good morning. We're looking for Brother Bernard,' said Daisy. 'He's expecting us. Brother Bernard Bellamy?'

The monk's face creased into a smile. 'We only have one Brother Bernard. Come in. I'll tell him you're here.'

They entered a dark-panelled hallway. Above the panelling, the walls were painted hospital green and hung with pictures of saints. There was a faint smell of incense.

'Would you mind waiting in the visitors' room?' The monk ushered them into a low-ceilinged room lined with austere, straight-backed chairs. It looked like a doctor's waiting room, only with copies of the Bible and leaflets about religious retreats instead of *Country Life* and *TV Quick*. These walls were bare apart from a crucifix above the fireplace.

'It's not at all like I expected,' said Daisy. 'Less churchy, more institutional.'

'They do have a church. I expect that's quite churchy. And now who's whispering?'

'Sorry. You're right. It has that effect, doesn't it?'

The door burst open. 'My dears!' cried Brother Bernard, shattering their self-imposed hush. 'Thank you so much for coming at such little notice.' He took both their hands as they stood up to greet him. 'Some tea, after your journey? Or coffee? And a biscuit, of course!'

They said yes to coffee and biscuits, and he led the way along a corridor to a large kitchen with antiquated Formica units and wood-effect plastic worktops. He asked about their drive – was there much traffic? had his directions been easy to follow? – while he made them instant coffee in mugs. Hannah's had a picture of the pope on it, Daisy's a cartoon rabbit. 'You each take your mugs, I'll bring the biscuits and let's find somewhere to talk where we won't be disturbed.' He picked up a tin and guided them further down the corridor, then along another one at right angles, as far as a door marked Quiet Room. 'This will do. Close the door behind you, my dear. That's it. Now we can talk freely. Do sit down.'

They did as he said, and Hannah could restrain herself no longer. 'Look, I'm pretty sure I know what this is about.' She deposited her steaming pope mug on the low table beside her. 'It's my cousin, isn't it? He was in a tight corner and he made up a load of things about St Edmund's life that just aren't true, then he made up fake sources as well, to cover his tracks. I'm truly sorry he did it, but I honestly didn't know about it at the time, and Daisy and I only realised the full extent of what he'd done very recently. I know it's no excuse, but I can assure you he's suffered for it, as it has all come back to bite him. He deserves all he gets, without a doubt. The only thing I don't understand is why you said lives depend on it. Whose lives? How?'

Throughout this speech, which she delivered at breakneck pace with barely a pause for breath, the old monk had been looking at Hannah in bafflement. He held his hand up to stop her, shaking his head. 'That really isn't it at all. If only it were! What you say is news to me, although it doesn't surprise me.

But it has nothing to do with why I asked you to come here.'

'Oh,' said Hannah, suddenly feeling very foolish. Daisy raised an eyebrow at her, which seemed to agree she ought to feel foolish. 'So if that's not the reason, why did you ask us here?'

'Give him a chance, and I expect he'll tell us,' said Daisy.

'Thank you, my dear,' said Brother Bernard. His expression, normally so jovial, was disconcertingly serious. 'I confess, it's difficult to know where to begin. What I'm going to tell you is likely to sound far-fetched, but it is, I fear, very real.'

Hannah and Daisy exchanged glances. What on earth was coming?

'I should start by telling you something of the cult of St Edmund. As you know, I have some position as an Edmund scholar, but I suspect you may not realise what that scholarship involves. I don't restrict myself to St Edmund's life. If I did, there would be precious little to study, because there is such a shortage of material. Most of it is guesswork and your own naughty cousin' – he nodded at Hannah – 'was not alone among Edmund chroniclers in making up the facts to suit his own agenda. A monk of Bury Abbey called John Lydgate did much the same thing in the fifteenth century, so young Mark is in exalted company.'

'So, if not his life, what do you study?' said Hannah.

'His death. Not the manner of it. I don't fixate on his execution or anything like that. Rather, I study him *in* death. I am a necrobiographer, if you will. You see, we Catholics have always believed the saints are much more powerful in death than they ever were in life, because they have the ear of God. That's one of the things that makes them saints. Nowhere is this more true than in the case of St Edmund. In life, he was no warrior. At least, not an effective one, because he lost his kingdom to the Vikings. In death, by contrast, he was the saint whom all medieval warrior kings wanted on their side, because he had such an impressive record in helping them thwart their enemies.'

'Record?' said Daisy. 'You mean…there's evidence?'

'There are stories, and stories counted as evidence in the medieval mind. They started with the legend of Swein Forkbeard, the first Viking king of England. He invaded three times, and at the third attempt he managed to drive Ethelred the Unready into exile. The reason you've probably never heard of him – although you have heard of his more celebrated son, Canute – is that he only ruled for five weeks. Then he died suddenly. Some people think he fell off his horse but, in the Middle Ages, everyone believed he was killed with a lance by the ghost of St Edmund. This was either revenge for Edmund's own death at the hands of the Danes a century and a half earlier, or it was Swein's punishment for trying to levy taxes on the town of Bury St Edmunds, which was meant to be exempt for religious reasons.'

Hannah blinked. 'You don't really believe he was killed by a ghost?'

'No, perhaps not. All I know is that many miracles were associated with the shrine, and I do believe in those, or at least the possibility of them, because miracles are central to the Christian faith. In St Edmund's case, some of them were the sort of thing you might expect – sick pilgrims suddenly healed – but others showed a vengeful saint whom one displeased at one's peril. There is a notable story of thieves trying to rob the shrine of its ornaments, who were frozen to the spot until morning, when they were arrested and sent for execution. Another tells of an abbot of Bury – one of the most

senior and powerful men in the country, you understand –
who had the temerity to see if St Edmund's head really was
attached to his body, and was struck blind and dumb for his
pains. Then there was Prince Eustace, son of King Stephen
and great-grandson of William the Conqueror, who sent his
men on a rampage to plunder the abbey and died at his own
table as soon as he got home – poisoned, so everyone believed,
by St Edmund himself. In the twelfth century, Edmund
was widely believed to have come to the aid of Henry II in
putting down an armed revolt and, a century later, to have
helped Edward I in his campaigns against the Scots – those
journalists aren't wrong about that. The kings themselves
certainly believed in St Edmund's powers, which is why so
many of them spent so much time at his shrine, pretty much
until the time of Henry VIII, when it was dismantled, along
with the abbey, and the cult of St Edmund came to an end.'

He paused to take a sip of coffee.

'These are all very interesting stories,' said Hannah. 'But
what relevance do they have to us?'

'I fear it's all horribly relevant, if you will only open your
minds to the possibility. Cast your minds back, if you will,
to the day of the re-enshrinement. I know neither of you
were there, but you saw the reports afterwards. What was the
predominant image from that occasion?'

Hannah shrugged. 'I can think of several. The bishop in
his pulpit, the Archbishop of Canterbury at the door of the
cathedral, the crowds outside...'

'Nothing else?'

'Marina Spencer kneeling at the shrine.'

'Thank you, Daisy. Exactly so. The culture secretary,
as she was then, dressed in the colours of St Edmund, was
photographed praying beside his tomb. For me, it's the most

striking and memorable image of the day. And of course you recall what else happened that day?'

Hannah cast her mind back. It was the day she first spoke to Daisy, while out walking Ringo. Then, returning her four-legged charge to Frances, she had learned the shocking news that had knocked St Edmund out of the headlines. 'Morton Alexander's death, you mean. Wait, surely you can't mean...?' The idea was too preposterous to put into words.

Daisy jumped in. 'Come on, Brother B, that's just coincidence. A tragic one, but these things happen. The poor guy had a weak heart. Imagining a causal link between two unconnected events simply because they happen in sequence is a text-book case of medieval superstition.'

'I understand completely why you should say so, my dear. If it were the sole instance, I would agree with you. But it is not. Does the name Campbell Murray mean anything to you?'

'He's the guy from *Newsnight*, isn't he?' said Hannah. 'The Scottish academic. And yes, hang on, didn't I read he's just died? Some kind of tragic accident?'

There was mockery in Daisy's eyes as she turned to Brother Bernard. 'You're surely not going to say this character died because Marina Spencer put some kind of Edmundian hex on him? Sorry, Brother B, I don't mean to be rude or to insult your beliefs, but that's ridiculous.'

'Is it?' said the monk quietly. 'On the day Professor Murray died, the prime minister visited Scotland, where she made a speech at a distillery. It received a great deal of media attention because she wore a tartan coat in St Edmund's colours, and I believe she quoted artfully from a film I haven't seen.'

'*Braveheart*,' said Hannah. 'It was quite something.'

Daisy was shaking her head. 'For that guy to fall under

a lorry was awful, and I guess it was an irony of sorts that Marina made a speech fighting back against his arguments on the same day…'

'And only a few miles down the road.'

'All right, but what are you actually saying? That there was foul play of some kind? Or St Edmund tampered with his brakes?'

Hannah laid a restraining hand on her friend's arm. While she was equally embarrassed by the far-fetched nature of these claims, she was conscious that they were Brother Bernard's guests, and all this revolved around fundamental beliefs to which he had devoted his life. 'I'm sorry we're not being more receptive,' she said gently. 'But this is quite hard to believe.'

He looked at them calmly. 'Do you know where the prime minister went on the morning of that visit, in conditions of great secrecy? No? I'll tell you. She went to pray at St Edmund's shrine, arriving very discreetly and wearing a veil so she wouldn't be recognised. I heard it from a friend at the cathedral who was party to the arrangements. He only told me yesterday, which was when I contacted you. You will tell me prime ministers criss-cross the country all the time, so perhaps she dropped in while she was passing through. But not on this occasion. She was not in Bury St Edmunds for any other reason. She made a special trip, travelling some distance out of her way, just to visit the shrine, before continuing to Scotland. Do you think now that I may have a point?'

Daisy was looking at him in open derision. 'So your point is that Marina Spencer – who is famously a really nice person – consciously went to St Edmund and asked him to kill off Morton Alexander, her political ally and friend, because she wanted his job? And because that worked so well, she went back to St Edmund and asked him to bump off some Scottish academic who'd been rude about her? I mean, even if we thought St Edmund could do all this stuff – which for Hannah and me is a pretty huge if – you're asking us to believe that the country's best-loved politician is some kind of secret psychopath.'

'I'm not saying that, because I don't believe that's what happened. I think we are dealing with a sincere misunderstanding. Let me try to explain.' He took his glasses off, breathed on them and polished them on a corner of his habit, before resuming. 'The last time the leaders of the land came to St Edmund and prayed for his intercession on their behalf, in the five hundred years or so from the reign of King Canute to Henry VIII, the world was a very different place. It was violent and brutal, by our standards – a place where conflict was resolved at the point of the lance or the sword. Nowadays our way of doing things has changed, but St Edmund himself doesn't know that. He is back in his shrine after an interval of five hundred years, he is once more receiving the most powerful figures in the land, and he is giving them what he thinks they want.'

'And he thought Marina wanted him to kill Morton Alexander?' Hannah was by no means convinced that a long-dead skeleton could think anything, but she was doing her best to approach the matter from Brother Bernard's point of view.

He shrugged. 'Of course I cannot tell you exactly what passed between them. I suggest merely that, now he's back in his shrine, St Edmund is keen to resume business as normal, as it were, and may have been a little too eager to show favour to the first political leader who came to pay him court. We cannot know the content of Marina Spencer's private prayers.

But is it really so implausible that she harboured personal ambitions, and that St Edmund perceived them, even if she did not give voice to them?'

'So you're saying he was trying to ingratiate himself by doing what he thought she wanted?' said Daisy.

'If you want to put it like that, yes, I suppose I am.'

'But that's just wild conjecture, predicated on the enormous hypothetical that the bones in the shrine have thoughts, feelings and powers.'

'I would never reduce the spirit of St Edmund to his bones, and it's not hypothetical for me. It's part of my faith. I believe St Edmund had powers when he was last in his shrine, so I have no reason not to believe he has them once again. That would be the height of modern arrogance. The fact remains that Marina Spencer paid two visits to pray at the shrine and, on each occasion, someone who might be viewed as an obstacle in her path died within hours.'

He was beginning to get heated, and Hannah was keen to steer the conversation in a less contentious direction. 'I'm puzzled about why she went there at all. Not the first time, obviously, when she was a guest of honour. But the second? In a secret visit, early in the morning, disguised behind a veil? Are you absolutely sure your friend isn't mistaken? I mean, that it wasn't just someone who looked like Marina Spencer?'

Brother Bernard shook his head. 'It was definitely her. There was security, and advance notice from the prime minister's secretary, whose name, I believe, is Priya. There can be no room for doubt.'

'Odd that she would want to go there. I don't mean the praying: if she wants to do that, good luck to her. But given how much trouble her association with St Edmund has caused her, I'm surprised she wanted to go anywhere near his shrine.'

The old man was calmer again now. 'I agree, my dear Hannah. On the face of it, it's peculiar. The prime minister is not, I think, a particularly religious woman. She was certainly not raised in the Roman Catholic Church. So the business of shrines and genuflection is new to her. I can only hazard this guess: she has a lonely role and, even though her connection with St Edmund has caused her great difficulty, she has drawn solace from her time alone with him. It is a time when she can be free in her thoughts, without fear of betrayal, which I imagine is a rare luxury for her. As a result, he has become her guilty secret, if you will. She cannot reveal to the world that she is visiting him, because it will fuel the controversy still further, but nonetheless he exerts a pull upon her. You will say, perhaps, that I'm indulging in pop psychology, but this sort of thing is not uncommon among those with great burdens on their shoulders.'

Daisy opened her mouth to speak, and Hannah braced herself for more discord. But her friend's tone was less confrontational than before. 'Can I just ask one thing?'

'Go on, my dear.'

'You said lives might depend on this. That means you think this will carry on happening?'

'I'm afraid I do.'

'And you think we should do something about it?'

'My fear is this. If the prime minister visited the shrine once when she was anxious about a forthcoming event, she will do so again. It's very hard for us to know in advance what that event might be, not least because we have no clear idea what is in her diary. But we can do some intelligent guesswork. She is unlikely to seek Edmund's spiritual support in advance of humdrum engagements, such as the opening of a new school or hospital. She will be more inclined to come at times of political stress, when she has an antagonist to deal with. It could be another political rival or opponent, or a media critic. And there could also be an international dimension to the problem. For example, it was announced only yesterday that she will shortly receive the president of China in London, along with a large business delegation, for crucial talks about trade.'

Hannah nodded. 'The news bulletins have been full of it.'

'In normal circumstances, those discussions ought to be amicable, but consider this: if the prime minister came to the shrine in search of reassurance before her visitors arrived, she might give St Edmund the impression President Wu was her adversary.'

'And Wu would keel over a few hours later?'

'You may scoff, Daisy, my dear. But can you not at least entertain the possibility? And if you can, surely you agree we ought to try to prevent it happening, if it's within our power?'

Daisy managed not to laugh out loud until they had reached the main gate, scraped the wooden door closed behind them and were safely in the car, but it was clearly an effort. 'I love Brother B to bits, but he's off his rocker,' she cackled as Hannah started the engine. 'I was trying so hard not to be rude to him or to mock him, but it was difficult.'

'I'm not sure you had a complete success on that score.'

'I ask you, though. That stuff was utterly loopy. How else were we meant to react?'

'By listening politely?'

'Do me a favour! Wait…you're not saying *you* think there's something in it? Please don't. I'm not sure I can cope with everyone around me losing their minds.'

'No, not exactly.'

'Then what?'

Hannah slowed to avoid a craterous pothole on the unmade road. 'I just don't know what to make of it.'

'It's stupid, that's what. Silly, credulous, medieval nonsense, dreamed up by someone with far too active an imagination. Maybe that's what comes of locking yourself away in a monastery your whole adult life: it's so dull, you end up living in a fantasy world just to compensate.'

'Now, now, let's not get personal. And it may be silly and medieval but…' She trailed off.

'But what?'

Hannah waited for a lorry to go past before pulling back onto the main road. 'I don't know. He just got me worried when he said it would happen again. What if it does, and we were the ones who could have done something about it, only we were too busy being rational and modern about it?'

'What can we do, though? I mean, I don't think for a moment it's going to happen again, and if it does, and some minor Chinese functionary chokes on a fish bone at a banquet during the president's visit, it will just be a coincidence. But even if we did believe there was a connection and we wanted to prevent it happening, what could we do? If Marina wants to pray at that shrine, there's nothing we can do to stop her.'

'I don't know. Maybe not.'

They drove on in silence as it started to rain. Hannah was surprised to find herself so conflicted. Everything Daisy said made complete sense, by contrast with everything Brother Bernard had said, which sounded like nonsense. So why did she feel so uneasy about dismissing it?

On an impulse, she said: 'You know what I fancy doing on the way home?'

'What?'

'Let's stop off at the shrine.'

'Do you want to pray to St Edmund too? Maybe ask him to go easy on visiting foreign heads of state? Or have you got some enemies of your own that you want bumping off?'

'I'm curious to see it, that's all. Neither of us went to the ceremony so we haven't seen the shrine, have we? Since we've been talking about it all morning, it seems like a good moment.'

'If you say so,' said Daisy, but she was laughing, so she was not unwilling.

They parked on a meter in Crown Street, right opposite the cathedral entrance. It was raining heavily now, and they put their coat collars up as they ran across the road.

'In here,' said Hannah, ducking inside the doorway of the tourist information bureau.

'But that's the cathedral along there.'

'You can get in through here. It joins up with the cloisters by the west door. We'll get less wet this way.'

The bureau opened out into the cathedral gift shop, which had the usual array of commemorative china, local honey and jam, expensively packaged soaps, chocolate and tea-towels, and then a few shelves of books, both religious and secular. Hannah stopped to pick up a slim volume on the stand nearest the cathedral entrance: *The Passion of St Edmund* by Abbo of Fleury. It had a modern introduction, followed by ten or twelve bite-sized chapters of no more than a couple of pages each.

'Look at this,' she said. 'I've heard of it, but I've never seen it before. It's the very first version of the Edmund legend, written in the tenth century. I'm pretty sure some of the stories Brother Bernard was telling us this morning come from here.'

'Treat yourself.'

'I think I will. It's very short. I like that in a book.'

Hannah paid for her purchase at the till while Daisy headed into the cathedral. When Hannah caught her up, she found her standing just inside the west doorway, gazing up at the bright-painted angels on the hammer-beams of the nave roof.

'You know, I've never actually been in here before,' said Daisy.

'You really avoid churches don't you?'

'It's not that. I just don't particularly go for buildings of any kind. I've always been more excited by the idea of the secrets the earth can give up if you dig for them, rather than the structures standing on top of it. I like this, though. I love all the colour up there.' She tipped her head right back to examine the gaudily painted scheme running all the way along the nave roof and into the chancel.

'I think the shrine's at the far end. See those gates? I'm pretty sure it's behind there.'

They walked the length of the north aisle, their footsteps echoing around the cavernous interior. At its eastern end, the gates to the St Edmund Chapel stood open, and there inside them was the simple, polished limestone tomb, sitting on an equally plain marble base. Its lack of ornamentation contrasted with the exuberance of the colours on the roof or the elaborate Gothic spires on the canopy of the bishop's throne beside them.

They stood contemplating the shrine.

'What now?' said Daisy. 'Is he speaking to you? Are you going to pray to him?'

'You're scoffing, and I don't really believe in it either. But if you think it's all such nonsense, why are you whispering?'

'Like you were earlier in the monastery. Out of respect? Maybe just because that's what you're meant to do in these places. So why are *you* whispering?'

'Because you are.'

'Don't laugh. You're the one who isn't being respectful.'

It was true, Hannah was having an attack of the giggles, having tried and failed to feel the holy aura of the shrine. 'Come on,' she said. 'It's not doing anything for me, so let's get out of here. We haven't had any lunch and I'm starving.'

'Can I have a quick wander around first, now we're here?'

'Of course. Take your time. I've got Abbo of Fleury to keep me company.'

Hannah sat in a pew at the front of the nave and opened the book at random. There were chapters headed 'The Coming of the Danes', 'Martyrdom' and 'Aftermath'. Then, nearer the end, 'Life After Death', which described the cult of the saint, as Brother Bernard had called it. And there was the story of the eight marauders who, according to Abbo, 'had determined to gratify their crazy cupidity' by stealing everything they could find within the precincts of the monastery. The monk related the story of their concerted attack on the church from various directions: 'One laid a ladder to the door-posts, in order to climb through the window; another was engaged with a file, or a smith's hammer, on the bars and bolts; others with shovels and mattocks endeavoured to undermine the walls. The work being thus distributed, whilst they vied one with another in the most strenuous exertions, the holy martyr bound them fast in the midst of their efforts, so they could neither stir from the spot nor abandon the task upon which they had entered; one on his ladder hung aloft in mid-air, another was displayed to view with his back bent in digging, who had stolen unobserved to the guilty deed. At length morning came, and then the thieves, still persevering with the work which they had begun, were arrested by a number of people and, after being firmly secured by chains, were finally committed for trial.'

It was a lively tale, culminating in the miscreants all being hanged together, but there was a coda: the bishop who sentenced them to death regretted doing so for the rest of his life, because it was 'highly unbecoming that a minister of the heavenly life should yield assent to the death of any man whatever'. He sought atonement by cleaning St Edmund's body, giving him fresh robes and building him a new and better shrine.

It was somehow reassuring to know that the cult of the saint had its softer side.

She looked up to see Daisy wandering towards her, having completed her circuit of the cathedral. She was still gazing above her head, clearly captivated by the faux-medieval colour scheme.

Hannah stood up. 'Have you seen all you want?'

'Yes, thanks. I'm pleased we stopped here.'

'Good.'

They started back towards the west door.

'So what shall we do?' said Daisy.

'About what?'

'About Brother B and his fear of our friend here bumping off Marina's political opponents.'

Hannah sighed. 'You were right. It's superstitious claptrap. Even if it isn't, there's nothing we can do about it.'

'Although…'

'What?'

'There is one thing we could do.'

'And that is?'

'We could have a word with your cousin, just to pass on Brother B's concerns.'

Hannah laughed. 'An hour ago, you were ridiculing the whole thing and making me feel an idiot for wondering if we ought to consider it. Now you want to tell Mark about it. What's come over you? Is it this place? One whiff of Gothic revival bling and you've come over all medieval?'

'I don't know. There is an atmosphere in here, I have to admit, even if you can't feel it. And I don't mind calling your cousin if you don't want to. I ought to apologise to him properly for my part in our little Elspeth McAdoo trick. Why don't we go for a sandwich, and I'll call him on your phone?'

'I want more than a sandwich,' said Hannah. 'It may have to be egg and chips. But if you really want to talk to my cousin, be my guest.'

In the event, the fall-out from the death of Campbell Murray focused entirely on road safety. He had been cycling across a busy roundabout when a truck taking the first exit cut straight through him. Visibility was good, he was wearing fluorescent gear and the driver was completely at fault (although Murray's choice not to wear a helmet kept the story going for an extra couple of days, as outrage-peddling columnists batted that controversy back and forth). The deceased's recent tangle with the prime minister over thirteenth-century English imperialism barely came up.

Mark followed Stewie Hunter's advice and drafted a brief public statement in Marina's name, plus a longer, private one to be sent to the family on Downing Street notepaper. A message came back to say the prime minister's condolences had made a difference at this terrible time, and there the matter ended. There was some further discussion as to whether flowers should be sent to the funeral, but that was judged excessive and in danger of looking opportunistic.

They had done all that was required and the episode was over.

When his phone rang a week or so later and he saw it was Hannah calling, he almost did not pick up. Privately, he was prepared to admit he deserved the whole Elspeth McAdoo prank, but it stung nonetheless and left him uncertain where he stood with his cousin. She had assured him she was on his side, but the fact that she had taken it upon herself to investigate his own contributions to the myth of St Edmund – and had taken at least two of her friends into her confidence – was disturbing, to say the least. That was actually why he did pick up. It was worth knowing what she wanted, just to keep tabs on her.

It was not Hannah, though. 'Mark? It's Hannah's friend Daisy. We, erm, met on the phone the other week?'

'As if I could forget.' Deliberately stony, he was not ruling out hanging up.

'I'm sorry about that. It was a mean trick and I hope you can forgive us. Listen, I'm with Hannah now. We've just come back from visiting Brother Bernard in Norfolk. Do you have five or ten minutes to speak? It's not about that Elspeth stuff, or anything you did, I promise. It's still about St Edmund, though, and I'm afraid it's quite weird. We both thought it was nonsense at first, but I reckon you need to know about it, just in case there's something in it. Brother B says it could be a matter of life and death, which we both think sounds crazy, but he also thinks one of the people in the firing line could be the president of China, which is why we thought…'

'Whoa! Slow down, Daisy. You're not making any sense. What do you mean, "a matter of life and death"? And what the hell has the president of China got to do with St Edmund?'

'Sorry, I was babbling. It's all mad, and I'm not explaining it well. I'm a bit nervous too, to be honest, because I've never called 10 Downing Street before. You are in Number 10 at the moment, aren't you?'

'I am, but I was just going out to get a sandwich. If you give me a moment to put my coat on and get out in the street, I can listen to what you have to say, as long as it really is only five or ten minutes.' If any further nasty revelations about St Edmund were in the offing, he would rather hear them away from the office.

'Thank you, Mark. I really appreciate it.'

'Just give me two seconds... Right, I'm leaving the building...and now I'm in the street, walking towards the park.' A detour through St James's Park would mean less traffic noise. 'Fire away.'

'Good. Here goes.'

It took her longer than ten minutes to tell her story. He listened to it sitting on a bench, with a pelican pecking at the tarmac around him. It was indeed bizarre.

First off, it confirmed his suspicion that Marina's top-secret destination on the morning of their Scottish trip had been St Edmund's shrine. That, in itself, was hardly sane behaviour for someone who had never shown any sign of being especially religious and who had openly blamed Mark for the pictures beside 'that blasted tomb'. The fact that she had been at such pains not to say where she was going to any of her team, including Karim and Giles, reinforced the impression that she had something to hide. Did he believe she was colluding with St Edmund to nobble her enemies, or that St Edmund was volunteering these favours because he thought they were what she wanted? Since working for Marina, Mark had become used to a world where the truth was frequently stranger than fiction. Even by those standards, however, this was a stretch. He could see why Brother Bernard might believe it, but he was not sure anyone else ought to.

Of far greater concern was a more prosaic problem. 'Who else has Brother Bernard told about this?'

'No one except Hannah and me, as far as I know.'

'What about the other monks in the place where he lives? Or his contact at the cathedral – the one Priya dealt with?'

'I don't know. From the way he was talking to us, I got the impression he was sharing it for the first time and he was treating it as highly secret, so I wouldn't have thought he's told anyone else. Why do you ask?'

'The tabloids would have a field day if it got out. *Marina's killer curse…* It wouldn't have to be true for them to make hay with it, and then there'd be no stopping it. That alone is a good reason to prevent her going there again.'

'I see what you mean. I hadn't thought of it like that. So I was right to tell you about it?'

'You were indeed. But swear to me you won't tell anyone else. The same goes for Hannah. And make sure Brother Bernard doesn't, either.'

'I promise we won't. I've got a number for Brother B now, so I'll call him as soon as I get off the phone. What are you going to do?'

'Not sure yet. Leave it with me.'

'Will you let me know, so I can report back to Brother B? Otherwise he's going to get agitated.'

'Fair enough. Text me your number, and I'll get back to you later.'

Ending the call, he started on a circuit of the park, feeling conspicuously native among the crowds of European and Far Eastern tourists feeding the ducks and posing for pictures, as he tried to think the matter through.

If it was essentially a media problem, as his instinct told him it was, the overriding priority was to prevent any meddlesome hacks getting wind of a connection, fantastical or otherwise, between Marina's visits to the shrine and the deaths of Morton Alexander and Campbell Murray. That meant everyone who had discussed it so far must keep quiet. He was prepared to accept that Hannah and Daisy would do so. The real danger was Brother Bernard: if the monk grew frustrated that no one was taking him seriously, he might decide to shout his mouth off, as a kind of monastic whistle-blower. If he did so, the red-tops would lap his story up.

The risk of that would be even greater if Marina returned to the shrine. For that reason alone, it should be a priority to stop her going back. How was Mark to do that, though? He could hardly contact the cathedral authorities and ask them not to let the prime minister in. Why would they take any notice? They would never turn her away if she turned up with her two burly protection officers. And what reason could he possibly give them, without telling them the whole daft yarn?

He had arrived back at the pelican pond, having made a complete loop of the park. He embarked on another circuit.

If he could not plausibly persuade the cathedral to stop Marina coming in, there was only one logical alternative. The sole person he could tell without any risk of the story leaking was Marina herself.

He tried to imagine how that encounter might go. 'Prime Minister, you remember the elderly monk who spoke just before you at the Bury St Edmunds press conference? You'll laugh, but he thinks you and St Edmund are jointly responsible for the death of Morton Alexander...' She would not laugh, though. Marina Spencer was not the laughing type. 'Prime Minister, there's a delicate matter I need to raise with you. You'll find it shocking at first, but do hear me out, because it's important you should know about it…' He could not see that working either. Marina was not a hearing-you-out person. 'Don't misunderstand me: I don't believe for a moment that you're a supernatural double murderer. The problem is that other people might…' The prospect made him feel physically ill.

Nevertheless, telling Marina was the key to the whole thing. If she was unwilling to hear it from Mark, he would have to enlist the help of someone she actually trusted. And there, finally, was the kernel of a plan. It would not be easy, but he would have to tell Karim or Giles.

Which of them to choose? Karim had Marina's ear more than Giles did. If Mark could only get the message across to him, it was more likely to reach its intended target. That was easier said than done, though. Karim hated Mark even more than Marina did. It was hard to imagine him having the patience to hear the story through to the end. It would be easier to tell Giles, who at least behaved with a veneer of civility, so Mark did not always feel on the defensive with him. He would therefore be able to explain the situation more persuasively, which was obviously a good thing. But a nagging voice told him that choosing Giles was the cowardly option…

By the time he walked over the threshold of Number 10, he had decided: he must swallow his pride and tell the whole story to Karim, however difficult and humiliating it was. The life of the government depended on it, and it was his own fault for landing Marina in this mess in the first place. His own discomfort was of minor importance within that bigger picture.

Giles was at his screen when Mark approached his colleagues' desks, but there was no sign of Karim.

'Is he around?' said Mark, in as casual a tone as he could muster.

'He's with the cabinet seecretary. It's going to be an all-afternooner. Can I help?'

'No, you're all right…' Then he wavered. Giles was being affable – he was actually smiling – and here he was, willing and available. How different his attitude was to anything Mark could expect from Karim. Bravery and the greater good wilted in the face of expediency. 'Actually, Giles, yes, thanks. There is something you can help me with. It's pretty important.' He glanced around the room, where three or four other young staffers were tapping at keyboards. 'Would you mind taking a stroll outside? There's something I need to share with you, and it's very much for your ears only.'

Giles looked at his watch, then shrugged and picked up his coat, phone and vape. 'What's on your mind?' he said, as they emerged into the weak afternoon sunshine and turned right towards the park.

Now he had taken the plunge, Mark was not sure how to begin. 'It's complicated, it's highly sensitive and it relates to St Edmund,' he said, playing for time.

'I thought it might.'

'Whatever you're thinking, that's not it. This is a bizarre story. It takes a bit of explanation, and a good deal of it will sound insane, but I hope by the end of it you'll see why I need to share it.'

Giles exhaled an aniseed-flavoured cloud. 'Sounds intriguing. I'm listening.'

'Do you remember the elderly monk who was one of the speakers with Marina at the press conference at Bury St

Edmunds abbey?'

'The one you whisked away because you thought he might be trouble? What was his name? Bradshaw?'

'Bellamy. Everyone calls him Brother Bernard.'

'Let me guess. He's turning out to be trouble.'

'You have no idea! He's got it into his head that St Edmund is working miracles now he's back in his shrine. And not in a good way.'

'He's a Benedictine monk, isn't he? That's the kind of stuff they believe. It's none of our business. Just ignore it, buddy. It's not our place to tell people what they should and shouldn't believe. Not the religious stuff, anyway.'

'It is our business if they start believing Marina murdered Morton Alexander.'

Giles had a coughing fit as his vapour went down the wrong way.

Mark waited for him to recover. He had not meant to deliver the news so abruptly. 'That's the implication of it,' he added.

Giles had regained the power of speech. 'Your monk is saying' – he dropped his voice to a strangulated hiss as they walked past a benchful of office workers eating sandwiches from takeaway boxes – 'that Marina *murdered* Morton?'

'Not in so many words. But he is connecting Morton's death to Marina's prayers at the shrine on the day of the service. And he's saying it's no accident that Campbell Murray, the guy who got knocked off his bike, died on the day of her second visit.'

'Second visit? Where?'

'Yes, that's the other thing. Brother Bernard found out where Marina went on her hush-hush trip in the morning, the day we travelled to Scotland. She went for secret prayers at the shrine.'

'In order to ask St Edmund to kill off some obscure academic historian? Sorry, but that's batshit crazy.'

'No. The way Brother Bernard sees it, St Edmund is trying to please Marina by taking down anyone he thinks is standing in her way.'

'You're not saying you believe this crap?'

'Of course not. But I'm scared it will get out. The tabloids would have a field day if they got wind of it. Obviously they wouldn't dare accuse Marina of collusion with a medieval saint. There are limits, even for *The Sun* and the *Star*. But a killer curse? They'd love it.'

'You could be right there. What are the chances of it getting out?'

'Low, at the moment. Brother Bernard is naturally discreet, and the only other people he's told are my cousin, who was a member of the original dig team, and her friend, who was also on the dig. I've sworn them to secrecy.'

'In that case, why the big panic? It's one old nutcase with a crazy theory, who isn't going to go anywhere near the press with it. That seems pretty low-risk, compared to the risk of dignifying it by taking it seriously.'

'The problem is these secret visits to the shrine. More people know about those, because Priya has to set them up in advance, with the dean or the verger or someone. If Marina has already snuck off there once without telling anyone, what's to say she won't carry on going? Brother Bernard reckons she's most likely to go there at times of greatest political anxiety, when she's under major pressure or she has a high-level meeting coming up. The way he sees it, every visit will result in a death.'

'But you've already agreed that's rubbish. Or are you

actually starting to believe this juju?'

'Absolutely not. But Brother Bernard is more likely to run and tell tales if he thinks there's an ongoing problem. From his point of view, lives will be lost – perhaps some very important lives – if he doesn't speak out.'

'So what do you think should happen, going forward?'

'We need to tell Marina to stop going to the shrine.'

'You tell her, then, if you think it's so important.'

Mark paused. This was the most awkward part. 'I was hoping you might do it. She hates me, and she won't give me a proper hearing. I'd be out on my ear before I could finish the first sentence.'

'Whereas she'll be sweetness and light if I tell her she has been accidentally murdering people and she needs to stop it?'

'That might not be the best way of putting it. Can't you just have a quiet word with her? Not to alarm her or to blame her, but to let her know the seriousness of where we are.'

'You know what I think, buddy?'

'What?'

Having completed the same circuit of the park that Mark had made earlier, they climbed the steps from Horse Guards back towards Downing Street.

'You're out of your mind. If you want to tell her all this, good luck with that. If you're expecting me to do it, you need your head examining.' Giles gave him a gentle clap on the shoulder as they entered Number 10. 'Let me know what you decide.'

As he returned to his desk, Mark found he was less discouraged by this rebuff than he might have expected. Giles had knocked him back, but his reasoning was sound enough – that Marina would be no more disposed to hear this story from him than from Mark – and it was also the closest they had come to bonding. His own isolation at work ground him down, however much he made light of it, and the chance that it might ease made him feel uncharacteristically chipper.

Daisy had, as promised, texted her number, and he drafted a message. *Mark here. I've discreetly raised the matter with a close colleague. He thinks any attempt to stop the PM making future visits will do more harm than good, so we won't be doing anything at this end. Pls try and talk Brother B down. I hope he'll see sense and this will all blow over. Mx* He read it through, decided the final *x* was too much – he had forgiven her, but she need not know that yet – so he changed it to a simple *M*, and hit send.

The reply pinged back a few minutes later. *That's fine by me and Hannah. We thought it was all nonsense anyway. Wish me luck trying to convince Brother B!*

He sent her a laughing face to make up for the deleted *x*.

This new scare aside, the Edmund problem seemed to have gone off the boil. After the favourable reception the media had given to Marina's *Braveheart* speech, it had lost interest in the controversy, and the received wisdom within Number 10 was that the Alliance's coalition partners in Scotland, Wales and Northern Ireland were equally happy to see the furore die down, because the last thing they wanted was grief from their own supporters. As the fuss abated, they could get on with working harmoniously in government with Marina and her party.

The new hobby-horse for the press was Sino-British relations. Suddenly every second hack was a keyboard expert on international trade policy, the security hazard of dealing with Huawei and the sources of the Covid pandemic. It was all-consuming, and even Marina seemed to have let go of her fury towards Mark. She actually invited him to sit down if he went into her study.

In a further sign that he was back in what passed for favour, he was called upon to rejoin the team prepping her for Prime Minister's Questions. On his first week back in the tent, on the first day of March, he gave her a good line about the opposition whipping up prejudice against the forthcoming guests from Beijing – 'playing Chinese whispers on social media' – and he was also responsible for a gag concluding with her catchphrase 'Yeah, no, I really wouldn't' which brought the House down. The government side of it, at any rate.

He and Karim were in the prime minister's room behind the Speaker's chair, watching the proceedings on BBC Parliament, as the leader of the opposition finished his allotted six questions. This was the newsworthy centrepiece of the weekly occasion, and the heat was off as the focus moved to questions from backbenchers. Mark was only half-watching as the Speaker called Lowri Edwards, the Plaid Cymru MP for Gwynedd North. A middle-aged woman in a bright red suit with a determined expression, she opened her mouth to speak, but her eyes registered surprise as no words came out. She tried again to ask her question, but she had no more success on the second attempt: her mouth moved, but no sound emerged. Visibly embarrassed, she sat down again. 'I'm sorry to see that the cat has got the honourable lady's tongue,' said Marina, and most of the chamber laughed.

'Ohmigod!' said Karim. 'Did you see that?' The incident was so striking, he was prepared to lift his veto on civil engagement with Mark.

'Amazing,' said Mark. 'It's like she's got sudden-onset laryngitis. Is that even a thing? Look at her. She's gutted.'

'She's right to be. She's going to be a viral sensation. How long before she's trending?'

'An hour?'

'More like half.'

It was the longest-lasting pleasantry they had ever shared.

Five minutes later, Marina was back with them and it was business as normal as they headed back to Downing Street, Karim close by her left flank, receiving confidences and whispering earnest counsel, with Mark an obligatory couple of paces behind. Turning a corner, they saw Lowri Edwards at a distance. 'Go and speak to her, Mark,' said Marina. 'Tell her she has my sympathy. These attacks of nerves happen, and she mustn't let that unfortunate incident get to her. Make her feel better and find out what she was trying to ask. She's meant to be on our side, after all, so we ought to be nice to her.'

Without waiting for an answer, she turned on her heel and she and Karim strode away.

'Lowri!' Mark called, waving the sheaf of papers in his hand. She turned and waited. 'Marina says she's so sorry about what happened,' he said as he caught her up. 'She asks if there's anything she can do. Don't try to talk, if it's an effort. If necessary, we can book you in for a chat at Number 10 when you've got your voice back.'

'I've got it back now,' she said, and it was true, there was nothing wrong with her voice – its nasal, North Walian lilt so much more singsong than his father's Glamorgan accent. 'It was so odd. I was literally struck dumb, in a way I thought could only happen in the Bible. You know, like Ezekiel or someone? The minute I sat down I could speak normally again. Nobody can understand it.'

'That is indeed very strange.' Talk of the Bible made Mark

uneasy. 'Tell me, what was it you wanted to ask the PM?'

'She wouldn't have liked it. Here, I've got it written down.'

She passed him a sheet of House of Commons paper with her own name on it, on which a short paragraph had been printed out. It read: *To mark St David's Day, can the prime minister reassure the people of Wales that she has abandoned her misguided plan to force upon them an English patron saint, St Edmund, under whose banner King Edward I subjugated Wales to English rule?*

The words landed with a smack in Mark's solar plexus. He hoped the shock did not register on his face. 'Lowri, do you mind if I hang on to this? Then I can pass it directly to the prime minister.' He wished his hand holding the paper would stop shaking. Fortunately, the MP was too caught up in her own trauma to notice.

Leaving her at a walk in order not to attract suspicion, but breaking into a run once he was round the corner, he dashed to the prime minister's room, which now stood empty, and pulled out his phone.

Before making the call, he closed his eyes and forced himself to think calmly. Was he going mad, and wildly over-reacting? He wished he could believe he was. What to do for the best, though? If this were a movie, it would be an open-and-shut case of supernatural intervention, which only the stupidest characters – those destined for an early, gory exit – dared to ignore. But this was real life, where the supernatural was not meant to exist. Except when it was called religion, of course. Then it was officially sanctioned, not least by the House of Commons itself, which began every day with prayers. If the institution within whose walls he now sat officially believed in Christianity, with all its miracles, was it really so outrageous to believe that a Christian saint might be exercising his miraculous powers, albeit misguidedly?

His mind was made up. 'Giles,' he said, when his colleague answered on the third ring. 'It's worse than I thought. That St Edmund business, I mean. Something has happened, and it's really shaken me. I hate to say it, but I'm beginning to wonder if Brother Bernard may be right after all. Did you see PMQs just now?'

'Yes, of course, buddy, but…'

'So you saw that Plaid woman dying on her feet?'

'Hilarious! Poor Lowri. She's trending on Twitter already, and that's all she'll ever be remembered for. But what's it got to do with Bellamy? You're worrying me, Mark.'

'Good. I want to worry you. Do you know what Lowri wanted to ask? Listen to this.' He read out the text of the question. 'And you know what else? As soon as she sat down, she was right as rain. I've just spoken to her now, and her voice sounds completely normal. She says she was struck dumb the moment she got to her feet, like something out of the Bible. Those were her very words. She said it was biblical.'

'What are you trying to say?'

'You know what I'm trying to say, Giles. I don't want to say it and I don't want to believe it, and if anyone else said it I'd they think they'd totally lost the plot. But I think Brother Bernard may be right to say there's something weird going on. Proper, old-school biblical weird.'

'So you're saying you now think Marina was responsible for Morton's death?'

'Not at all, no. Well, maybe. Causally, anyway. I just don't know, but I don't think we can rule it out. Campbell Murray, too. And the thing is, it may happen again. Imagine if she goes to the shrine before the Wu visit. That's Brother Bernard's greatest fear, apparently, and I think we might be wise to listen to him. I mean, if he's wrong, that's brilliant and no harm done. On the other hand…' He tailed off nervously, and there was a long silence. 'Hello?'

'Yeah no, I'm still here. Look, you did the right thing by telling me about this. Leave it with me. Don't worry, mate. I'll do what needs to be done.'

'You'll raise it with Marina? She's on her way back with Karim now.'

'Leave it with me.'

'Brilliant. Thanks.'

'Oh, and Mark?'

'Yes?'

'What are you doing now? Are you coming straight back, or…?'

'No, there are some hacks I need to buttonhole. Not that I can concentrate much.'

'Do that. Try to take your mind off it. Take your time.'

'Thanks. Will do. See you later.'

Giles ended the call and Mark sat on in the empty room, wondering if any of its previous occupants had ever had to deal with anything as crazy as this. He was pleased, at least, that the conversation with Giles had gone well. That was all down to his own groundwork, in initiating their discusssion the other day. He could congratulate himself on that.

Two hours later, he returned through the gates and hurried along Downing Street. He had managed to brief a few friendly journalists with some snippets about the Chinese bilaterals, but now he was keen to touch base with Giles.

The door of Number 10 swung open to admit him. As soon as he stepped inside, the police officer on duty in the hall stopped him.

'Mr Price? I've been told not to allow you into the building unaccompanied.'

'Why? What's wrong?'

'I can't tell you that, sir. I've just been asked to come with you to your desk where you're to collect your personal effects, and then I'll have to escort you out of the building.'

'You can't do that! I work here. Look, here's my ID. I work for the prime minister!'

'I'm only following my instructions, sir. Now, if you'll come with me calmly, it'll be easier for both of us. And I'll need that ID, I'm afraid.'

'Tell me what's happening! What am I supposed to have done? Am I under arrest?'

'No sir, you're at liberty to go on your way once you've left the building. But you'll have to do that as soon as possible.'

His cheeks were burning as they trod the soft carpet towards his cubby-hole. Had Marina reacted so badly to Giles' revelations that she had ordered Mark to be thrown out on the spot? Had she sacked Giles too?

Sitting on his desk was an empty cardboard box, clearly intended for his belongings, and a sealed envelope with his name on it. He ripped it open. It was a letter on government notepaper, signed by the head of human resources for Number 10.

'Dear Mr Price,' it read. 'It has come to my attention that you have lately made a number of serious and slanderous allegations against the prime minister, in the light of which it is no longer possible for you to remain in your post. I am suspending you with immediate effect, pending urgent psychiatric evaluation. Your email account has also been suspended with immediate effect. You will be required to surrender your government ID pass on departure from the premises. I remind you that you are still bound by the terms of the Official Secrets Act. Accordingly, any repetition of the slanderous allegations you have made will be met with the full force of the law.'

He read it in a daze. The copper was still standing over him, waiting for him to pack up his stuff. In truth, there was nothing he wanted. He had an emergency toothbrush, razor and tube of toothpaste in his top drawer, as well as some cough sweets, paracetamol and half a packet of fig rolls, but someone else could deal with all that.

'I'm ready to go,' he said, with as much dignity as he could manage.

Whether the policeman was following protocol or had taken pity on him, he did not lead Mark out of the front door where, cardboard box or not, his humiliation would be instantly obvious to the waiting hacks, but via the back corridors that led through into the Cabinet Office and out of a much more anonymous exit onto Whitehall. As they followed this route, a door from one of the side rooms opened and Mark found himself face to face with Giles, whose eyes registered a moment of panic, but not surprise. It was the look of someone who had not expected to confront Mark directly. In that moment, it was clear Giles was not a fellow victim of a swingeing authoritarian clampdown, but his betrayer.

'What have you done, Giles? I thought you understood this was a matter of life or death. I trusted you.'

Giles avoided looking him in the eye. 'I told you I'd do what had to be done, and that's what I did. I genuinely hope you get the help you need.'

Before Mark could respond, his escort was nudging him onwards. Perhaps it was just as well. Now they had decided he was a headcase, all his possible parting shots – from 'you'll regret this' to 'you've got to stop her before she kills the president of China' – would hardly make him look sane.

So he kept these thoughts private and, thirty seconds later, found himself standing on the pavement. He was an ordinary civilian now, no longer a Westminster insider, with little to distinguish him from the stream of tourists buffeting him as they crocodiled from the gates of Downing Street towards Trafalgar Square.

What the hell was he meant to do next?

ﬔannah had not spoken to Mark since the day of their prank call. Daisy seemed to have taken charge of all communication with him. First he messaged Daisy to say he thought the Brother Bernard problem, as they all now thought of it, was best ignored. When, a couple of weeks later, he changed his mind and was promptly sacked, he chose to call Daisy with the news rather than Hannah.

It was strange to be sidelined in this way, but Hannah knew she had no grounds for complaint. It was not as if she and Mark had any great prior relationship of their own. Her own petty jealousy also seemed indulgent alongside the shock of his losing his job.

She had already seen the clip of the poor Welsh MP in the House of Commons. The whole country was laughing about it. Probably the whole world, for that matter, because the look on Lowri Edwards' face was funny in any language. It was not so funny when Daisy called to explain what the hapless woman had been trying to ask.

250

'Wow,' said Hannah. 'I'd love to call it coincidence, but I'm not sure I believe that.'

'I know, right?'

'Have you told Brother Bernard?'

'I didn't feel I had any choice.'

'And?'

'You can imagine. It confirms everything for him.'

'One thing, though…'

'What's that?'

'The way Brother Bernard told it, bad things would only happen if Marina went to the shrine. Does this mean she's been there again?'

'He mentioned that too. Not as far as he was aware, and he was sure he would have heard. He thought maybe she's taken to praying to St Edmund privately, from the flat at Number 10, or wherever. At least Lowri Edwards didn't keel over and die, which he thought she might have done if Marina had been to Bury.'

'It's all so crazy. I feel like we've left the real world behind and stumbled into some kind of Indiana Jones film.'

'*Brother Bernard and the Shrine of Doom*? I know. I can't get my head round it.'

And that was where they had left it, neither of them knowing how to adjust to this bizarre parallel universe into which they seemed to have stepped. At least, that was how Hannah felt, and she assumed it was the same for Daisy, hence the radio silence since that night. It was all so hard to deal with; it was easier to pretend it was not happening.

It was only when Mark's mother called one afternoon that she began to realise there might be another reason.

'Hi Pauline, how are you doing?' she said.

'Oh, you know,' said her aunt. 'I'm afraid I haven't got time to talk. I hope you don't mind, but could I speak to Mark? I've been trying to get hold of him. Whenever I ring his phone, it always sends me straight to the answering machine.'

'Of course I don't mind. But he's not here. What made you think he was?'

'Isn't he? He said he was going to Suffolk for a few days, to detox from Number 10, as he put it, and I naturally thought he meant with you. I was pleased you were getting on so well.'

'No, sorry, definitely not with me. I haven't actually heard from him since…well, for about two weeks.' She was not certain how much Pauline knew about Mark's departure from Downing Street. A thought occurred to her. 'I do have one idea where he may be, though. Leave it with me. If I track him down, I'll tell him to call you, all right?'

She dialled Daisy, who picked up on the first ring.

'Hey, Hannah! How are you?' She sounded breezy. Too breezy.

'I'm fine, thanks. How are you, more to the point? Sorry I haven't been in touch. What have you been up to? Anything special?'

'Oh my God, Hannah, you know, don't you? I'm sorry, I was going to tell you, I just haven't got round to it. How did you find out?'

'Call it a lucky guess. I didn't have any inkling until five minutes ago, when his mum called me, trying to get hold of him. He told her he was going to Suffolk, so she naturally assumed he was with me. More fool her, eh?' She forced her mouth into a beam, in the hope it would come through in her voice. 'Crikey, Daisy, that was fast work. All in the space of three weeks?'

'I'd noticed him from afar, on the day of that press conference, to be fair. The night after he was sacked, we talked on the phone for ages, and then we Zoomed, and then, well…'

'Spare me the details. To be honest, I always assumed he was gay.'

'He's not gay, trust me.'

'I repeat, spare me the details.' She now felt thoroughly foolish about those hopes of her own… 'Just tell him to call his mum. She's worried about him.'

'I will, but he's all right, honestly. They did him a favour. He says he's relieved to be out of there, and he would never have jumped if he hadn't been pushed.'

'I'm pleased to hear that. What about the Edmund difficulty, though? It still hasn't gone away.'

'The way Mark sees it, he tried to warn them and they wouldn't listen. What more can he do? It's not his problem any more.'

'I wish it were that simple. What happens if the president of China really does keel over and die during his state visit? How are we going to feel?'

'Vindicated?'

'Well, maybe. I think I'd also feel pretty wretched. We knew it was coming and didn't do anything.'

'What can we do? Mark tried, and they sacked him for it.'

'I know, but we've got to try harder. Shouldn't we get together with Brother Bernard again, to see if he's got any ideas? Maybe he'll know how to exorcise the shrine or something.'

Daisy laughed. 'I think you may be mixing up your movies there. But I don't mind contacting Brother B, if it's so important to you. How about I ask him to come to mine, so all four of us can discuss our options? If there are any, that is. Will that make you feel better?'

Daisy lived in an eighteenth-century cottage with a Dutch roof and a façade of rough flint, on the main road to Bury St Edmunds. Here, the four of them convened in her narrow sitting room three days later.

'How long do we have until the Chinese visit starts?' asked Brother Bernard, who had driven himself down from Norfolk in an ancient Morris Minor.

'The talks start in eight days, so the delegation will probably arrive one day before that,' said Mark. 'Exactly a week, in other words.'

'If the prime minister comes to the shrine, she will do so in advance of the visit,' said the monk. 'We may only have five or six days.'

'Can I just clarify,' said Hannah, 'why precisely you think Wu is in danger? The Chinese are meant to be our friends nowadays. That's the whole reason they're coming, isn't it? Why would St Edmund wish them any harm?'

'You're quite right to raise it, my dear. This Chinese delegation is not the classic enemy of the kind that might have been vulnerable to St Edmund's intervention in times past, and it's certainly true that the prime minister wants them to become amicable trading partners. Remember, though, that such a trading relationship will only happen at the successful conclusion of the negotiation. During any such negotiation, the person across the table is an opponent until hands are shaken and an accord is signed. Also, to reiterate, I believe St Edmund is offering the kind of assistance he thinks the prime minister needs. If she comes to him to calm her nerves on the eve of an arduous day of talks, I'm convinced he will pick up on her anxiety and act in the only way he knows.'

'In that case,' said Mark, 'the real test of whether Wu is in danger or not is whether Marina comes to the shrine in the run-up to his arrival. If she doesn't come, it means she isn't fretting about it, Edmund won't think she's appealing to him, and the Chinese guy can sleep safely, right?'

Daisy was frowning. 'If she comes, she'll do it in secret, won't she? I mean, we won't know one way or the other, especially not with you on the outside, so we have even less idea of her movements. Unless there's someone who might tip you off?'

Mark shook his head. 'Forget it. Travel arrangements are top-secret. Leaking her movements is an absolute no-no, because of terrorism, so nobody would do it, even if they were well-disposed towards me. Which they aren't.'

'I'm confident I can find out if a VIP visit is imminent,' said Brother Bernard.

'From the same person who tipped you off last time?' said Hannah.

'Exactly so. The greater difficulty I anticipate is the timing. Today is Monday. The talks start next Tuesday. If the prime minister does come to the shrine, it could be as early as Sunday. On the experience of my last tip-off, we won't have much warning, and therefore very little time to act. So I suggest we prepare a plan we can put into action if we know for certain she's coming.'

'What plan?' said Daisy. 'Personally, I don't see what we can do.'

Hannah had hoped this would be the moment when Brother Bernard unveiled a perfectly crafted scheme. Instead, he sighed. 'Me neither, I fear.'

'See?' said Daisy.

Hannah ignored her. 'In that case, let's approach it logically.

The essential problem is that, when the prime minister gets together one-to-one with St Edmund, bad things happen. If we want to prevent that, we have to keep the prime minister and St Edmund away from each other. Mark has tried persuading her not to come, which didn't end well. So we have to stop her entering the town, or at least the cathedral. Or maybe allowing her into the cathedral but making sure St Edmund isn't actually there when she arrives.' Her eyes widened. 'That's it! We steal in and remove the remains, then put them back after she's gone. Nobody would even know we've done it. She would just kneel to pray beside an empty shrine, and no one would be any the wiser!'

Brother Bernard coughed delicately. 'I don't think I could ever sanction grave-robbing...'

'Me neither,' said Daisy. 'I'm meant to be a professional archaeologist, remember?'

'...Quite aside from the obvious physical danger.'

'Danger?'

Mark cut in. 'I think Brother Bernard means St Edmund wouldn't take it lightly. If we believe he's capable of striking his enemies dead – and we all must believe that's possible, otherwise we wouldn't be having this conversation – then it would be rash to mess with his body.'

Hannah bit her lip. 'I see what you mean. No, maybe that's not such a good idea after all.'

'You're right about the two options, though,' her cousin said. 'If removing Edmund isn't possible, we can stop Marina going into the cathedral.'

'How?'

He looked at all of them in turn and smiled. 'I reckon a simple phone call should do it.'

For the rest of the week, Hannah tried to go about her normal life as best she could. She visited Frances, who was always glad of an offer to take Ringo out. She baked a batch of fruit loaves for a tea party for the church roof appeal. She even took all her curtains down and washed them, in her most rigorous spring clean for years. None of this calmed her jitters.

Having agreed on a plan, they had divided most of the tasks between Daisy and Hannah, because Brother Bernard was providing the key intelligence, and it seemed unfair to ask Mark to get too closely involved, since he had already paid a heavy price.

Daisy's first task was to buy a pay-as-you-go phone and SIM card in Argos, which she aimed to do on the most blustery, rainy day of the week. That gave her good reason to wear an enormous parka with its hood up, which would make her harder to recognise if anyone checked back over the CCTV. She also sourced a voice-distorting app and used it to record a message.

Hannah's job was to phone this message in at the optimum time and then get rid of the burner phone, as Mark insisted on calling it, and destroy the SIM. The risk was tiny, Mark and Daisy kept assuring her. Still in the first flush of romance, the pair of them clearly thought it was all a thrilling adventure. Without any such amorous excuse of her own, nor Mark's excitement at being released from a job he loathed, Hannah was free to dwell on less romantic considerations, such as the fact that they proposed to commit a serious crime centring on the prime minister.

Then again, she was the one who had insisted they do something.

She clutched at the hope that none of it would prove necessary. If Brother Bernard's source at the cathedral was as reliable as the old man claimed, the best possible outcome would be silence. Maybe Downing Street would realise they had a problem, even if they refused to admit it, and there would be no more trips to the shrine. Was that completely impossible?

She buried herself under a further mound of domestic tasks as Sunday dawned. By late afternoon, she was putting all her pillows in the washing machine and shampooing her rugs. Her phone was lying screen upwards on the sofa as she passed the cleaner over her tasselled kilim, so she could not hear it ring, but she saw Brother Bernard's name flash up clearly enough, calling via WhatsApp. She stopped the machine and picked up the phone. 'Does this mean it's on?'

'I'm afraid it does, my dear. I've just heard from my informant. The visit is scheduled for seven tomorrow morning. I've told Daisy and Mark already. Let's not say any more about it over the telephone.'

She dragged the carpet cleaner into the kitchen and poured herself a large glass of wine. She wished she could call Daisy to talk it all through once more, but there was no point, because her friend was so caught up in the excitement. Besides, it was best to keep communication to a minimum, especially on the phone. Now she just had to wait until the early hours, when she would drive to the darkest, most CCTV-free spot she could find, call the message in and immediately destroy the SIM. Then her role was done.

She returned to the living room, keeping clear of the soggy rug, and put the television on. In extremis, there was solace to be derived from Antiques Roadshow.

She must have nodded off, because she woke with a start as her phone rang. It was Daisy. Was this wise? Surely they had said no contact?

'Hello?' She was still groggy with sleep.

Her friend was hissing in an urgent whisper. 'Hannah, it's all messed up. We can't go through with it. You mustn't make the call.'

'Sorry, I've just woken up. What are you saying? I don't understand.' She wanted nothing more than to be absolved of her duties, but was it safe to abandon the plan? 'What about President Wu? Anyway, I'm not meant to be making the call yet. We said not until one or two in the morning.'

'I know, but you can't do it then either, because we'll still be here.'

'Here? Where are you?'

'In the cathedral, with Mark. We're locked in.'

'You're *what*? What are you even doing there? And how the hell did you manage to get locked in?'

'I can't go into that now. The point is, our plan is stuffed. If we hoax-call the police to say there's a bomb in the cathedral, the first thing they're going to do is come and look, and then they'll find us. We'll be sitting ducks, and Mark will be completely finished. He's already meant to be under psychiatric evaluation. If they catch him in here, they'll put him in some secure unit and throw away the key. Do you see? That's why we can't go through with it. I'm really sorry, but President Wu will just have to take his chances.'

If Mark had been asked to rank recent events in his life in order of improbability, attempting to check a spree of political assassinations by a confused medieval saint would have featured high on the list, but not as high as getting together with Daisy.

It had started with a series of conversations on the evening of the day he was marched out of Number 10. They softened the blow of that humiliation and, as they looked set to develop into something else, more than compensated for his sudden change of circumstances.

His romantic life had been non-existent for several years. After a string of indifferent relationships in his twenties, he tried online dating, with limited success, but that became impossible once he arrived at the court of Marina Spencer. Aside from the new-found need for discretion (the classic 'how would this look if it ended up in the *Daily Mail*?' test), the demands of the job made any kind of personal life impossible. Now, at last, that barrier was gone and happiness beckoned. He could not believe his luck.

Since he had not been formally sacked, there were meant to be procedures relating to his suspension, including the psychiatric evaluation stipulated in his parting letter. He ought to have got himself a solicitor, or at least put in a call to his union rep, but the idea of pleading his case, or having contact with anyone associated with his job, filled him with horror. Daisy suggested he might be suffering from post-traumatic stress. While he outwardly dismissed the possibility, he privately conceded there might be something in it. He certainly felt much better to have escaped to East Anglia, where everything about life – pace, rhythm, setting – was light years away from Downing Street.

He would have been happy to walk away from the whole Edmund issue and let Number 10 deal with it in whichever way it chose. When Hannah insisted they could not let the matter drop, he reluctantly admitted to himself that he did bear a good deal of responsibility for the entire fiasco, so the moral obligation endured, even if his job did not. When he suggested a hoax bomb-threat to scupper Marina's visit to the shrine, he was prepared to make the call himself, but Daisy persuaded the rest of the group it would be too risky for him. Hannah said she was happy to do the deed, although she did not look it, and Mark worried for her. He was painfully aware she was only involved because of him.

Daisy, having been reluctant to get back involved, had thrown herself into their plans. She was fired up, and her enthusiasm was infectious. It became an exhilarating game, more *Tomb Raider* than *Indiana Jones*, where he actually got to have sex with Lara Croft.

They decided to step up their initiative after Brother Bernard and Hannah went home.

Mark was opening a couple of bottles of beer when Daisy said, 'I'm not sure a call is enough.'

'What do you mean? Why not?'

'Think about it. All they'll do is seal the place off, search it thoroughly and then allow her in once they've discovered it's a false alarm.'

'Maybe so. But what else can we do?'

'If we really want to stop her coming, wouldn't it be better to plant something that actually looks like a bomb? That way, they'll have to do a controlled explosion, and there's no way they'll let Marina in. Apart from anything else, it would take too long, and presumably she'll have to go back to London to get on with the rest of her schedule.'

'Something that looks like a bomb? You mean wires, circuit boards and stuff? Are you sure you're not getting carried away? I've seen plenty of armed protection officers in real life, and I know what kind of kit they carry. You really don't want someone like that to think you're a terrorist.'

Against his better judgement, they agreed on a compromise: they would leave a rucksack near the shrine, filled with innocent day-tripper paraphernalia. That way they could argue, if it came to it, that they had simply mislaid their bag on their visit to the town's newest and most famous attraction. It was no fault of theirs if, entirely coincidentally, some random nutter had called in a bomb threat. Mark doubted the police would buy it, but a jury might.

Daisy made a recce of the cathedral, nosing around every corner, admiring the craftsmanship high and low and, crucially, using her phone to film everything she saw. Since the great glory of the building was its painted ceilings, she naturally did a lot of her filming in an upwards direction. Back home, she made a thorough search for CCTV cameras, intending to map the blind spots like a bank robber planning a heist. There was no need. The exercise revealed there were no cameras at all.

Next, she found a battered old maroon rucksack in a charity shop, which she decided was a safer place to buy from than Tesco or Argos, with their computerised records of every sale. She wore gloves to buy it, as she did to pick up the tourist information map to go inside it, and to swipe a half-empty litre bottle of water from a recently vacated table at Starbucks. Mark was impressed by her attention to detail. She had clearly missed her calling as a criminal mastermind.

From the outset, they had resolved not to tell Hannah or Brother Bernard about this unilateral element of their mission. Mark did not want his cousin worrying any more than she was already, and it seemed fairest to keep the old monk's involvement to a minimum. Even though he was a reluctant party to this initiative, Mark did rather like the idea of himself and Daisy going out on a limb as a daredevil twosome: the Bonnie and Clyde of Bury St Edmunds. Hopefully they would not fall in a blaze of gunfire at the end.

Once they received the call that Marina was expected at the shrine the following morning, they swung into action. They dressed carefully in hats and scarves, leaving visible as little of their faces (and Daisy's hair) as possible. Fortunately it was cold and wet enough for the layers of extra clothing to seem natural. Daisy placed the maroon rucksack carefully inside a larger, blue one, which Mark slung over his shoulder.

They set off in the late afternoon, allowing themselves half an hour inside the cathedral before closing time. This was long enough for a plausible visit, but also gave them a realistic chance of being the last to leave. In order to pass as genuine tourists, they began by following the visitor route, admiring the gaily decorated font and the carving of St Edmund's head in a wolf's paws. They avoided the south-west corner, where a volunteer guide pressed visitors to buy a brick for a Lego scale-model-in-progress of the cathedral.

It was only when they approached St Edmund's Chapel, which they had deliberately left till last, that their problems started. At this late hour, they had assumed the chapel would be deserted, allowing them to walk around the shrine and make a show of paying it suitable attention. Then Mark would pull the maroon bag out of the blue one and leave it at the head of the shrine, out of view of the entrance to the chapel, so it could not be seen by whoever locked up for the night. It would only be discovered in the early hours, once Hannah had made her call.

As they drew closer, however, they realised the chapel was occupied. A black-robed figure was kneeling beside the shrine, head down. Now the head rose a little, revealing a tangle of thin white hair around a weathered pate.

'I don't believe it,' hissed Daisy. 'It's Brother B!' They both stopped in their tracks.

'He didn't say he was planning to come here.' Mark started to walk forward, but Daisy pulled him back.

'We shouldn't let him see us. He'll try and talk us out of it.'

'In that case, come up here.' They were at the bottom of the steps to the little private gallery where he had sat for the re-enshrinement service. Taking her by the elbow, he ushered her onto the staircase, glancing around to check no one was watching them, as he followed her up to this hidden perch.

'Damn,' said Daisy, as she reached the top. 'I don't know what he thinks he's doing. I get that he likes to pray a lot, but couldn't he have done it at his priory? Besides, he's meant to be a Catholic. Why does he even want to pray here?'

'There isn't a shrine to St Edmund at his priory.'

'Maybe not, but this afternoon is a terrible time for him to show up here.'

'He could say the same to us.'

'Yes, but we've got a sound plan which we know will keep Marina away. What's his excuse?'

Mark put his head cautiously out over the front of the gallery and looked towards the chapel.

'Is he still there?' she said. 'Can you see?'

'I'm not sure. Hang on. I can't see him, so maybe he has… No, I can see his feet. He's still there.' He pulled his head back in and they stared at each other hopelessly.

'He'll have to leave soon. It's nearly closing time. Have another look.'

Brother Bernard had not moved. This time Mark stayed where he was, elbows on the ledge, leaning out from the gallery. The minutes ticked by. How long did it take to say a prayer? Still focusing on the old man's feet, which were all he could see, he thought he detected movement, but it was only a minor shift in position. 'Come on, come on…' he muttered. Finally, the feet disappeared. A moment later, there was Brother Bernard's white head, with its back to Mark. It bowed, and now the monk turned to leave the shrine. Mark pulled his own head in. 'He's leaving. Let's give him a couple of minutes, then the coast should be clear.'

'We haven't got long.'

'I know, but we don't want to run into him.'

They listened to the sound of receding footsteps and a door closing.

'Come on,' said Daisy.

Mark took her elbow to hold her back and whispered, 'Hang on a minute.' There were more footsteps now:

someone else was walking along the north aisle below them, back towards the main entrance in the north porch. They waited again, until the sound faded.

'Right,' said Daisy. 'We can't afford to wait any longer. Let's get moving.'

It was reassuring to find the chapel empty. There was no time to linger, so Mark ducked down at the top end of the stone coffin, pulled out the maroon bag, left it propped against the limestone plinth, then stood up again, with his blue bag back on his shoulder. 'Right. All done. Come on, let's get out of here before we get locked in.'

They hastened towards the door into the cloister through which Brother Bernard had disappeared. Daisy turned the handle but the door would not budge. 'No! Please, no. We can't be locked in!'

'Quick, let's try the main door.'

They raced back along the north aisle. Half an hour earlier, they had entered through glass swing doors, but the doorway was now blocked by a pair of stout oak doors, unmistakably closed.

'I don't believe it.'

'Try the handle. It may not be locked.'

She tugged at the large wrought-iron ring, and the door swung slowly towards her.

'Relief!' said Mark. 'I was getting seriously worried there. I really don't fancy spending a night in this place.'

'Me neither. Come on.'

They emerged into the porch, then Daisy stopped short. In front of them, the pair of even larger, stouter oak doors onto Crown Street were closed. They had the same wrought-iron ring handles, but this time the door did not respond when Mark tried to turn one of them.

'What about the other way?' said Daisy. 'Through the cloister?'

'If you say so.'

She turned on her heel, leaped down a short flight of steps and dashed along the colonnade which flanked the north wall of the cathedral. Ahead of them, the barred gate that normally stood open was now shut. She shook it uselessly, but there was nothing to be done. They were indeed locked in.

'What do we do now?' said Mark. 'Call for help? Whoever closed up can't be far away.'

'We can't do that. It would be like giving ourselves up.'

'We're just visitors who got locked in.'

'So you want to give up on the whole plan?'

He shook his head as they both paused to catch their breath. 'No, not really. But how the hell are we going to get out?'

'There must be another way. Another door, a window, anything.' They went back into the cathedral itself and made a full circuit, but the search was fruitless.

'We're such idiots!' said Mark.

They climbed back up to the gallery, which felt like their own sanctuary. 'All right, let's look at the options,' he said, as they each sank into a pew. At least they did not have to whisper any more. 'We could try and bed down here for the night, then get out when they open in the morning. On the downside, it's hard to see how we can do any of those things and still carry out a bomb scare.'

Daisy opened her mouth to speak, then closed it again and put her head in her hands. 'There must be a solution. We've just not thought of it yet.'

'I'm sorry. I'm as frustrated as you are. I hate to say it,

but our only option may be to drop the whole idea and tell Hannah not to make the call after all. Then we can try and slip out without being seen when they open tomorrow morning.'

'We will be seen. You know we will. They'll come early to sweep the place, with or without a bomb scare, and the first thing they'll find is the prime minister's ex-adviser, last seen being frog-marched out of Number 10, camping out in what will look like some kind of ambush. It certainly won't make you seem any more sane, in their eyes.'

Mark had been trying not to think about that. 'What else can we do, though? All the doors are locked, and there are no opening windows. And we can't break one to get out, even if we were prepared to do that, because they're all made of tiny leaded panes. Short of calling 999 to see if the fire brigade will come and rescue us, I can't think of any other option.'

'Maybe we ought to do that,' she said miserably. 'Do you think they'd really come? It would be humiliating, but at least we'd be out of here before Marina and her party arrive.'

'They'd take our names, though, wouldn't they? I mean, they'd want to know what we were doing here, and they'd search us, to check we hadn't stolen the altar candlesticks, or whatever. So it would still get back to the police that someone who's meant to be under psychiatric evaluation because he's too mad to work for the prime minister was lurking suspiciously in the cathedral a few hours before she was due to arrive there.'

'I'm so sorry. It's all my fault. I talked you into coming here. If we'd stuck to the original plan, none of this would have happened.'

'I know. But I went along with it, so we're both idiots. In our defence, we did it for the best of reasons.'

'Maybe some things are just too big to stop. What's that

prayer? 'Grant me the serenity to accept the things I cannot change, the courage to change the things I can, and the wisdom to know the difference.' We weren't wise enough to know the difference, were we?'

'We ought to phone Hannah.'

'She'll be furious with us for messing this up. She was the one pushing hardest for us to do something.'

'At least she doesn't have to make the call. I don't think she was looking forward to that.'

Daisy pulled her phone out. 'No bars.'

'I remember now, from the day of the service: there's no reception up here at all. You'll have to go down into the nave and do it. Why don't you do that, while I go foraging to see if I can find anything remotely blanket-like for us to sleep under? It's going to get pretty cold in here tonight. And I'm trying not to think about how hungry we're going to get.'

'I'm trying not to think about what the hell I'm going to do when I need a wee. Thank your lucky stars you can do it in a bottle.'

They descended from their gallery and split up. As he scavenged for makeshift bedding, Mark tried and failed to stop fretting about how bad the consequences would be if Marina's security team discovered them inside the cathedral. Their only hope was to escape in the tiny window of opportunity between the cathedral authorities opening the doors and the security team coming in to do their sweep. It was a slim chance, but the only one they had. And somehow, in the meantime, they had to get through the night.

When he got back to their elevated refuge, Daisy was already there.

'How did Hannah take it?'

'She couldn't understand what we were doing here.'

'I'm with her on that one. But she understands she doesn't need to make the call? That she absolutely mustn't make it, in fact?'

'She said she did.'

'You don't think she'll be so desperate to save Wu, she'll make it anyway?'

'If she does that, she knows she'll be dropping us right in it.'

'She may not care, after all I've put her through. She doesn't have much reason to like me.'

'Maybe not, but she likes me.' She was smiling at that, at least. She nodded at the bundle in his arms. 'What did you find?'

'This is a bit wicked, but needs must.' He let the bulky bundle of fabric he was carrying drop onto a pew, then held up the first item to show her. 'The fanciest blanket you've ever slept under. Actually a tapestry. It's got scenes from St Edmund's life on it. It was hanging on the wall round the corner. Here's another one: a picture of his shrine in the old abbey. What could be more appropriate? And I picked up the rucksack from the chapel, so at least we've got a bottle of water.'

'You're welcome to that. I daren't drink a drop.' She stared at the tapestries. 'Isn't it, you know, sacrilegious to sleep under those?'

'We came here to carry out a bomb scare at a sacred shrine. If you're comfortable with that, you can sleep under a silk rug with a picture of a saint on it.'

'I guess so. You didn't find any food anywhere?'

'They really don't have food in cathedrals.'

'If we could only get into the shop. I was in there when I came with Hannah. They have fudge and oatcakes and stuff.'

'So what are we waiting for?'

'The shop is on the other side of one of those locked doors.'

'I wish you hadn't mentioned it. So near and yet so far.'

She looked at her watch and sighed. 'It's going to be a long night, isn't it? It's not even seven o'clock yet.'

'There's one thing we could do to pass the time…'

'Don't even think about it. We're in a cathedral.'

'I thought you didn't believe in all that stuff.'

'I'm not sure what I believe any more. But either way, the answer is no. I'm sleeping in this pew, and you can have that one over there. If I see you coming anywhere near me, I'll scream for St Edmund to come and rescue me.'

'Do you really think he's bothered? Hasn't he got bigger fish to fry?'

'Do you really want to put it to the test?'

He sighed and looked around for some distraction. 'I haven't even got anything to read.'

'You must be able to find a Bible lying around somewhere.'

'That wouldn't have been my first choice.'

'Go downstairs so you can use your phone. Have a fight with someone on Twitter or something. Isn't that what it's for?'

'I'm low on battery. We may need it in the morning, and I haven't got a charger with me. Can I use yours?'

'I'm quite low too.'

'The Bible it is then. Do you want one?'

'Can we not just play I Spy instead?'

'All right. I'll start. I spy with my little eye something beginning with…P!'

'Pew?'

'No.'

'Pulpit?'

'Yes! Your turn.'

'I spy with my little eye…'

They kept it up as gamely as they could, but they both found themselves short on ecclesiastical vocabulary, and there were not many non-ecclesiastical objects to choose. Eventually they gave up and attempted to settle down for the night.

Mark prided himself on his ability to sleep anywhere, but these long hours were an ordeal. The pew was too narrow, so he arranged a line of kneelers on the floor. They were well padded but slid apart whenever he made the slightest movement, so parts of him were always falling into the gap. Added to that, the silk tapestry was thin and surprisingly scratchy. And he was still beset with worry about what would happen when the doors opened in the morning. Such bouts of fitful sleep as he was able to get were full of armed search parties, snarling dogs and dripping dungeons. Karim was there, handling a team of panting Alsatians, and so was Marina, in her tartan coat, ordering Mark to be tied to a tree and shot with arrows. None of these killed him, but he looked down at the blood flowing from his naked chest and wished that, if he had to be humiliated in front of Karim and Giles (who had now turned up as well), he could have kept his clothes on.

This uneasy rest had finally resolved itself into a deep slumber by the time the alarm on his phone went off. Still dark outside, it was six-fifteen. Mark turned over to grope for his phone, but it had slid underneath the nearest pew in the course of the night, and he smacked his head on the base of it. He yelped in pain.

'What are you doing?' groaned Daisy from under her own tapestry. 'Can you make any more noise?'

'Don't worry about me. I'm fine,' he said, rubbing his forehead. He shivered.

'I'm glad one of us got some sleep.'

'Meaning you did? I barely got a wink.'

'Oh please, you've been snoring for hours. At one point St Edmund came over and asked you to turn on your side. He said it was a request from all the rest of the dead.'

He smiled in spite of himself as he got stiffly to his feet. 'Come on, we should get up. They could be here to open up any minute.'

'I can't begin to think about how badly I need a wee. I'm amazed it didn't happen of its own accord in my sleep.'

'You just said you didn't get any sleep.'

'That must be why.'

She emerged from her inadequate covers, stood up and stretched. She started smoothing the creases out of her tapestry. 'We should put these back.'

'Don't worry about that for now. Our priority is to be ready to slip out as soon as they open up.'

She compromised by folding both tapestries and leaving them in a neat pile on her pew. Mark was about to descend the steps towards the nave when she held him back. 'Wait, let's think about this properly. I reckon we're best staying up here.'

'Isn't it better to hang around by one of the doors, so we can get out as soon as they unlock it? That's what we agreed.'

'Hang around where, though? There isn't much in the way of hiding places down there. We're better up here. This whole place is so echoey, we'll hear as soon as the door opens, and we're high enough up to be able to look down without being seen. That way, it will be easier to pick our moment. Let's face it, we've only got a slim chance, but I honestly think we've got a better one up here.'

'If you say so.' Mark was still groggy with sleep, and his head throbbed after the crack he had given it on the pew, so he was willing enough to lie back down on his line of kneelers. He shivered. 'Give me my quilt back, then. If we're staying here, we may as well wrap up in everything we've got.' Back under the covers, he checked his watch. It was six forty-five. 'They're cutting it fine, if she really is coming at seven.'

Daisy grunted. She too was wrapped in her tapestry again.

Mark must have nodded off. Jerking awake, he sat up and looked at his watch again. It was five to seven. 'Where the hell are they?'

'Whassat?' Daisy had been asleep too.

By seven-thirty, white light was streaming in through the east window and the lantern of the tower. 'Do you think she isn't coming?' said Daisy.

He shook his head in bewilderment. 'I don't know what to think.' He lay down again, pulling the scratchy tapestry up to his chin. Having spent all night trying to second-guess plans to which he was not party, he had reached the point where it was easier not even to think about them.

At nine, Daisy shook him awake.

He sat up in a panic. 'What? What is it? Are they here?'

'No, not a sign. I think we can assume she's not coming. Maybe she changed her mind. It's a good job we never made that call.'

'Maybe it means Wu is safe too. No thanks to us.' He rubbed his eyes. 'I wonder what time they open up normally?'

'Half nine, maybe?'

'We ought to get ready to leave.' He started folding their covers once more. He had grown strangely attached to this gallery refuge. He wondered if this was how a prisoner felt, preparing to leave a cell that had become home over many years. 'I'll take these back where I found them. If we're not about to get arrested, we may as well tidy up after ourselves.'

He returned the two tapestries to their proper place, hoping that the overnight creases would eventually drop out of them, and lingered a moment in front of the high altar, which was now bathed in bright sunlight. It seemed to be a beautiful morning out there.

On his way back to join Daisy in the gallery, he heard the clank of the door handle. He ducked into the shadow of an aisle pillar. This was the moment of truth: if Marina was on her way after all and had simply delayed her arrival, black-clad security goons would now rush in to check for hidden devices and hostile intruders. He strained to listen, but all he could hear was one set of footsteps. He moved around the pillar to remain hidden, as whoever had opened the door made their way across the front of the cathedral. Now he could see them from behind. It was a solitary verger, jangling a set of keys.

Energised by the prospect of escape, he pulled his shoes off to avoid making any noise and raced back to the gallery, taking the steps two at a time. 'Hurry,' he hissed, grabbing his phone and the blue rucksack, into which he had already stuffed the maroon one. 'We've got about thirty seconds.'

She followed him down the steps and they ran on tiptoe, each clutching their shoes, to the door nearest the chapel. It yielded easily. Two seconds later they were in the cloister, where they slipped their shoes back on. They resumed a normal pace as they saw a cleric – it seemed to be the sub-dean who had dealt with Marina's tantrum on the day of the re-enshrinement – walking towards them.

'Morning,' he said as he passed them, as if it were the

most normal thing in the world to see a couple of dishevelled visitors emerging from the cathedral as soon as the doors opened.

'Morning,' they chimed back, then goggled at each other with glee, scarcely believing their luck at getting out without so much as a raised eyebrow. A few moments later, they emerged from the cloister into the crisp spring air, leaving the cathedral complex for the morning bustle of Angel Hill.

'Before we do anything else, I need the toilet,' said Daisy.

'How about Costa?' said Mark. 'I'll order while you pee. I could murder a latte and a triple-chocolate muffin.'

'Me too. Deal.'

As they passed the Art Deco fingerpost, Mark's phone pinged, and so did Daisy's a couple of seconds later. Then Mark's pinged again, and a third time, followed by Daisy's, in the same sequence. They both reached for their devices.

'Three missed calls from Hannah.'

'Me too. And two texts.'

'Yes, I've got a couple of texts as well. I'd forgotten there was no reception up there.' She dialled her voicemail and held her phone to her ear, and Mark did the same. As they listened to their messages, they turned to each other in amazement.

'I don't believe it!' they said in unison.

In Costa, Mark stood at the counter while Daisy hastened to the ladies'. He jumped from news site to news site on his phone. The entire media was reeling from the bombshell announcement, which had come at seven o'clock, while they had been quaking in their hiding place at the prospect of imminent discovery. The prime minister had resigned with immediate effect, for unspecified personal reasons, and asked for her privacy to be respected. The trade talks with China would be led by the chancellor and the business secretary, while the deputy prime minister would step in as interim premier. The commentators were universally baffled, hailing it as the biggest and most mysterious shock resignation since Harold Wilson's in 1976.

He dialled Hannah as he waited for his coffee to be made.

'Where have you been?' she demanded, picking up straight away. 'I've been trying you both for the past two and a half hours.'

'We were in a mobile dead zone. What stunning news, though. We've only just seen it, so we don't know what to make of it. We're blown away.'

'Join the club. The whole of the rest of the country could say much the same, including the entire media. One odd thing, though. After Daisy called me last night, I tried to get through to Brother Bernard, to make sure he knew we weren't going through with the plan. He wasn't at the priory, but I carried on trying and I managed to get him about an hour later. I told him what Daisy had said, thinking he'd be really bothered about it, because we were effectively abandoning President Wu to his fate. But you know what he replied?'

'What?'

'He said, "My dear, I suspect it won't be necessary anyway." When I asked him what he meant, he wouldn't say anything else. He just told me to be patient and wait and see. What do you make of that?'

Now at last I understand where I have erred. You came to tell me what was in your heart, old man, and by doing so you lifted the scales from my eyes. How I regret my conduct. I wish you could hear my voice and know that.

It took you some time, kneeling there, to make your case. You, a man of God in your monk's robe, feared to tell me what was on your mind, did you not? As well you might. You have spent your long life, as you told me, devoted to the study of my existence, in life and afterwards, so you know how terrible the wrath of St Edmund can be. I respect your courage, old man, in coming here and speaking as you have. Without your frank speech, I would not have known that my actions, which I thought so fine and noble, have brought shame upon my own name as well as that of the lady whom I sought to help.

You took care to keep reproach from your voice, for fear of driving me to anger, but there was reproof nonetheless in what you said. For me, it was chivalrous to champion the lady, but you told me that times and manners have changed. I must believe you, because I have fallen into ignorance during all my darkened centuries, and you are much better versed in these things.

What remedy should I make? If I could reverse those actions by which, unknowingly, I caused the mayhem you describe, I would gladly do it. But how? The stricken leader – he who stood in my lady's path – is in his grave, and I do not have the power to bring him back. What else can I do to make amends and convince you that I have truly harkened to your words?

You yourself seemed uncertain on that score. Was it that you did not know what to bid me do, or that you did know, but you dared not say it? Did you also fear to leave? You begged and begged me to desist from the path that I have taken, but still you tarried. 'I hear you, old man, and I will heed your counsel,' I told you. 'Leave me now in peace, I pray you, that I may consider what to do.' But you did not hear.

At last you clambered to your feet, slowly, because of your advanced years, and because you had been kneeling too long in that position. You brushed the dust from your black robe and kissed your hand to press it to the marble slab that lay above me. I thank you for the gesture. I am pleased not to have fallen so far in your esteem that your devotion has run out.

I listened to your slow, shuffling footfall as you departed, and I hoped you would come again. By then, perhaps, I would have worked out how to make amends.

Left alone, I began to consider how to do so. You spoke of a great leader, come out of the East, to whom my lady must pay homage, since the destiny of this whole nation depends on his good favour. My lady would be anxious about the conduct of this parley, and you in your turn feared I might smite the oriental potentate.

For my part, I knew it would be hard to resist the pleas of my lady's heart. I am a creature of olden, chivalrous times. I was not confident I would be able to stop myself granting her wishes. Better, then, for her not to come at all.

It would have been easy, if I wished it, to cause some accident upon the highway to block her path. As you know, I have been down that path before. But to do so risked harm to the lady herself, which could not have been further from my wishes. Therefore I decided on another course. I would visit her myself, and entreat her not to come.

So it was that I arose from this place, as once I arose to visit Forkbeard, although my mission now was not to slay the lady, have no fear.

I took myself to her chamber and came to her in her sleep. 'Be not afraid, fair lady,' I said. 'I have been your friend until now and I remain so still. It is most pressing that I speak to you, though, which is why I have come straight to you here and not waited for your visit at my shrine.'

She knew me at once, and at first indeed she had no fear, because she thought she was simply dreaming. For her, perhaps, it was nothing out of the ordinary to talk to saints in her slumber.

'Lady,' I said, 'you are not dreaming, for I am real.'

'Of course you would say that,' said she, 'but you are saying it in my dream, of which you are a part, therefore I am still dreaming.'

From here, I did not know how to proceed. In olden times, when a saint came to a mortal Christian in their sleep, that mortal quaked before them and showed a fitting regard. What has happened in your age, that such deference is gone? Having fretted that I might frighten her, my problem now was that she lacked the belief to be afraid.

Then I saw what I must do. Just as I woke Forkbeard to make him meet his doom, so with my lady I pinched her on the arm, bringing her out of her slumber.

'You are not dreaming now, my lady, and look, I am here before you,' I said. 'Thus you can be sure I am no figment of your dream.'

She rubbed her arm and looked bewildered but still she was reluctant to acknowledge me. 'I must be dreaming still, and my dream is telling me that I have woken with St Edmund pinching at my arm.' She rubbed at the place as she added: 'Although I own, if it really is a dream, it is the most vivid I have ever had.'

'It is not a dream, dear lady,' said I, knocking a book from a table to the floor, and giving her a pinch on the other arm, a little harder this time, for good measure.

'Ouch!' she cried. 'You are hurting me.'

There came a knocking at the door from her attendant, roused by her cry of pain. 'Good lady, are you in danger? Is aught amiss?'

'No, good man, it is nothing,' she called back, rubbing her other arm now. 'It was just a dream. I have no need of you.'

'Tell me you are satisfied it is not a dream, else I will pinch your leg next,' said I.

'I am satisfied it is not a dream. But how do I know you are really St Edmund and not some jokester come to make merry at my expense?'

'Touch me,' said I.

She reached out towards me, but there was nothing for her fingers to touch.

'See?' I said. 'I am real enough to knock that book to the floor, but not physical enough for your hand to touch. Do you now believe I am Edmund, come to talk to you here in your chamber?'

'I think perhaps I do,' she said. Now, at last, she began to tremble. 'I have never received such a vision before. What is happening to me?'

'I bid you again, fear not, fair lady, but know you only this. I have wrought ill deeds on your behalf when I thought they were your will, but I have come to understand they were not so. And some of these deeds were most dire.'

She asked what these might be, and I told her about the leader struck down on the day she visited my shrine, and the unruly Scot whom I silenced so he could torment her no more.

At this, she began to weep and wail. 'You believed you were following my wishes? But I never bade you do such things! Now I am to blame for these two murders? I did not wish anything of the sort to occur. How could you think it of me?'

I explained to her, as I have explained to you, how my own confusion had arisen.

She was scarcely listening though, as she began to beat her breast. 'Woe is me! What have I done? However can I make amends?'

'It is for me to make amends, not you,' said I.

She shook her head as she wept. 'I am unworthy of this great office I hold, or even of life itself,' she cried. 'I should forfeit my freedom for these crimes, even if they were done unwittingly.'

I was overcome by the force of her penitence, and I felt even greater remorse now, for the fault was mine much more than hers, yet she blamed herself above all.

'Fair lady, do not keen so,' I said. 'You are not the author of these deeds. All I ask of you is this: come to my shrine no longer, that no more blood be spilt. Do that for me, and it will be amends enough.'

She made that promise and also vowed she would take action forthwith to show her penitence. I told her it was not necessary, repeating that it was I who was at fault, not her, but she insisted. I could see she was not a lady for turning from a decision once she had made it.

I think, by now, she may have made a public sign of remorse. You will know this better than I, so perhaps you will tell me. If she has done so, perhaps I will have risen a little in your esteem.

There is one more thing I would have you know, old man, so you can see how I have changed my ways and am now much better fitted to this modern world of yours.

That very night that I went to my lady, there was some disturbance at my shrine: a ruffian of pretty looks, and a most strange-looking woman with hair the hue of the sky. This pair disported themselves naughtily around my precincts. They remained within the holy walls of that place all through the night and acted in a most suspicious way, very close to my person. My first instinct was to strike them down or freeze them where they stood, so they could be seized on the morrow and hanged by the neck, or whatever is your custom now. However, to show you how much I have changed and taken your guidance to heart, I left them free to do whatever it was they were about, and in the morning they left the place in peace.

Did I do well? I hope you will agree I did, for I cannot tell you how much I itched to smite them.

Hannah peered anxiously at the passengers streaming out of the station, then broke into a smile. 'Pauline!' she waved. 'Over here!'

Her aunt looked summery, in a sleeveless blouse and a lightweight floral skirt. She was wearing big, preppy glasses in bright red frames which Hannah had not seen before. They seemed to assert that seventy was the new fifty, if not forty.

'Let me take your bag,' Hannah said, after they had hugged. 'The car's just over here. Two minutes' walk, that's all. How are you? You look so well!'

'All the better for seeing you love. I'm a bit nervous, if truth be told. You know, about meeting *her*.'

'Daisy? There's no reason to be nervous. She's got blue hair, I should warn you, but apart from that…'

'I'm not bothered about her hair. It's just… I don't know. One moment Mark had the best job in the world, at the heart of the government, and suddenly he meets this Daisy and he packs it all in…'

'You think he left his job because of Daisy?'

'Well, didn't he? He's never explained it, so what else am I to think?'

'It's honestly not that.' She pointed her key fob at the car to click the doors unlocked. 'Have you got enough room? Hang on, let me put the seat back a bit for you... There you go. No, trust me, that's really not how it happened. Anyway, I'm not sure it was the best job in the world. He was miserable, you know he was, and he's much happier now. But I should let him explain. We'll go straight to Daisy's, if that's all right, rather than go all the way to mine and then have to come back again. Mark's doing the lunch, apparently. You're honoured.'

It was ages since Hannah had had her aunt to stay. Daisy had been pushing to meet Pauline, but there was not much room for a guest in her house, so Hannah stepped in and offered one of her own spare rooms – to her aunt's evident relief. 'I don't want to get under their feet or cramp his style,' she confided.

Hannah had not seen much of Mark and Daisy, either, since the fiasco in the cathedral. Mark had rented out his flat in Vauxhall, moved in with Daisy and was planning to train as a history teacher. One unexpected consequence of Marina's sudden resignation had been the cancellation of any disciplinary action against him, which was apparently one of her last directives as prime minister. Instead he had been offered a substantial pay-off to go away quietly. Hannah did not know how much it was worth, but it came with a gagging order. He risked losing every penny if he or anyone else was indiscreet, which was another good reason to let him decide how much to tell Pauline.

It was safer, therefore, to change the subject completely as they drove to Daisy's. Hannah chatted away about what she had been doing in the garden – her vegetable patch had come into its own this year, with bumper crops of chard, radishes and rhubarb – and Pauline added her own bits of news, about a singles' coach tour of the Lake District that she had just booked, and the saga of a next-door neighbour with early symptoms of dementia.

Daisy flung open her front door while they were still getting out of the car, which Hannah took as a sign of nerves. Monty jumped up at Pauline as soon as he saw her, prompting a stream of apologies from Daisy before she had even said hello. Pauline said she liked dogs and proved it by crouching to greet Monty properly. The ice was broken.

'Come through into the kitchen, Pauline,' said Daisy. 'Mark's doing the cooking, look. He could barely boil an egg when he moved in, but I've made him learn, what with all this time he's got on his hands. I hope you're all right with spicy food? Curry is his main speciality, I'm afraid. In fact, for "main", read "only". But he's getting quite good at it.'

Pauline pulled a face at Hannah which suggested Indian food might not be at the top of her wish list, but it would clearly not do to say that out loud.

Mark was wearing an apron and seemed to have flour in his hair. 'Hello, mum. How was your journey? Sorry I didn't come and meet you, but I was up to my elbows in paratha dough. Hannah, can you pass me the amchur powder? Just next to your left hand. That's the one. Have you done the introductions? Daisy, Mum. Mum, Daisy.'

'We've already done all that. I see that whoever taught you to cook hasn't taught you to wash up as you go along,' she added, surveying the carnage on the draining board. She winked at Daisy, and it was clearly meant as a show of solidarity rather than a dig.

The food was indeed impressive – tender chicken in a tangy, gingery sauce, with chickpeas and spinach flavoured with something sharp and unfamiliar that turned out to be tamarind paste, with plenty of yoghurt and mango chutney to cool it all down. Pauline asked for the tiniest of portions, saying she was not hungry, which Mark seemed to believe, not noticing how hungrily she attacked Daisy's fruit salad and the cheese and biscuits that followed. But the atmosphere was convivial. It was a proper family occasion, Hannah realised, of the sort she had scarcely ever known. That was an unexpected benefit of their Edmund adventures.

Of these, nothing was said. 'I won't pry about your time in Downing Street if you don't want me to,' Pauline said, stirring sugar into her tea as the others drank small cups of strong coffee. 'One thing I would love to know, though: what happened to Marina? Why did she leave so suddenly? And where is she now? Everyone I speak to wants to know. Do you? Or are you not meant to say?'

Hannah stared down at her empty plate, avoiding catching Mark's eye. It was entirely his decision what he chose to tell his mother, and she had no wish to add to the pressure.

'The simple answer is, no, I don't know,' he said. 'You know what they always say about a week being a long time in politics? Well, bear in mind I left three weeks before she resigned. I genuinely have no idea what made her go. I was on the inside until shortly beforehand, but I have no more information than you about what happened after I left. I have no love for Marina, because she was a demanding and ungrateful boss. But I do think she's a brilliant politician, so she's a loss to the country.'

Hannah realised how good at this he was. He had only supplied part of the picture, editing out the gravity of their fears about Marina's conduct in office; but nothing he said was false, which meant he could convey it with sincerity. And the central part of his answer was certainly true: the reason for her departure remained a mystery to them all. Only Brother Bernard seemed to have had wind of it, with his mysterious comment on the night in question, but none of them had seen him since then.

'And you don't know where she is now?' said Pauline.

'Honestly, no idea. She always had a nice house in her constituency. She has stood down as an MP as well, but I don't think she's sold it. She's probably holed up there, and she'll eventually make tons of money from a book or making speeches, and maybe she'll set up a foundation. That's what ex-prime ministers tend to do. What happened will remain a mystery, and we won't know the full story until other cabinet ministers start writing their memoirs. Or maybe they don't know either, and we'll have to wait thirty years until the official papers are published. For now, there's a new prime minister, so Marina's old news, and all the political journalists have moved on.'

'But aren't you curious to know?' pressed Pauline. 'You spent all that time up close with her. You must be dying to know why she did it.'

'Of course I'm curious, just like everyone else in the country. I'll never forget how amazed I was when I heard the news. I've moved on though, and the truth is I try to think of Marina Spencer as little as possible.'

Later, when they were driving back to her own cottage, Hannah asked her aunt: 'So what did you think of Daisy?'

'I liked her. You were right, I needn't have worried. Though I'm still none the wiser about why Mark left his job.'

'Get him on his own some time and ask him. I'm sure he'll talk about it when he's ready. The main thing is, he's much happier, don't you think? I mean, I barely knew him before, but even I can see how much he's changed.'

'He's more outgoing, you're right about that.'

'And he's learned to cook.'

Pauline groaned. 'If only he'd learned to cook something that didn't set your mouth on fire.'

'I think he's enjoying having his own area of culinary expertise.'

'I dare say, but I'd rather he became an expert at omelettes or bangers and mash.'

Hannah smiled, and they drove on in silence.

'One thing that's a shame, though,' said her aunt.

'What's that?'

'St Edmund. Have they dropped the idea of making him patron saint? Nobody seems to talk about it any more.'

The policy did indeed seem to have been quietly binned. Marina had been replaced by the home secretary, a stolid, uncharismatic toiler who had proved to be the safe pair of hands the Alliance needed in its time of crisis. As far as Hannah was aware, he had not mentioned St Edmund once, and she did not remotely blame him for kicking the scheme into the longest grass he could find. 'Yes, I think they have.'

'I was so proud you found him, and even prouder when Mark had the idea of championing him. I don't like to blow my own trumpet, but it was partly my doing, wasn't it, when I told him about it and then it became government policy? I felt bad when they were giving Marina a hard time for it in Wales and Scotland, but that blew over. It's a shame if they abandon it now.'

Hannah thought for a while before answering. 'You know

what I think?' she said at length, as they drew up outside her house.

'What?'

She hesitated, then shook her head and laughed. 'Actually, I have no idea what I think. I've had quite a lot of exposure to St Edmund in the past few months, in a variety of ways, but if you asked me to tell you all about it, I wouldn't know where to start, or how to separate fact from fiction, or from downright lunacy. All I know for certain is I'm glad he's stopped making headlines. We all need a bit of calm, including St Edmund himself.' She got out of the car. 'Hand me your bag, will you? Come on in, and I'll show you to your room. I'm guessing an early supper wouldn't go amiss. How about I do us both an omelette?'

The newest member of the community put her hand to her forehead to check there was no hair showing under her wimple, before knocking on the door.

'Come,' commanded a voice within.

That was what she herself used to say. She turned the handle and pushed the door. It was strange to feel nervous of authority once again, but oddly reassuring too. 'You wanted to see me, Mother Abbess?'

'Ah, Catherine.' That name! She was still trying to get used to it, having left her old one behind. 'Do come in. Sit, please, and don't look so worried. I merely want to ask how you are settling in.'

She sat on the hard wooden chair in front of the abbess's desk. 'Well, thank you. I've been made very welcome, and I'm grateful.'

'Of course you're welcome. We're pleased to have you among us.'

'It's good of you to accept me, given the obvious...

sensitivities.'

'Are there sensitivities?'

'Well, I'm nervous of the unwanted attention my presence may draw, if the media get wind that I'm here.'

'Need they? No one here will tell. This is not like the outside world, where every secret has a price. Here, we have no need of money, so we're much harder to corrupt. Besides, even if it does get out, what's the worst that can happen?'

Catherine glanced out of the window, which looked over the gardens towards the high perimeter wall.

'They would besiege us. Believe me, it can be frightening to be on the receiving end.'

'Let them. They can stay out there as long as they like, provided they don't try and scale the wall. Even if they do, they'll find we're more than a match for them. To tell you the truth, I think we'd all find it rather an adventure. But I don't believe it will come to that.'

'You're very kind, Mother Abbess. If it does happen, I'm deeply sorry for the disruption.'

'Don't be. Don't let them add to your troubles. I know you have many. You haven't yet told me what they are, and I'm comfortable with that. You may tell me in your own good time, or you may never tell me, as you prefer. When you came here, you assured me you weren't fleeing the law. I believed you then and I still believe you. Anything else is entirely your own business. It's between you and God.'

'I did tell you that, and it was true. It might have been easier if my misdeeds had been covered by the law. Then I could have been punished. But if I had confessed to them, nobody would have believed me.'

'If you're truly sorry for whatever it is you've done or you think you've done, the Lord will forgive you.'

The abbess fell silent. They were probably about the same age, Catherine thought. How strange that she herself was a novice, at this time of life.

As if reading her thoughts, her superior said: 'Now, on the subject of your instruction. Since you're not a member of the Catholic Church, you will need to be received into it. It's highly unusual for someone to be accepted into our community who is not yet a member of our faith but, given the strength of your wish to join us, and the particular circumstances…'

'I'm so grateful for that too. It had to be your Church, you see, because you're more likely to believe me than anyone else, if I tell you what I've done. I'm not sure any non-Catholic would.'

The abbess nodded, waiting for her to continue, but Catherine was not yet ready to unburden herself. She would not know how to begin.

'Well then,' said her superior, 'you will need guidance. I've asked a good friend of our community to come and instruct you. He lives not far away, in a similar house to this one. Not Franciscan, but we are of similar mind. He's waiting downstairs. Would you like to meet him?'

Catherine was not sure she was ready to meet anyone from outside the convent, but it was important to show willing, so she nodded and said she would.

'Good. Excuse me one moment.' She went to the door, and Catherine heard her say, 'Sister Monica! Would you ask our visitor to come to my room, please? He's in the morning room.'

They waited in comfortable silence, a state so rare in the outside world, but quite natural here. Then there was a knock on the door and an elderly monk entered. He wore a belted black robe and had a shock of unruly white hair around a shiny brown pate.

'Ah, Brother Bernard,' said the abbess. 'I want you to meet the newest member of our community, Catherine.'

She stood to greet him. She looked very different now, with her hair covered, no make-up and her eyebrows back in their right place, so she was not sure he would recognise her. Unless he had been told already, of course.

'Hello, my dear,' the old man said. 'In actual fact, we almost met once before. Don't worry, I don't expect you to remember, but we spoke on the same platform, in the Abbey Gardens. You didn't have time to say hello at the time, which I understood, of course...'

'I do remember. And I did have time. I wanted to meet you, but they said you'd gone.'

'How strange. No matter. It's a pleasure to meet you now.'

'Catherine is keen to receive instruction from you so she can become a Catholic,' said the abbess. 'She was not raised in our faith, but she believes only we can understand what troubles her, and therefore only we can give her comfort. I have assured her the Lord will understand, which is what matters.'

The old man smiled. 'It is indeed, Mother Abbess. All the same, Catherine is right to place her trust in us.' He had kind eyes, she noticed, which he now turned on her. 'Speaking for myself, I guarantee I will understand whatever it is you have to tell us. You know, there is an assumption among many people in the outside world that we who live the religious life are sheltered and unworldly. They would be surprised by how much we know. Sometimes the most remarkable things happen, do they not?'

In the warmth of his sympathy, Catherine felt calmer than

she had for years. She had been right to come to this place. Perhaps, one day, she might be able to tell this nice old monk what she had unwittingly done.

He might even believe her.

AFTERWORD

When I told friends my next novel was about St Edmund, a surprising number reacted by saying they had never heard of him. Yes you have, was my stock reply. You've heard of Bury St Edmunds, for sure. What you mean is, you've never asked yourself who he was.

In East Anglia, far fewer people would profess ignorance, not just because of the town that bears his name and boasts not one but two statues to Edmund. He's a big deal all over the region. In the Suffolk village where I live, he features in the medieval stained glass and the carved Victorian pulpit of our church, and one local historian even maintains he's buried under our Lady Chapel. (If he's right, Vernon, Daisy and the gang have been looking in the wrong place, but I don't believe he is.) A beautiful thatched church stands alone in a field on the supposed spot of Edmund's coronation, on the Suffolk/Essex border, while at least three villages in Suffolk and Norfolk make rival claims to be the site of his death. And if you want to explore Suffolk on foot, with a couple of diversions into Essex and Norfolk, you can do it on the eighty glorious miles of the St Edmund Way.

Even in these parts, though, nobody knows anything much about his life. As Mark Price discovers early on, that's pretty much a blank slate, and my hapless Whitehall aide is only the latest in a long line of fanciful chroniclers to flesh out the tale. That ought to make Edmund a fertile subject for a novelist, but I decided I didn't want to dramatise his life; two of my previous novels have been largely historical, but I had little desire to immerse myself or my readers in the Dark Ages.

Fortunately for his academic biographers, as well as for me, Edmund's story did not end with his death in 869.

The word 'necrobiography' was first coined, as far as I know, by Norman Scarfe, the celebrated historian of East Anglia, in an essay about St Edmund in the late Sixties. He neatly summed up the point of his new word – that the scope of biography may continue long beyond the subject's death – in his opening sentence: 'Unable to resist the Danish marauders who slew him, King Edmund of the East Angles made amends after his death by providing one of the most effective symbols of English resistance to the invader ever recorded in our history.'

I didn't come across that quote until some time after I'd starting writing my novel, so it would be wrong to call it my inspiration. But it does sum up the contradiction with which I've attempted to make merry: that St Edmund in death had a very different character, in the eyes of those who believed in his powers, to King Edmund in life.

The inspiration proper for my modern take on the cult of St Edmund was a bumper sticker.

In 2006, when the 'Edmund for England' campaign was launched by Radio Suffolk host Mark Murphy, I had just become a part-time resident of the county. Backed by the *East Anglian Daily Times* and the brewer Greene King, he and David Ruffley, the MP for Bury St Edmunds, delivered a petition to Downing Street calling for St Edmund to be reinstated as patron saint of England. They only had 2,500 signatures, so they can't have expected Tony Blair to take them seriously, but they did get a consolation prize, and St Edmund became patron saint of Suffolk County Council. Twelve years later, when I settled permanently in East Anglia, one of my new neighbours still had a faded 'Edmund for England' sticker on the back of their car.

The thrust of the campaign was that Edmund would make a better patron saint because he was English and St George wasn't. That makes it look pretty xenophobic to outsiders, rather than the outburst of East Anglian pride which I think it was primarily meant to be. The idea stuck with me. When I was playing with ideas in my head and wondering how the world might react if and when St Edmund's body is found, I began to imagine a well-intentioned liberal trying to frame him not as a patron saint of England, but for the whole United Kingdom.

I used a lot of books for my research. The one I returned to again and again was Francis Young's *Edmund: In Search of England's Lost King*. If this novel whets your appetite for further necrobiographical study, there is no better place to start. *The Passion of St Edmund* by Abbo of Fleury (first published c986) is also a surprisingly good read, as is Jocelin of Brakelond's *Chronicle of the Abbey of Bury St Edmunds*, still readily available in print. *The Sacred and Profane History of Bury St Edmunds* by Peter Bishop was also a good source. For my gallop through British medieval history, I was well-served by Simon Schama's *A History of Britain*, plus Robert

Bartlett's sumptuous *Medieval Panorama* (thank you to Nick at Long Melford Library for that recommendation). I also made liberal use of a certain online resource which I've given, as a mark of my appreciation, a starring role in the novel. (Please don't be like Mark and plant fakery on Wikipedia.)

I hope the timeline at the front of the book will help readers orientate themselves and place genuine historical figures as I canter through the centuries from Anglo-Saxon to Tudor England, with the occasional detour via medieval Wales and Scotland. Everyone else in the novel is strictly fictional, including the holders of offices which exist in real life. My fictional sub-dean, verger and bishop of St Edmundsbury Cathedral should not be confused with the real ones; nor have I met any of the archaeologists doing the real-life survey of the old tennis courts in the Abbey Gardens. Marina Spencer, the charismatic politician adored by everyone who has never met her, is a figment of my imagination and not to be confused with any existing politicians who may match that description.

Thanks for advice, help and input to Liz Curry, Barbara Segall, Cheryl Collins, Richard Titford, Francis Young, Maha Khan Phillips, Rose Shepherd, Tom Dawnay (whose excitement about medieval art proved infectious), and the staff of Moyses Hall Museum in Bury St Edmunds and Long Melford Heritage Centre. Cath Senker volunteered to read the manuscript and then, quite unbidden, did a full-scale copy-edit, shaming me with the amount she picked up. The irrepressible Jules Button at Woodbridge Emporium gave me valuable encouragement during lockdown by championing my writing. Scott Pack has proved, for the fourth time on the trot, an invaluable editor, while my publisher Dan Hiscocks is endlessly supportive. Thank you to Clio Mitchell for (official) copyediting and typesetting, to Hugh Brune for championing the book within the trade, and Ifan Bates for another superb cover. The central figure of St Edmund is from a silk tapestry by the late Sibyl Andrews; the tennis racket and balls are Ifan's addition.

Racing to finish a novel to be published in this, the millennium year of the foundation of Bury St Edmunds Abbey, I was nervous that the real archaeologists would find St Edmund's body too quickly – or worse, find nothing, and destroy my premise. The Covid-19 crisis put paid to that and, as far as I'm aware, everything is currently on hold. I very much hope the search will resume and the real St Edmund will be discovered, so that he is one day enshrined in the cathedral where Mark and Daisy spend the night. If that happens, I hope he doesn't bear any grudges against novelists who have made mischief with his story.

I also strongly advise against any attempt to make him patron saint of the United Kingdom.

By the same author

The Hopkins Conundrum

Tim Cleverley inherits a failing pub in Wales, which he plans to rescue by enlisting an American pulp novelist to concoct an entirely fabricated 'mystery' about the poet Gerard Manley Hopkins, who wrote his masterpiece *The Wreck of the Deutschland* nearby.

Blending the real stories of Hopkins and five shipwrecked nuns with a contemporary love story, while casting a wry eye on The Da Vinci Code industry, *The Hopkins Conundrum* is a highly original mix of page-turning fiction, literary biography and satirical commentary.

I love this novel. It pulls off the three-card trick of being entertaining, touching, and a fascinating insight into Gerard Manley Hopkins' poetry
Harriett Gilbert

A compelling and captivating debut
Laurie Graham

A deft fusion of genuinely funny writing and deeply poignant drama bound artfully around the vividly imagined character of Gerard Manley Hopkins, who is long overdue a revival and deservedly takes centre-stage
Jennifer Selway, Daily Express

Edge keeps things enjoyably straightforward and the result is a pleasurable literary thriller. This is thoroughly enjoyable hokum. Edge wears his Hopkins learning lightly, sprinkling the book with snippets while avoiding didacticism or handholding...it's a merry page-turner
The Spectator

A witty satire... By turns gripping and laugh-out-loud funny
Press Association

A comedy with a touching emphasis on the importance of truth in human relationships
The Tablet

The Hurtle of Hell

Gay, pleasure-seeking Stefano Cartwright is almost killed by a wave on a holiday beach. His journey up a tunnel of light convinces him that God exists after all, and he may need to change his ways if he is not to end up in hell.

When God happens to look down his celestial telescope and see Stefano, he is obliged to pay unprecedented attention to an obscure planet in a distant galaxy, and ends up on the greatest adventure of his multi-aeon existence.

The Hurtle of Hell combines a tender, human story of rejection and reconnection with an utterly original and often very funny theological thought-experiment. It is an entrancing fable that is both mischievous and big-hearted.

A sparkling mixture of domestic and celestial comedy. A conflicted gay man meets his bungling creator in an ingenious take on It's A Wonderful Life
Michael Arditti

Simon Edge has given us a creator for our times, hilariously at the mercy of forces beyond even his control
Tony Peake

Part philosophical quest, part redemptive religious exploration, this is an original and witty look at religion and society seen through the eyes of a hapless and confused young man. The result is a clever and enchanting fable of self-discovery
The Lady

An unorthodox, comical and often deep story of rejection and reconnection with daft, challenging and fun plot twists. It's not what it seems, but then what is? Edge delivers a warm-hearted narrative of redemption that's never judgemental but is inclusive, funny and undoubtedly heretical. Read it or burn it, depending on your sense of humour
Gscene

A Right Royal Face-Off

It is 1777, and England's second-greatest portrait artist, Thomas Gainsborough, has a thriving practice a stone's throw from London's royal palaces. Meanwhile, the press talks up his rivalry with Sir Joshua Reynolds, the pedantic theoretician who is the top dog of British portraiture. Gainsborough loathes pandering to grand sitters, but he changes his tune when he is commissioned to paint King George III and his large family. In their final, most bitter competition, who will be chosen as court painter, Tom or Sir Joshua?

Two and a half centuries later, a badly damaged painting turns up on a downmarket TV antiques show. Could the monstrosity really be, as its owner claims, a Gainsborough? If so, who is the sitter? And why does he have donkey's ears?

Mixing ancient and modern as he did in his acclaimed debut, *The Hopkins Conundrum*, Simon Edge takes aim at fakery and pretension in this highly original celebration of one of our greatest artists.

A glorious comedy of painting and pretension
Ryan O'Neill

The rivalry between Thomas Gainsborough and Sir Joshua Reynolds is at the heart of this larky novel
Saga Magazine

I loved this book, a laugh-out-loud contemporary satire, skewering today's tired reality TV formats, married with a tale of vicious rivalry in the world of 18th-century royal portraiture. Simon Edge manages to pin asses' ears onto the lot of them, to great comic effect
Liz Trenow

I enjoyed this beguiling book very much. The interwoven strands between 1780s and the 2010s are beautifully managed and brilliantly resolved
Hugh Belsey

If you have enjoyed *Anyone for Edmund?*, do please help us spread the word – by posting a review on Amazon (you don't need to have bought the book there) or Goodreads; by posting something on social media; or in the old-fashioned way by simply telling your friends or family about it.

Book publishing is a very competitive business these days, in a saturated market, and small independent publishers such as ourselves are often crowded out by the big houses. Support from readers like you can make all the difference to a book's success.

Many thanks.

Dan Hiscocks
Publisher
Lightning Books